TRUST

Sasha Greene lives in Glasgow and regularly travels to the Scottish Highlands for hiking, snowboarding and to enjoy the amazing scenery. She first started writing when she was a child and her books were full of things like witches and magic houses. These days she is more fascinated by the real world, especially people and relationships.

Trust is her second novel.

Other books by Sasha Greene:

Something Like Happy

To Isla

many thanks for
everything you do

Trust

SASHA GREENE

Sasha Greene

Published in Great Britain in eBook and paperback format by Sasha Greene in 2021

Copyright © Sasha Greene 2021

Cover design © Fully Booked 2021

Sasha Greene asserts the moral right to be identified as the author of this work

ISBN:
9781739936907 (Paperback)
9781739936914 (eBook)

This book is for all the people who have ever spoken out for equality. You form a ladder with which we will eventually reach the stars.

It's also for all the people who didn't speak out because they couldn't or because it was just too tiring to do it one more time.

And for my mother and all the other strong women who helped me find the power of my own voice.

Author note

This book contains depictions of PTSD and a character who has experienced sexual assault and coercive control. I have made every effort to handle this appropriately and sensitively.

I have included these topics because they are a part of so many people's lives, and love doesn't always appear at the most convenient time.

Chapter 1

The day Jenny left London sheets of rain were coming down, but Katie still insisted on seeing her off at the airport. Jenny's fingers twisted around the handle of her suitcase as they waited at check-in, the hard plastic cold beneath her skin. 'I feel like I'm running away.'

'Don't be ridiculous. Anyone would need a break after what you've been through these last ten days.' Katie squashed her in a hug. 'So just go and make the most of it. I can't believe you'll be away for a whole month! I'm so env, darling.'

'Env? That's the first time I've heard you use that one. Is it the latest word of the moment?' Jenny couldn't help smiling as she teased her flatmate. She loved Katie's expansive personality. It meant she could fade into the background when she needed to. Whenever things got a bit too much.

'Sure.' A wicked laugh escaped Katie. 'I mean, totes, sweetie.'

She gave Jenny another hug as they parted. 'I'll see you in three weeks! You'd better arrange some fantabulous things to do while I'm up.'

'You have fun with the lodger.' Jenny fished out her phone to bring up her boarding pass. 'If you find out she's a serial killer then call me, OK?'

Katie just left her with a cheery wave.

Jenny passed through departures in a bit of a daze. Shopping was out of the question; she would have to be careful with her savings now that she was out of a job. She did treat herself to a copy of Vogue though, and it wasn't long before she was settled into a window seat on the plane with the glossy magazine open on her lap.

'What a nightmare.'

Jenny looked up as a tall man slid into the seat beside her. He might have been good-looking if there wasn't such a scowl on his face.

She sneaked another peek to the right. Despite his casual jeans, he looked like a typical businessman, with clean-cut dark hair and a smooth-shaven chin. He seemed quite young; not much older than herself. His shirt sleeves were rolled up, showing off a nicely toned set of muscles, so he obviously worked out too.

Something about him looked vaguely familiar and she tried to work out what it was, but came up blank. He probably just had one of those generic types of faces. Or maybe he was an actor in a TV show or something, one of those extras who you don't really notice. She smiled at her flight of fancy. If he had looked less bad-tempered then she might have asked.

His long legs were squashed against the seat in front of him, and as he shifted to try and make himself more comfortable, his knee brushed against hers. Startled, she pulled her legs together and inched herself closer to the window. The small plane suddenly felt very claustrophobic and she closed her eyes, fighting the panic.

Breathe. Slowly. In. Out. She curled her fingers around the edge of the seat, gripping the rough fabric to try and anchor herself in reality. Counting slowly as she took measured breaths, she waited for her hammering heart to return to something more like normal.

By the time she had recovered her composure the plane was ready to go and she dutifully watched the cabin crew go through the safety demonstration. Her neighbour glowered beside her all the way up to cruising altitude, while Jenny tried to ignore the blatant invasion of his legs into her personal space. It was a small plane with just two seats on each side so he could have easily put them out into the aisle.

As soon as the seatbelt signs had been switched off, she made her move. 'Sorry, could I just get out?'

He let out a tired sigh, not even bothering to look at her, and Jenny decided it was time to do some scowling of her own. 'Are you always this rude, or is it just when you get on a plane?'

There was a quiet snort of laughter from a white-haired lady across the aisle. The guy's head snapped around in her direction and Jenny's breath caught. Deep brown eyes drilled into her own, and she saw ice flash beneath the cool exterior. Then it was gone in an instant, and he grinned apologetically.

'Sorry, I'm not normally such a grouch.' He made a miniature sitting bow, and held out his hand. 'I'm Nadeem.'

His voice was mellow and pleasant, with just a hint of a Scottish accent. As Jenny took his hand it closed over hers, strong and capable. She was surprised to find that it was also slightly calloused, something she definitely hadn't expected.

'Jenny. Nice to meet you.' She reluctantly let go of his hand and collected her scattered thoughts, motioning towards the front of the plane.

'Oh yeah, sorry.' He got up to let her out, and as he did so Jenny caught a hint of his aftershave; it was clean and fresh, and a surprising hint of a vaguely floral scent reminded her of summer days in the park.

When she returned from the toilet he was peering out of the window, as if hoping to get a glimpse of the ground below. 'I fly quite a bit, but somehow I can never get used to the idea,' he said when she had settled herself back into her seat. 'It seems so amazing, just so...'

'Improbable?'

He smiled again, a warm smile that did funny things to her insides. 'Exactly! A small metal box, thirty thousand feet up in the air, flying at three hundred miles an hour...'

'Don't.'

He sobered instantly, creasing his features into a frown. 'Sorry. If you're afraid of flying, that was out of line.'

'I'm not, but I still don't like to think about the improbability of the behaviour of a little metal box while I'm actually in it.' She smiled back at him, just to make sure he knew she was joking.

Nadeem rubbed his chin. 'I seem to be spending the first five minutes of our acquaintance continually apologising; it's not a good start.'

'Well.' Jenny gave a slight quirk of her lips. 'You actually spent the first twenty minutes of our acquaintance scowling ferociously, so I'd say it's a definite improvement.'

'Pff – if you'd had the morning I did...' Nadeem raised his eyebrows.

'Why, what happened?'

He ran his fingers absently through his hair, glancing down the plane. 'I was flying out from Gatwick this morning, sat on the plane for twenty minutes and then my flight was cancelled due to some kind of bloody technical error. The only other flight today was this one. I had to trek all the way across London and almost missed the plane. And now I've got to put up with this cattle car of a seat and paying a fortune for a bottle of water.' He crossed his arms defensively.

'Ooh, big deal.' She couldn't help teasing him a little. 'Some of us plebs do this budget airline stuff all the time, you know.'

He shifted in his seat, looking back at her. 'It's not that. There's a party tonight for my sister's eighteenth birthday and if I missed it my family would never forgive me. I was supposed to be there yesterday, but I got caught up in some stuff going on at work.'

It did sound like quite a stressful morning. Nadeem looked back up towards the front of the plane, and Jenny suddenly noticed how large his nose was in profile. It suited him though. It somehow fit into the rest of his face in a very pleasing way.

Jenny laughed inwardly at herself. Here she was having a perfectly polite conversation with a stranger on a plane, while at the same time making internal judgements on his physical attributes. Still, it was good to know that even after her recent trauma she could still find a guy attractive. It wouldn't do any harm to be nice to him. Although it really was a bit awkward having a conversation in such a confined space; normal body language rules just didn't apply.

'What do you do for work?' This was her chance to place him. If he was an actor he would definitely mention it.

'Me?' He pointed at his chest. 'I work in logistics. Pretty boring stuff for most people. What about you?'

'Oh, just working random jobs.' There was no way she was going to tell him about her latest work fiasco. And there too went her theory of him being someone famous. 'I'm trying to save enough money to pay for my LPC – that's Legal Practice Course. It's the one that will finally let me qualify to be a solicitor.'

Nadeem raised his eyebrows appreciatively. 'Oh, great. What area of law?'

'Family law. It's the one that interests me most.' Jenny realised she was clasping her hands together tightly and released them slowly.

'Why's that?'

Jenny hesitated and looked across at him, but he had sounded genuinely interested. However, despite the surprising feeling of intimacy that was created by sitting so close to him, she had no intention of sharing the exact details. Revealing just how shitty her teenage years had been tended to be a real conversation killer.

She tried to keep her voice casual. 'It's a long story. Let's just say that I went through quite a bad time when my dad died, so if there's anything I can do to smooth the way for kids in that sort of situation, then I want to be able to do it.'

'Sorry to hear about your dad. That must have been hard for you.' He leaned his head back on the seat.

Discussing her family with a stranger was definitely not going to happen, so Jenny just smiled politely at him and changed the subject. 'What do you actually do in your job?' She looked down at her hands, wondering if she should just leave him alone and get out her magazine again. She definitely needed a manicure soon. Not that it was a problem. There would be plenty of time to spare while she was on holiday.

'Sorting out unexpected problems, mainly. Meetings. Managing stuff.' There was a note of pride in Nadeem's voice.

'It sounds like you love it.' Jenny was surprised. That sort of job would be her worst nightmare.

He turned his head, shooting a quick look at her. 'You're right, although sometimes I miss being at the sharp end of the action. I spent six years in the Army at one point.'

Jenny smiled at him. 'Ah, so that's where the muscles came from.'

He raised one eyebrow. 'Were you ogling them?'

She laughed, then ducked her head, suddenly shy. 'No! Anyway, if you weren't so busy glowering about your terrible hardships, you might notice more when women swoon over your steely arms.'

Nadeem laughed. 'Are you flirting with me?'

Startled, she crossed her arms defensively. 'No! Not at all!' And the exchange thrust her back into the very memory she was most afraid of. The smell of whisky. The stark whiteness of office walls, and the insistence that she'd been flirting...

Someone was gently shaking her shoulder. Jenny focused on a concerned pair of eyes and a worried frown. 'You're scowling again,' she said weakly, trying to free herself from the memory of a hand moving up her thigh. Her heart was racing and she felt like she desperately wanted to have a shower.

'Damn right I am, I was worried!' Nadeem's voice was quiet, but with a definite note of concern. 'You just zoned out there for a few seconds. Is that normal for you? Are you alright?'

'I'm fine.' Jenny did her best to sound firm, but underneath she was really shaken. She had kind of expected the nightmares, but losing some moments like that? What was happening to her?

Nadeem looked at her suspiciously, as if he knew she wasn't telling him the full story. She crossed her arms and stared out of the window, not wanting to meet his eyes.

Nadeem rubbed his chin thoughtfully. There was definitely something going on that she wasn't saying. In his years as a combat medic, he had come across all sorts of conditions, and he could swear that what he had just seen looked like some kind of absence seizure. Epilepsy maybe. But it would be rude to ask. If she didn't want to tell him it was none of his business.

His brain poked him. *You know what else looks like that? Post-traumatic stress. Raised heart rate, blanking out...*

Something inside him stirred at the possibility that he might be sitting next to someone who had experienced similar things to him. Who could understand what he had been through.

He shook his head to rid himself of the thoughts. Just because he'd experienced PTSD himself, and seen a lot of other cases, didn't mean he had to see it everywhere. It probably was epilepsy. And yes, in either case it would be insensitive to press for more details.

He looked at the lovely woman sitting next to him. One soft brown curl had fallen out from behind her ear, and his fingers itched to smooth it back in place. He stifled the urge; that sort of thing would just creep her out. But he couldn't leave the awkward silence hanging between them.

'Don't worry about it.' He spoke cheerfully, to try and break the tension. 'I am intensely intrigued about why you're flying to Inverness though.'

Jenny raised one eyebrow, and he saw her face relax a little. 'Intensely intrigued...really? What are you, a walking crossword?'

Nadeem shrugged, happy that she had taken the diversion. 'I just can't help myself. Now spill the beans.'

She leaned back in her seat and let out a breath. 'Nothing too gripping I'm afraid. Some long-standing friends of my father recently moved back to deepest darkest Scotland and I thought it would be interesting to visit them for a while. They live about an hour's drive north of Inverness.'

'Sounds good. And have you got any plans?' He smiled at her.

She shook her head. 'Not much. Just relax, sit by the fire, walk their dog, maybe do a few day-trips to places like Loch Ness and so on. I've not been up to the Highlands before. Plus, I really just need a rest.'

'Sounds great. Is someone collecting you at the airport?'

'Oh yes, Alison's coming down to meet me in the car. She said it was a good excuse to stock up on a few things she can't get locally.'

'So you're all set.' He found himself unexpectedly disappointed that he wouldn't be able to offer her a lift.

Jenny nodded. 'Can't wait to have a proper lie-in on Monday morning and think about all the poor people who actually have to work.'

'You hard-hearted woman.' He couldn't help teasing her, and he knew his eyes showed his suppressed laughter, even though he did his best to keep his face straight. She did give him a smile, but he also noticed how she wrapped her arms around herself, as if there was something else on her mind.

He carefully steered the conversation towards impersonal things after that, by giving her a list of good places to go sightseeing. They then fell into a discussion about Scottish politics that kept them busy for the rest of the flight.

As they taxied towards the incredibly tiny airport terminal, Jenny turned to Nadeem again. 'It was good meeting you; I had a fun flight. Thanks for sharing it with me.'

Nadeem smiled back. 'Guess I'm glad that my other flight was cancelled.'

She felt tiny shivers run across her skin at the obvious warmth in his voice. She waited to see if he would ask for her number, but all he said was, 'Have a great holiday.'

'Hope you have a good time tonight.' She wasn't really disappointed, she told herself. He was just a random guy on a plane, and they'd had an interesting conversation.

Nadeem winked cheekily at her as he left the cabin, but by the time she made it into the terminal building he had disappeared. Travelling light, maybe. Or, she thought with a flash of cynicism, he probably still had clothes at his parents' place. She envied pampered guys like that; mainly because they reminded her of the deficiencies in her own family life. Still, the few good friends she had went a long way towards making up for what she had lost.

The bags came out in record time, and Jenny found Alison waiting at the exit. Alison seemed to have changed very little since Jenny last saw her; she was still the same hardy reliable character she had always been.

Jenny kissed her on the cheek, noting as she did so the extra grey strands in the dark brown hair, cut in Alison's usual sensible short style. 'One of the things I love about meeting you is the fact that I don't have to stand on tiptoe to hug you like I do with everyone else.' She smiled happily.

Alison laughed. 'How was the flight?'

'It was fine, I had an interesting conversation with the guy next to me. He seemed a bit grouchy at first but he turned out nice enough once we got talking.'

They reached the tiny blue car and Jenny hauled her bag into the back and clambered into the front. 'How long is the drive going to take?'

Alison backed the car out of the parking slot. 'Not more than an hour and a half, if we don't run into traffic or get stuck behind any lorries.' Her voice was slightly muffled by the ticket in her mouth.

Jenny looked over at her. 'Great, it'll give us some time to catch up. Is David back at home?'

Alison nodded. 'Yes, he didn't want to leave Scotty on his own.'

Jenny rubbed her hands together in excitement. 'That's the dog, right? I'm looking forward to meeting him.'

'I love the new hairstyle, by the way.' Alison reached out and fed the ticket into the machine.

Jenny tugged at a curl unconsciously. The day after her nightmare in the office she had gone to the hairdresser and asked them to cut it into a practical bob, to try and banish the image of fingers winding through it. It was something she would have never considered before; her hair was something she had taken such pride in, and hours of straightening and styling were her usual norm. But now that it was done, she quite liked it. Plus, her natural curls were more manageable this way.

'I needed a change.' She was surprised by how calm her voice sounded. She would tell Alison about what had happened, but now was not the right time. So far, all she had said was that she was between jobs, which was entirely the truth. 'Tell me what it's like living up at the croft.'

'Well, it's nothing like it was in Geneva, but it is stunningly beautiful. It's amazing to think that we've been there almost a year already. We've put in a small vegetable garden and managed to grow some spinach and beans but we think a greenhouse might be a good option for next year.'

'And you don't miss the Swiss high life?'

Alison shook her head. 'Not really. You know the social scene was never my thing, or David's either. And the people who really matter will always come to visit. Klara and Svein came this summer and had a great time, do you remember them?'

Jenny shook her head. She had been too deeply mired in her own problems to really take much in during her Switzerland visit. 'And what sort of work are you doing these days? You mentioned some flexible commitments. I take it you've given up the human rights work?'

Alison nodded. 'These days it's mainly just legal advice for people trying to fight the wind farms up here. We don't charge much unless we know they can afford it; I feel bad asking local people for money. We've both got a pension coming in these days so we do pretty well for ourselves. I do occasionally get requests for advice from my old colleagues, but only on the odd case now and again.'

Wind farms were a divisive topic in the Highlands. Some of the local people were very negative about them, saying they would put off the tourists, while others said they brought employment to the area and were vital for a greener future. Jenny could see both sides of the argument, but she knew Alison was firmly against them, so she kept quiet on the topic.

The rest of the journey flew by as they chatted and Alison filled Jenny in on the history of the area. The road followed the coast for most of the way, and even with the overcast weather the gentle swell of the of the sea was beautiful. The hills rising up to their left were dotted with farmhouses and white cottages, and at one point they crossed a bridge over an estuary where sea birds floated on the calmer waters. Halfway through the journey, the sun finally broke through the clouds and turned the sea into a deep green-blue that took Jenny's breath away.

'I'm so glad you sent me that random postcard last week!' Jenny looked warmly across at Alison. 'It came just at the right time.'

'So I see.' Alison smiled back. 'It's great to see you again.'

Just before they reached Helmsdale Alison pulled off the main road and up a driveway with an old stone cottage at the top. The original house looked as if it had been pretty tiny, but there was a dormer window in the roof, and it boasted a decent extension and a smaller outbuilding which looked like a garage. A grassy garden looked out down the hill over the sea. Part of the lawn was neatly cut, but the edges straggled away into bushes and beyond the hedge was heather and moorland.

The front door opened and a small bundle of brown and white came racing out, followed much more slowly by a lanky grey-haired man.

'Hi David.' Jenny reached up as he stooped for a quick peck on the cheek.

Scotty bounced around them, desperate to be part of the fun. Jenny knelt down to pet him, admiring the Jack Russell's glossy coat while David collected her things from the car.

'I've been telling him how many walks he's going to have while you're here.' David gave her a smile.

Jenny's bedroom was in the roof on the first floor, with sloping ceilings and windows on both sides. The bed – a traditional one with both headboard and foot-board - was covered with a soft white puffy duvet and thick tartan wool blankets to keep out the cold. A luxurious blue carpet covered the floor.

Alison smoothed a hand over one of the blankets. 'I'll give you the rest of the tour.'

It was no time at all before they were sitting out in the glass-roofed conservatory on comfortable chairs with generous glasses of Malbec, while Alison filled David in on Jenny's news.

'I really like what you've done with the space.' Jenny waved a hand. 'This conservatory is great for summer, and that little enclosed lounge with the fireplace must be really snug in winter. And I love the Aga in the kitchen; it must make that quite cosy too. Is it hard to cook on?'

'It takes a bit of getting used to, but I actually like it better for some things.' To Jenny's surprise it was David who spoke. He laughed when he saw her face. 'I may be an old codger, but I do like a bit of cooking now and then.'

'Dad would have loved it.' Jenny smiled. 'You know how he always liked the old-school stuff.'

'Oh yes.' Alison turned to David. 'Do you remember that time when he bought that ridiculously old Citroën and spent ages repairing the engine, only to have it fall out the bottom because of the rust?'

David laughed. 'Yes. We all called him Rusty for ages after that.'

Alison, David and her dad had all been together at university, Jenny remembered. She tried to picture David as a young student and completely failed. She yawned suddenly; the wine and the depth of the cushions were getting to her. 'It'll be an early night for me tonight I think.'

When dinner was over Jenny made her excuses and gratefully sank into bed with a book picked from the bookshelves downstairs. It was a guide for the local area and she thought that she could start to plan out some trips. Her phone showed a weak signal but no internet, so research into other things would have to wait. It would probably do her good to be cut off from the real world for a couple of days anyway.

When she settled back on the pillows, thoughts of the man she had met on the plane found their way into her mind, and instead of opening the book she turned off the light and lay there musing about how strange it was to meet someone and then never see them again.

I wouldn't have minded seeing him again. She hugged herself at the idea, realising that given how dirty that horrible day at work had made her feel, even this thought was a small but important thing to hold on to. She would tell Alison about everything tomorrow. No doubt her older friend would have some useful words of advice, as she had always done in the past. With that comforting thought Jenny drifted off to sleep.

Chapter 2

Nadeem stood in the corner of the main lounge, watching the ebb and flow of the guests as they chatted and sipped at their drinks. Even though there were close to fifty people, the private family party still felt reassuringly intimate. He could see exactly how his mother had managed it using subtle arrangements of furniture and lighting, strategically placed throughout the two main rooms. She was a real pro. He wasn't surprised that she still personally supervised the arrangements for all the major company events, despite the fact that both his parents had taken a step back from the day-to-day running of the family business.

He looked over to where his two sisters were chatting with his mother over glasses of champagne, no doubt catching up on family gossip.

His mother had been the one who had managed the foundation they had set up, while his father took care of the logistics business. Did she regret swapping the challenges of running a charity for taking care of his father? Perhaps, but then his parents were just as much in love as they had ever been. He couldn't blame her for wanting to spend as much time with her husband as she could, given the scare they'd all had with his father's heart attack. So now Nadeem was running himself ragged trying to fill their shoes. Thank goodness his cousin was also helping out; he'd be lost without Derek and all the other people who had stepped up to try and fill the gap while his dad recovered.

He couldn't help his mind slipping back to the woman he had met on the plane that afternoon. The image of those stunning grey-green eyes was stuck in his head, and the protective spark he had felt for her had surprised him. He shook his head at himself. *You should have got her number.*

Mia, his youngest sister, skipped over to him. 'What are you all glowery about?'

Nadeem grunted. 'I met this gorgeous girl on the plane coming up. And I never asked for her details.'

Mia put her hand to her mouth in mock surprise, her eyes teasing. 'You mean that she didn't fall swooning at your feet like all the others? It's probably a good thing anyway, when she found out what a moody bastard you really are, she'd run away screaming.'

Nadeem just glared at her, then couldn't help a laugh. 'Nothing like family to make you feel better.' He nodded towards the other two. 'Are they talking kids again?'

Mia rolled her eyes. 'Of course. But you've got to forgive Dina; the baby's such a new thing. In six months she'll be back to her dentistry again and kids will be old news.'

She took his hand and pulled him towards a small couch that stood against one wall, sinking down gratefully, her long green dress pooling gracefully around her ankles. 'We're doing all the pregnancy rubbish this coming year. There's no way it's going to be as cool as the anatomy and dissection stuff we've already done though.'

Nadeem smiled, knowing that while Mia liked kids as much as anyone, she had her heart set on being a surgeon. It seemed that medical careers ran in the family, which wasn't surprising given that both their parents had been doctors.

He snagged another glass from someone passing with a tray and settled back comfortably into the couch. 'Go on sis, cheer me up. What's the latest local gossip?'

Mia grinned. This was one of her favourite subjects. How she managed to get her information he never knew, although he suspected a lot of it came from their foster brother Jamie, who was still living locally. 'Well, firstly, the wind farmers are trying again.'

Nadeem rolled his eyes. 'What, in the same place?'

Mia shook her head. 'No, a bit further down the coast. Lots of people are fighting it though. And Mrs Morrison is married again.'

'I assume those bits of information aren't connected.' Nadeem couldn't prevent himself from laughing. 'What is this, her fourth?'

'I think so.' Mia ticked off things on her fingers. 'OK. The cafe in the village has been taken over by a couple from Kent, they've gone all organic but still do a great cooked breakfast so that seems to please everyone.'

Nadeem closed his eyes and leaned his head back as she rattled through a list of births, deaths and weddings, mainly involving people who he was unfamiliar with.

Mia leaned towards him, lowering her voice. 'Oh, and apparently the Campbells have some young woman staying with them for a few weeks, so I was thinking someone should see what she's like and maybe we could invite her to the charity gala. I heard she's from London, so she's probably going to be pretty bored up here unless she likes the great outdoors.'

Nadeem's eyes shot open and he sat bolt upright, almost spilling his drink in the process. 'Not Jenny?'

Mia looked at Nadeem strangely. 'Yeah, I think it was, how did you know?'

'I think she might be the one I met on the plane coming up. She'd be great; do you want me to run across tomorrow and check if it's her?'

Mia clapped her hands in excitement. 'Ooh! Yes, do. I want to find as many young people as I can to offset all the old fogeys that Mum and Dad have invited.'

He elbowed her in the ribs. 'Some of the old fogeys are nae too bad, you know.'

Mia sighed. 'I know, I know.' She looked at him with a wry smile. 'And what about you? Are you OK?'

Nadeem frowned. 'What makes you say that?'

She shrugged. 'You're just not yourself today. A moody bastard, like I said. All I've had from you since you arrived is a Happy Birthday and complaints about your cancelled flight. And you turned up a day late. What's that all about?'

Her turn of phrase made him laugh again. 'I'm fine, honest. The reason why I didn't make it here yesterday was because we heard we've won that massive government contract we were bidding for. You know, the one that nobody expected us to.' He had almost been hoping they wouldn't win it, just because of the extra burden it would place on his shoulders, but he would never have voiced that thought aloud. 'We won't have it officially confirmed for another couple of weeks, but I had to make sure some things got sorted before I left the office. So I'm just a bit stressed trying to fill some very big shoes right now. Or two pairs actually. But it's all good.' It had to be. He had no other choice.

He pulled her to her feet. 'Let's get back into the fray, sis. Great as it is chatting to you, we should probably get on and circulate. This is your party after all.'

'But you haven't told me yet about your Tanzania trip.'

'Tomorrow, I promise. I'll tell you everything.'

Mia just stuck her tongue out at him before disappearing off into the hall.

Jenny was woken by the smell of frying bacon. She blinked; the first part of the night had been taken up by the nightmares that were a common theme now and her brain still felt fogged and confused. She rubbed her eyes with her fingers and stared up at the ceiling, which looked a different shape from normal. Then she remembered where she was and a small thrill of excitement sped through her.

There was a faint chill in the air; she was glad of her soft cotton pyjamas and the thick duvet above her. Her stomach grumbled. She jumped out of bed into borrowed slippers and raced downstairs, stopping only to grab the dressing gown that was hanging behind the door.

Alison laughed when Jenny appeared. 'I knew the bacon would do it.' She laid two rashers on Jenny's plate, just as David clumped through the front door with Scotty hard on his heels.

Jenny looked at the kitchen clock; it was almost half past nine. 'I can't believe the time. That's more than eleven hours I've slept.'

'Well, you obviously needed it.' Alison turned back to the cooker and carried on dishing out food.

Scotty was begging silently for something to eat from his place in the corner, a piteous look in his eyes.

'Pay no attention to him, he's had breakfast,' David warned around a mouthful of toast. 'Did you have any idea what you might want to do today?'

'Not sure really,' Jenny mused. 'Not too much. I'd quite like to go into the village to have a look though.'

Alison sat down at the table. 'It's only a twenty minute walk to the village and there's a nice path along the beach. David and I would really like to get some work done in the garden since the weather is good, but if you don't mind being by yourself then you could go this morning. You could take Scotty with you for some company.'

'That sounds great, it also means I can get him out of your hair for a bit.' Jenny cut a thick slice of bread and lathered on a generous layer of honey. It was heavenly.

When they had finished breakfast, Alison rose to do the washing up but Jenny lingered at the table, nervously rolling the edge of the tablecloth between her fingers.

'Alison.' At Jenny's voice the other woman turned around. 'I need to talk to you about something.'

David looked up from his newspaper. He must have seen something in Jenny's expression, because he folded it up and placed it on the table. 'I'll be out in the garden, m'dear.' He kissed his wife gently on the cheek and disappeared out the back door, Scotty right behind him.

Alison came to sit down next to her, looking concerned. 'What is it?'

Jenny felt her heart thudding in her ears, and took a couple of deep breaths to calm herself down. This was Alison she was talking to. The woman who had rescued her at eighteen, when she had left home with a hundred quid in her pocket and no plan as to what she was going to do. Alison wouldn't judge her. She had been more like a mother at that time than Jenny's own mother, who was totally useless.

No, she corrected herself. Her mother wasn't useless, just had her own problems. Eight years of separation had made her realise that, but it didn't hurt any less.

'I've got something I need to tell you.' She leaned forward, bridging the gap, and grasped Alison's hand. The story of the assault at work and how she had subsequently been fired from her job made tough telling, and by the time she finished there was a small pile of tissues on the table in front of her.

To her surprise, Alison's reaction to the story wasn't one of disbelief, but weary acceptance. 'It's more common than you think.'

'For goodness sake, I know.' Jenny shook her head. 'I've read the statistics. I just never thought it would be me. But the way I froze when it was happening still makes me so ashamed. After all you taught me. I feel like I've let so many people down. Including myself.'

Alison squeezed her hand tightly. 'You haven't let anyone down. Especially me.'

'Thanks.' Jenny gave her a half-smile. 'But it's weirder than that. In my nightmares it seems to have got tangled up in all the stuff from before. You know, all that other stuff. That my stepfather did.'

Alison's eyes widened. 'He never did anything like that to you, did he? Because if he did, I swear-'

'No, no.' Jenny interrupted her quickly. 'It was purely mental abuse, nothing sexual. It would probably be classed as coercive control these days.' She had to put a name to it. It was in the past, and he couldn't reach her now. 'But he never touched me like that. Or Bella.'

It was a long time since she had spoken of her sister and the thought brought an ache to her chest. She took a deep breath to try and push it away.

The painful grip on her hand relaxed. 'Thank goodness for that.'

Jenny found herself folding the edge of the table-cloth again. 'But what happened, it's sparked off my panic attacks again. And I seem to have picked up a fear of small spaces.'

Part of her wondered how she could sit here dis-cussing it so rationally, but she knew from experience that the best way to deal with it was to talk about it and Alison was exactly the right person. A career at the forefront of prosecuting human rights abuses meant she wasn't shocked about anything, and that was ex-actly what Jenny needed right now.

'The bit that really worries me, though, is that on the plane, on the way here, I had a flashback. To the exact point where that creep had his hand up my skirt. It was really weird. And really scary.'

Alison frowned, crossing her arms. 'That doesn't sound good at all.'

Jenny tugged a hand through her hair. 'I know.' She paused, searching for the right words. It was so hard to voice her biggest fear. 'I've been going over it in my mind, and I can't help worrying. You hear so many sto-ries about people who push away memories, just be-cause they're too traumatic to think about. What if that sort of thing did actually happen to me when I was younger, and I just don't remember? What if that's the reason why this is all affecting me so badly?'

Alison was silent for a few moments, and then she sighed, twisting the tea towel she was holding around her fingers. 'You really want to know my opinion? I just don't think now is the time to start questioning yourself. Surely something would have come out when you had all that therapy way back when?'

Jenny shrugged. 'Honestly, I just don't know. Nightmares and anxiety are old ground for me. I feel like I can deal with them. But the flashback? It scared the shit out of me. I felt like I was losing my mind. Losing myself somehow.'

She rubbed her arms, as if by doing so she could brush off the memory of how it had felt. 'I saw the doctor before I left anyway, and she's given me a referral to mental health. I just have to wait for my appointment, I guess, and tell them about everything. See what they can do.'

They sat there in silence for a while, Alison obviously mulling over what had been said. 'Do you think you might have PTSD?'

That was one of the reasons why Jenny loved Alison; the older woman was not one to shy away from difficult topics. 'I just don't know. I was wondering if it was something like that, but I need to do some research into it. They did make us read a bit about it at university, just so we'd be aware of what clients might be dealing with, but not in any depth. If it is something like that, then if I can identify the triggers for it then it will really help. My guess is that it's all tied up with this confined spaces thing and feeling trapped. It came on when...' She thought about exactly what had happened on the plane, trying to set aside the emotions and focus on the facts, although she could still feel her heart rate rising in response to the memories. 'Yeah, when that guy asked me if I was flirting with him. So maybe a combination of feeling trapped and unwanted sexual attention, mixed with leftover stuff from feeling totally trapped in an unpleasant situation when I was younger?' She tugged at a curl again. 'Sorry, I'm just thinking aloud.'

'It could be.' Alison nodded. 'I actually put together quite a lot of resources on PTSD a while back for one of my cases. I could see if I still have the details. I'm not quite sure what I got rid of in the move, but I'll have a look. And you can definitely use my laptop to do any research you need; it's all connected to the Wi-Fi.'

'I should have guessed you'd have internet. I totally forgot to ask last night.' Jenny laughed, glad to be able to lighten the mood somewhat.

Alison smiled at her. 'In terms of mental health, there is someone up here you could see if you want. He's very well-regarded locally. You could go private and he'd see you pretty much straight away.'

'A man?' Jenny couldn't imagine describing the intimate things that had happened to her to someone who would have no idea of what it felt like. 'I don't know if I'm going to feel comfortable opening up to a man, particularly about this.' She winced. 'I know that sounds really judgmental. But it's true.'

'Not all men are the same, as you know. And I've heard some very good things about this therapist. He's a lovely person.'

'Let me think about it.' She would, but probably not for very long.

'I do have to also ask, did you go to the police at all?' Alison picked up her tea towel again.

A memory came to Jenny of the last time she had tried to get the police to help her. Her anger still burned at how all the concerned looks from both the officers and social services had turned to pitying smiles once they talked to her stepfather. He had seduced them with his lies and his fake concern for their family and her only hope of escape had evaporated. Not that she blamed them at all; her stepfather could be very convincing. He had used those very same skills to worm his way into her mother's heart and take total control of their family.

She could still hear his voice in her head. *Jennifer is a little troubled. She watches too many horror films, you know.* Things had only got worse after that. So much worse for both her and her sister.

'I just couldn't.' Even considering the idea had given her a full-blown panic attack on her way home from work after the incident, but she wasn't going to worry Alison with that piece of information. 'The thought of having to strip off for forensics, that they might take away my phone…it was all just too much. The most I could manage was to put the clothes away in a plastic bag in case I ever feel capable of doing it at some point in the future.'

Jenny stood up, trying to project confidence. 'I'll do a bit of research later on today. And I have to try and fill in the forms the lawyer sent to file my complaint. I'll get through this, I know I will. Resourceful is my middle name.' She attempted a smile. 'At least my direct boss believed me. He was the one who gave me the details for the lawyer. I like him a lot. He's said he'll give evidence if I need it.'

Alison pulled her into a hug and then touched her cheek gently. 'Just let me know if you need any help with anything; I'd be happy to look things over. Now, you get out and enjoy the sunshine. You really deserve it.'

Back upstairs in her room, Jenny flopped onto the bed and stared up at the ceiling. It was such a relief to have got it all out in the open so Alison knew what was really going on. It was maybe something to do with her childhood, but she found herself instinctively expecting people to judge her when she told them what had happened, and her body reacted accordingly. Thankfully she'd had nothing but support from her friends so far.

The sparkle of sunlight through the trees was really beautiful and she lay there watching it for a few minutes. Alison was right. It was time to enjoy her holiday. Time to get some real clothes on and get moving.

Chapter 3

Jenny dressed simply in her faded blue jeans with a soft peach-coloured cashmere sweater that brought out the sea-green tint in her eyes. Reminding herself that she was on holiday, she settled for a quick swish of mascara and a touch of lip gloss. She dragged her waterproof hiking shoes out of her suitcase, and bounded down the stairs, eager to be off.

Scotty was waiting for her at the door with his lead in his mouth. Jenny grabbed her jacket from its hook by the door, and set off down the drive, waving to Alison and David, who were now both out in the garden in their wellies. She crossed over the main road and as soon as they were well away from it let the dog off the leash. He was quite happy sniffing around by himself as she walked, investigating the rabbit holes that were dotted all over the landscape, only occasionally returning to check up on her as if to make sure that she was still alright.

Jenny was also enjoying herself. To her right stretched the sea, a swathe of never-ending blue, and to her left the hills rose up in a large ridge, brown with heather and green with grass. The clouds scattered shadows along the hillside in the sunshine, and the air was fresh; so fresh indeed that her lungs almost hurt. She drank in deep breaths of it, feeling the difference from the London pollution. A stiff wind at her back made her very glad for the warm sweater she had put on.

She had just started to see Helmsdale appearing in the distance when she noticed a lone figure walking along the path towards her. From the height it had to be a man, probably someone out for a morning walk. He had his head down against the wind, and didn't notice her until they were less than ten yards apart, when he lifted his head and she found herself looking into a familiar pair of deep brown eyes.

'Nadeem?' Her voice was incredulous.

Nadeem looked no less surprised to see Jenny, but instantly a big grin split his face. 'Well, who'd have thought!'

Striding towards her, he swept her up in a big hug and round and round until she was dizzy, Scotty yapping excitedly at his heels until Nadeem set her down.

'Seems like fate wanted us to meet again.' Nadeem gave a smile and a quirk of one eyebrow. 'Are you off into Helmsdale?'

'Yes.' Jenny tried to regain both her mental and physical balance. It was almost as if she had conjured him up from her own thoughts. *You know they always say, be careful what you wish for...*

'Are you sure I'm not dreaming?' She pretended to pinch herself.

'Nightmare, maybe.' Nadeem shrugged, still smiling.

Jenny laughed. 'I was off into Helmsdale to have a look around. I know there's not much there, but apparently it's really pretty.'

'Right on both counts. Would you like me to give you the tour?'

'Weren't you heading in the opposite direction?'

'I was, but now that I've found you then I'm happy to turn back. Since this is my home turf, I'd be glad to show you around.'

Jenny suddenly remembered. 'Of course, your parents. How was the party last night?'

'It was great. It's always good to see family. And not one single argument, which with my extended family is quite an achievement. I spent a bit of time chatting to my sisters; haven't seen one of them in a while.'

Jenny was still struggling to get her head around Nadeem's surprise appearance. 'But seriously, what are you doing here?' She narrowed her eyes suspiciously. 'You didn't follow me from the airport, did you?'

Nadeem laughed out loud. 'No, I didn't. Although I did wish afterwards that I'd got your number. But no, my parents live a few miles away over that hill.' He gestured towards the other side of the village.

'So it really is just a coincidence.'

Nadeem looked a bit guilty. 'Well, kind of. Local gossip has it that there's a good-looking girl from London staying with Mr and Mrs Campbell. I put two and two together and was just walking up to see if it was really you.'

Jenny gaped. 'But I've been here less than twenty-four hours!'

Nadeem just laughed again. 'That's how it is in small villages. Doesn't take long for word to get around.'

Noticing her worried look, Nadeem laid a hand on her arm. 'Don't worry, I wouldn't go blabbing about your personal business. Besides, I wasn't sure it was really you.'

'So you risked a forty minute round trip just to check? That's some hunch.' Jenny couldn't stop herself smiling. His thoughtful care on the plane, and now his obvious consideration for her feelings, touched her very deeply.

'Yeah, well, I'll go a long way to prove that I'm right.' Nadeem's reply was offhand, but when she met his eyes there was something deeper in them that she couldn't quite read. 'Actually, it was sort of my sister Mia that sent me. She wanted to invite you to the charity gala we're having in a couple of weeks.'

Jenny suddenly laughed out loud. The whole situation was so surreal she could hardly believe it, and yet in some way it just felt so right. At Nadeem's enquiring glance, she shook her head. 'I'm just laughing at all of this. You, me, meeting like this, being on holiday in such an amazing place, it's great.'

Nadeem swept her an exaggerated bow, and elegantly proffered one arm. 'Now we have made each other's acquaintance, madam, will you allow me to escort you to the village?' He completely spoiled the effect by giving her a suggestive wiggle of his eyebrows.

'Why certainly, kind sir.' Jenny took his elbow with a silly grin on her face.

As they strolled along next to the white-tipped sea, Nadeem looked down at Jenny. 'Would you mind if I ask you what really happened on the plane?'

Jenny swung her gaze up to meet his, surprise on her face.

'I was a combat medic.' Nadeem shrugged. 'I'm just curious about things like that. I wasn't going to ask at the time, but now that we've met again...'

He must have seen the expression on her face. 'Don't worry, if you don't want to talk about it then don't. I'm not going to make you if you want to keep it private.'

Jenny let out a breath. 'There's not much to tell. I've got some history and I'm suffering for it. I think I had a flashback on the plane.'

'Ah.' Nadeem just nodded. 'I was wondering.' He paused, clearly considering something. 'You think you had one? Are you not sure?'

'It was my first one. I'm still trying to work out exactly what's going on. The events which probably caused it happened less than two weeks ago, so it's all a bit new.'

He nodded again, and she couldn't help liking him more for the way he didn't make a big thing of it. 'I had flashbacks too, you know. After I came back from Afghanistan. Replays of things that happened, things I'd hoped to forget.'

So that explained why he had asked. She breathed a sigh of relief. Here was someone, even though he was a man, who might really understand what she was going through, and even better, be able to give her some insights into what was happening. 'The army...I'm not surprised. Being in a war zone you must have seen a lot of things.'

He nodded fractionally. 'It doesn't affect me as much as it used to. I got some good help and have some great coping mechanisms, so my trauma responses are pretty rare these days. But as you know, not all ugly things happen in war. If you ever need someone to talk to, I'm happy to, but no pressure either way.'

Jenny shrugged. 'I don't really like talking about it. I had a bad experience at work. One of the male bosses.

It was kind of...' She trailed off, her throat closing with emotion.

Nadeem's jaw tightened. 'What a bastard. Let me assure you that if he was here right now, I would have no hesitation in punching him into the sea.'

He placed his free hand on hers where it rested on his arm. 'I offer you a heartfelt apology on behalf of all the male tossers on this planet.'

The feel of his skin against hers made her insides do a quick flip. The thought of her attacker getting a soaking made Jenny giggle, surprising herself, but Nadeem's serious expression also warmed her heart. She placed her hand on top of his, and hugged his arm more closely.

His mouth split in a grin. 'So here we are, two strangers on a beach. Two dodgy damaged deviants, deviously daring to get to know each other...'

Jenny had to laugh at that, and she reluctantly pulled her hand away. 'I knew it. I always sit next to the weirdos on planes.'

'Oh yes.' He laughed. 'Would you rather have some normal conversation?'

That made her smile again. 'Not really.'

The harbour in Helmsdale was lovely and the old stone bridge which ran across the small river was very impressive. A couple of fishermen who were sorting out their boats waved to them cheerily as they strolled by. Despite the attractions of the village the cold wind soon made Jenny wish for a cup of tea, and she mentioned it to Nadeem, who nodded.

'We could go to the cafe at the end of the harbour.'

'How about the pub in the hotel?' Jenny pointed to the one she had noticed as they strolled by. 'It looks nice and cosy. I'm sure they'll do a good cup of tea too.'

'Oh no, you don't want to go to the pub.' Nadeem replied swiftly – too swiftly, Jenny realised.

'What's wrong with the pub?'

Nadeem just shrugged, his face carefully blank.

Light dawned. 'Don't tell me you're barred! What did you do?'

'Not really.' A wry smile turned up the corner of Nadeem's mouth.

'OK, the cafe it is. But only if you tell me why.'

Jenny had meant it as a joke, but Nadeem looked uncomfortable, hesitation written plainly across his face. He leaned back against the harbour wall, a gesture that was supposed to look casual, but Jenny wasn't fooled.

Nadeem cleared his throat, looking directly into her eyes. 'When I first came back from Afghanistan, I pretended to myself that I was OK. I thought the memories I had would fade over time. But every time I closed my eyes they were right there. So I started drinking, and things got a bit out of hand.'

He shrugged, with a nonchalance he clearly didn't feel. 'I wouldn't say I became an alcoholic or anything, but a couple of my most embarrassing moments happened in that pub, and I don't really like to remind myself of them. There's a couple of regulars who always look at me with condescending smiles whenever I go in.'

Jenny moved to rest against the wall beside him, looking out over the harbour and the seagulls drifting overhead. She watched the blue water lapping against the rough stonework, feeling the warmth of the sun on her face. Then she looked up at Nadeem and gave him a tentative smile. 'Thanks for telling me. I think the café will be just fine.'

Over coffee they spoke about their lives in London. Scotty sat happily at their feet with a donated bone, thumping his tail occasionally. Jenny revealed her secret passion for dressmaking and was surprised when Nadeem knew more about it than she would have expected.

'When I was little my mum used to make all our clothes, or alter things she bought from charity shops.' He took another sip of his cappuccino. 'We never had that much money, and with three kids she had to scrimp and save as much as she could while my dad got his business off the ground.'

Jenny sighed. 'I've made quite a few pieces for friends and everyone says that I should do it professionally. But I think it's too much of a jump for me; I don't think I could deal with the stress of not knowing when work is going to come in. Besides, I'd have to save some more money first to set everything up.'

Nadeem leaned back, stretching his elbows out sideways. 'I've been working too hard recently. I used to be a real party animal, but since I started my current job the only evenings I've been out on are with clients.'

'Good-looking clients at least?' Jenny teased.

'Not even that.' Nadeem sighed. 'Most of them are old and boring and very male unfortunately. Although you didn't hear that from me.'

'Not to your tastes then?' She couldn't help teasing him a little further.

'Not at all.' Nadeem's eyes met hers with a gaze that showed he knew exactly what he wanted, and it was sitting right in front of him. She felt her skin tingle.

'So how long are you here for?' Jenny hoped her tone sounded casual.

'I'm here until Wednesday actually. I can do some work from here and to be quite honest, I need a bit of a break.' His voice sounded slightly weary.

'Are you the oldest in your family then?'

Why was she sitting here asking these inane questions? A frisson of fear knotted in her belly. She was so clearly attracted to this man, which some people would have said was weird, given her recent experiences. But she had read about this too. It was a well-known phenomenon; survivors of trauma feeling an intense connection with people they felt they could trust. People who felt safe.

She had missed Nadeem's reply. If she swooned any more she'd end up in a melted puddle on the floor.

As if he could sense her thoughts, Scotty shifted and got up, looking hopefully at her. Jenny checked her watch gratefully. 'I really must be going, it's almost one and I still have a bit of a walk back. They'll be wanting to have lunch soon.'

Nadeem rose in one fluid movement. 'I'll drive you back in the car. I parked it here in the village before I walked up to yours.'

'You don't mind taking Scotty? He's pretty muddy. He won't ruin your upholstery?'

Nadeem erupted in a massive burst of laughter that had her smiling too. 'Believe me, when you see the car I'm driving, you will laugh at the fact that you even asked that question.'

Sure enough, when they rounded the corner into the car park, there stood the most battered white Landrover that Jenny had ever seen. She did laugh at the sight of it. Actually, it was only white if you discounted the large patches of rust and the massive splodges of mud.

'Yes, my parents won't trust me with anything else.' Nadeem put on a woeful expression. 'Something to do with the time that I took their car on an off-roading session when I was only seventeen.'

She had to look carefully at his face to check that he was joking, although she suspected that the story about his escapade was actually true.

Jenny clambered up into the passenger seat, while Nadeem lifted Scotty into the back. She was surprised about the fact that she felt absolutely no qualms about accepting a lift; in London she would definitely have hesitated. But the friendly atmosphere in the village and Nadeem's total honesty had made her feel completely different about it.

At her insistence he dropped her off at the bottom of the drive, and got out to stand beside the car while Scotty raced off up the path. 'I'd love to take you out for the day tomorrow, if you don't have any other plans.'

Nadeem's request made made her turn back towards him. 'That would be nice. I think Alison and David said they had some errands to run so I'm sure they won't mind.'

'Great, would about ten suit you?' He ran a hand through his hair.

Had she just agreed to a date? Was that what she really wanted from all this? And to her surprise the answer was yes. Her eyes met his. 'I'll be ready.'

'Good.' He stood for a second longer, and Jenny thought he might try to kiss her. What would she do if he did? But instead, his hand came up unexpectedly to touch her face, and she felt the warm roughness of his palm caress her cheek just for an instant. Then, flashing a blinding grin, he jumped in the car and roared off down the road.

Jenny looked down to find Scotty staring up expectantly at her, tongue hanging out. 'Don't you even think about saying anything.' She set off up the drive towards the smells of an excellent lunch.

Chapter 4

After a couple of hours on Alison's laptop Jenny had to conclude that PTSD was looking more and more likely, but she was very reluctant to actually self-diagnose. Better leave it to the professionals. Still, being self-informed never hurt, and it would hopefully allow her to make better choices as she went through the mental health system. What was also interesting was that flashbacks weren't a requirement for a PTSD diagnosis, which left the possibility that she had been suffering from it since her childhood, and what she had now was just a more extreme form in some way.

On some strange level it was all very interesting. The habits she had built up over the years to compartmentalise things enabled her brain to analyse everything dispassionately, even though part of her somewhere was screaming in horror at what had happened. It was the only way to carry on. She had a life to be lived, and things that she wanted to do with it, so what other option did she have?

The preparation for her legal submissions came next. The lawyer had warned her that it all had to be done online, and had sent her a list of what she would need when submitting the form. Name and date of birth were easy. But when she looked at the clock and saw that twenty minutes had passed in staring at the place where she was supposed to write the details of what had happened, she realised she had a problem. A big problem.

'Look, work with me here. We need to do this.' She spoke out loud, hoping it would crystallise her words into actions, but it was no good. Every time she looked at the heading, her mind just went blank. Even the words she had used with Alison that morning had completely gone.

If she was really honest with herself, all this was tied up with what had happened in her teenage years. She had learned the lesson very early that avoiding conflict was always easier. Her stepfather had been fine when she had done what he wanted. Being good had been easy; fighting against him had consequences. She shuddered as the careful box she had built around the worst of the memories started to creak open, and she shoved them back down where they belonged. They had no place in her life any more. She couldn't change the past, but she might just be able to change the future.

Sighing, she folded away the laptop and went to join the others. She still had time. Tomorrow was another day. Besides, if she was going to have something to wear for this gala she would have to get cracking and actually sew together the pieces of her latest project that she had brought from London.

Nadeem ran up the front steps and opened the door to the house.

'We're in here,' his mother's voice called out from the dining room.

All of his family were sitting around the big pine table with what looked like a simple lunch of cheese and salad. His parents sat in their usual places at the ends of the table, with his sisters on either side of them. Mia's plate was already empty, which was no surprise; she always inhaled her food like it was going to disappear at any moment.

This table was one of the few things that had come with them from the old house. He could remember doing his homework on it, and countless family meals just like this one. His parents had always been very insistent that they eat together as a family whenever they could.

Nadeem sat down on the high-backed chair next to Mia and took a slice of bread. 'Where's the baby?'

He addressed the question to Dina, but it was his mother who replied. 'Having a nap upstairs. That's why we decided not to wait for you.'

'Never mind the baby, where have *you* been?' Mia turned to him. 'We were just about to send out a search party.' A knowing smile quickly spread across her face. 'Oh. *I* know where you've been. Did you find her? Did you give her the invite?'

'Yes.' Nadeem couldn't help a small smile curving his mouth too.

'Ooh! Deem's in lurve!' Mia made a heart symbol with her fingers and pumped it theatrically against her chest.

'Shut up. Am not.' Nadeem shook his head definitively.

'Am.'

'Am not!'

'For goodness sake, just because you're all back here doesn't mean you have to act like kids again. Break it up.' Their mother's voice was stern, but he could hear some humour in there too.

'Sorry.' They both subsided, although not before Mia had stuck out her tongue at him. He responded by good-naturedly flipping her the finger.

'So what are you all going to do this afternoon?' Their father reached for a slice of the chocolate cake that sat in the middle of the table.

'Weather's pretty nice. I was wondering if anyone would be up for a walk.' Nadeem buttered himself another slice of bread.

Mia groaned. 'Can't, I'm afraid. They sent me my pre-reading for the new semester this morning. It's a total nightmare. I have to sit down and work out a strategy for getting through it all.'

'Dina?' He turned to her but she was staring out of the window, clearly not listening to the conversation. He touched her arm and she swung her head towards him.

'Sorry? What did you say?'

'I said I thought I might go for a walk this afternoon. Do you want to come?'

She gave a small shake of her head. 'Sorry. Not really feeling like it.'

'Oh, come on.' He gave her a gentle poke. 'Don't be such a wimp.'

He was expecting a pithy retort, but instead she just stared at him with a stricken face for a couple of seconds and then burst into tears and fled the room.

Their mother rose to go after her, but Nadeem waved her down. 'I'll go. It was my fault.'

He found Dina outside, sitting on the wooden bench by the herb garden. 'I brought your coat. Didn't want you to get cold.' He held it dangling from one finger.

She climbed gratefully into it. 'Thanks, bro. You're the best.' Her face wobbled again, and then she swallowed and got herself under control.

Nadeem put an arm along the back of the bench so it was sitting around her shoulders. 'What's going on, sis? That's just not like you.'

Dina let out a long sigh. 'I don't feel like me at the moment. I didn't want to tell you because you've got so much else going on, but post-natal depression is biting hard, and every day is a struggle. Medication is helping, but things are still not great.'

'Oh, Dina.' He pulled her closer to him. 'You know it will pass eventually, right?'

'I know. That's the only thing keeping me going right now. The trouble is, I was hoping coming up here would make me feel better, but seeing how capable Mum is with the baby just makes me feel even more inadequate.'

He couldn't help a laugh escaping him. 'I'm sure by the time you get to your third you'll be just the same. You're barely three months into your first. Give yourself a bit of a break.'

She shuddered. 'God. I don't think I could do another one, let alone three.'

He squeezed her tightly. 'I'm glad you told me, anyway. I've been far too tied up in work to really notice what's been going on. Sorry I've not been there for you more.'

Dina shook her head. 'I can't blame you for that. You and Derek have taken on the bulk of the work supporting Mum and Dad, which takes a massive weight off my mind too.' Then she looked across at him. 'Mia was right, you know. You did have a look about you when you walked in. A sort of glow or something. I can't really find a better word for it.'

He shook his head, not sure what to think of this information. 'I do like her. But it's never going to be a thing.'

'Why not?' Dina's face was puzzled.

He bit his lip, struggling to find the words for what was in his head. 'It's hard to say. As much as I try to pretend I have a normal life, I'm still dealing with the fallout of everything that happened in Afghanistan. I feel like I just can't trust myself with someone else's life given how much I ballsed it up last time. And if I can't trust myself, why would they trust me? I know that's not logical, but it's what I've got to live with.'

'Everyone deserves love though, and when you find the right person they will love you in spite of everything.' Dina rested her head on his shoulder. 'In fact, that's one of the other reasons I had to come up here. When I'm at home then Mo just keeps - well - *hovering*. With this stricken look on his face. I just couldn't sit there and watch what it was doing to him. But he loves me just as much as he ever did. Even through all of this shit that's going on.'

Nadeem blew out another long breath. 'It's a different situation though. The two of you met while everything was fine. And of course Mo's not going to give up on you now, he's a good guy.'

'He is, isn't he? He told me yesterday he's coming up for the party, and I know the only reason he's doing that is to take care of Kami so I can have a good time.'

'I'm so glad you've found someone who loves you.' Nadeem kissed the top of her head gently. 'But it doesn't mean that everyone gets to have a happy ending. And I just don't think there's going to be someone out there for me.'

Monday morning was warm, but the forecast was for sunshine and showers, so Jenny made sure she dressed in her hiking shoes and her grey waterproof jacket, stuffing a small umbrella into her rucksack. She took a couple of apples and a banana from the kitchen just in case she got hungry, although she was hoping that Nadeem was going to take her somewhere that she could have a proper lunch. She was starting to get her appetite back, and had ravenously eaten both lunch and dinner the previous day. It must be all the fresh air. She did love London, but it was so nice to get away from the bustle of the city just for a while.

Alison and David had already set off to see some potential clients further up the coast, Scotty with them in the car. When Jenny had told them her plans for the day, Alison just nodded. 'His parents ran the medical centre down in Brora until a few years ago. I'm not sure exactly what they're doing now, but I've never heard a bad word about them. I'm sure you'll be fine with him.' It had reassured Jenny that her earlier instincts were correct.

When she heard the Landrover drive up to the house Jenny felt a small thrill of excitement. Grabbing her bag, she carefully locked the door and turned to face him as he stood by the car. He was dressed in practical clothes; dark green waterproof jacket, blue combat trousers and outdoor shoes. He smiled warmly when he saw her. 'I do like a girl who knows how to dress for all weathers.'

Jenny felt a warm glow inside at the note of appreciation in his voice. He opened the passenger door for her, waiting while she climbed in, and shut it after her, then climbed into the driver's seat and buckled his seatbelt.

'I do like a boy who knows how to act like a gentleman.' Jenny couldn't keep the laughter which was bubbling up inside her from showing in her voice.

Nadeem laughed, putting the car in reverse. 'Good, I'm glad we've got that sorted. I wasn't sure if you'd be the kind of person who would rather slap a man in the face than have him hold open a door.'

Jenny looked over at him, noting the capable way he handled the wheel. She wondered about the callouses she had felt on his hands and where they came from. 'Wow. You sure do take some risks. How did you know I wasn't the violent type?'

His eyes met hers. 'I didn't. I just figured that I'd be able to handle whatever you threw at me. It's a skill I learned in the Army.' Then he shrugged, pretending to look resigned as he pulled out of the driveway and turned south along the shore road. 'Sometimes these are just risks a man has to take in the pursuit of chivalry.'

Jenny rolled her eyes. 'Oh, purlease. Isn't that all a bit old-fashioned?'

Nadeem glanced across at her, eyes sparkling, but when he spoke his tone was deadly serious. 'Not chivalry in the traditional sense, I guess, but I do believe in treating women properly. Well, treating everyone properly really. I've seen enough bad things happen to want to try and do things right.'

Jenny sobered as she thought about some of the things he must have seen. 'Is Afghanistan really as bad as the media makes out?' She twisted her hands together in her lap.

Nadeem nodded. 'Yes, although it's also a place of amazing beauty with some incredibly generous people, so it's not all bad. But I didn't mean just over there, I mean everywhere. I see far too many people not treating other human beings with respect, when it doesn't actually take that much effort.' He dipped his head, obviously slightly embarrassed. 'Sorry, I didn't mean to start with a lecture first thing.'

'It's fine.' Jenny waved a hand. 'I mean, I've spent my life trying to do the right thing. Especially with my family. I just wish that they'd realise it.'

Nadeem glanced over at her. 'Tell me about it. Families are always tricky.'

Jenny wrapped her arms around herself. 'From what you've said though, you seem to get on well with yours. Mine just seemed to all go down the pan after my dad died. It's almost as if he was the one holding my mother together and she just lost it after that.'

'Yeah, love is pretty important.' There was a note of warmth in Nadeem's voice.

Jenny glanced at Nadeem, surprised. 'I hadn't pegged you as a romantic.'

He frowned. 'The love I'm talking about isn't really romantic. It's the one that makes you keep on trying, even when you're so frustrated with the other person that you really just want to slap them.'

Jenny laughed. 'Sounds pretty romantic to me. I just had to give up on my family. The whole situation was just sucking too much out of me and I had to call it a day.'

Nadeem looked over at her, clearly shocked. 'You cut them off? Isn't that a bit extreme?'

Jenny shook her head. 'The situation was pretty toxic. My mother suffers from depression and it seemed that the more I tried to support her, the more dependent she became on me. My stepfather is a pretty horrible man too and it all just got too exhausting.'

Nadeem looked as if he was going to argue with her, so she tried to divert him, ignoring the brief flash of irritation that she felt. 'Where exactly are we going?'

He smiled. 'Well, I thought you might want to see a proper Scottish castle. It has suits of armour and everything.'

'Wow.' Jenny was excited. 'That sounds great.' And she breathed a sigh of relief when he didn't ask anything more about her family.

It wasn't long before they turned off the road and swung through an impressive set of gates with a lodge on either side. They drove up a tree-lined avenue and into a large gravel car park. The sight of the castle took Jenny's breath away; it was like something out of a fairy tale. She had been expecting a medieval style castle, but this looked more like some kind of French château, or the pictures she had seen of Neuschwannstein in Germany.

Jenny looked up at the sky, which had clouded over. 'Shall we do the house first, then hope for some sunshine while we go round the gardens?'

Nadeem nodded in agreement. They paid for their tickets and took their time going through the opulent rooms. There were a few other visitors, but it wasn't busy, which gave her the chance to really soak up the atmosphere of the place. The thick stone walls made the inside feel very secure, and Jenny couldn't help thinking about all the people who must have occupied the castle since it was built. Some of the windows had stunning views looking out over the sea. Her favourite room was the library, although she wasn't so sure about the two lion skin rugs on the floor.

They came to a bathroom with antique plumbing and magnificent green and gold tiles, and a huge old-fashioned porcelain bath. Jenny pointed at it. 'I wouldn't mind having that in my bathroom. If I could squeeze it in.'

Nadeem considered the bath for a minute. 'I wouldn't complain. It looks like it might be big enough for two.'

Her face heated. The thought of her and Nadeem, naked in the bath together, skin to skin, made something tighten in her belly and an unexpected wave of longing swept over her. To hide her thoughts she turned away, pretending to read the leaflet they had been given. Her heart was beating uncomfortably fast and her palms were moist. 'I think we're almost done in the house. We should probably go and have a look at the museum.'

They strolled through the castle grounds to the small museum, and Jenny admired how neat the gardens were. The sun had come out, and was glinting off a deep blue sea. Nadeem took off his jacket and slung it over one arm.

The museum was a jumble of animal heads mixed with African artefacts and although Jenny had a good look, she felt it was a bit of a strange collection of objects, and wondered how many had been taken from their far-off lands without consent. She was starting to lose interest when she came across a couple of very impressive suits of armour, intricately engraved and jointed.

Seeing her interest, the warden hastened to explain exactly where they had come from, and which family members had worn them. 'As you might guess, back then might was right. It wasn't much fun being a woman. If you weren't rich enough to have your own castle, you'd be stuck wondering which army would be through next to rape and pillage to their heart's content.'

Men taking advantage of women. It was a common theme, as Jenny knew all too well. The memory that the day's distractions had pushed from her mind suddenly threatened to overwhelm her and she put a hand to her mouth, feeling sick and dizzy. She prayed it wasn't the onset of another flashback; not here, with people watching. Nadeem suddenly appeared at her elbow and glanced at her, frowning. 'Are you alright?'

She shook her head, not trusting herself to speak. She didn't know whether to close her eyes to stop the dizziness, or keep them open to minimise the chance of unwanted visions.

Nadeem put an arm around her waist, hugging her close. Given the memories threatening to engulf her, she had expected to be repulsed by his touch, but instead his warmth felt like a light in the darkness. He guided her out of the museum, waving away the concerns of the warden, and sat her down on a nearby bench, kneeling down beside her and taking one of her hands.

He rubbed her wrist, looking worried. 'You've gone deathly pale. What happened?'

She shook her head, gesturing to the small group of gathered onlookers. 'Not here, not like this.' The last thing she wanted was an audience. The warden must have seen Jenny's gesture, because she quickly guided people back into the museum and left them alone.

The sunlight gently warmed Jenny's skin. She sat for another few minutes, staring into nothing, while Nadeem waited on the bench beside her. He wrapped her hand in one of his, and she let him do it, taking strength from how warm his felt in comparison to hers. Finally, she glanced over at him. 'Could we walk a bit?'

'Sure.' Nadeem helped her to her feet, dropping her hands as they started off slowly along the hedge-lined path.

They found a secluded grassy slope that looked out towards the sea and sat down. Jenny picked a blade of grass and rested her arms on her knees, staring out to sea. She twisted the green strand between her fingers, not knowing where to start. Did she really want to share her story with this man?

She looked over at Nadeem, and saw the warmth and concern in his eyes. In a flash she realised that if she wanted them to have any type of meaningful relationship, whatever form that would take, she had to be honest with him.

'I got a new job just a couple of weeks back.' Her voice sounded uneven, even to her, and she swallowed a couple of times to compose herself. She looked back out to sea, knowing that if she didn't, she had no hope of carrying on. 'I was so happy to find it, because it actually used some of my legal training and it paid much more than my supermarket job. All my colleagues were great and my boss was brilliant. But the head of the company was a total sleazeball.'

It felt easier to tell it in the past tense, as if it was a story that had happened to someone else. She twisted the grass around her fingers, not daring to look at Nadeem's face.

'At first it was just the odd sexist comment, which I ignored, but it got steadily worse. He would ogle me from his office doorway, and stand too close to me when we were talking.' She stopped, trying to calm her breathing again as the memories flooded over her. Nadeem shifted beside her, as if he was going to say something, and she hurried on, anxious to get it all out before she lost her nerve.

'I didn't know what to do. I really needed that job – no, scrap that, I really wanted that job, I loved working there – so I thought I could handle one jerk. It was always just so subtle, so hard to pin down.'

She laced her fingers tightly together, fighting to keep control of her voice. 'Until the day he called me into his office and I fell for the oldest trick in the book.'

She couldn't stop the words now, couldn't stop them tumbling over each other as she carried on, and the movement of her hands twisted the green strand she still held into a knot. 'He trapped me against a filing cabinet and shoved his tongue down my throat. And violated me.'

It was still hard to believe that he had really had the nerve to do that in an unlocked office where anyone could have walked in on them.

The blade of grass finally snapped. She heard Nadeem swallow next to her, and didn't dare to look at him. He cleared his throat, and spoke very quietly.

'And did you nail the bastard?' She could hear the barely controlled fury in his tone.

It made her feel good to know that he felt the same burning anger as she did. It warmed her heart and made the sunshine seem just a little brighter.

She shook her head. 'Not yet. I'm trying. They fired me for complaining about it, so I'm having to put in a legal claim. And I seem to have a mental block at the moment about putting it down on paper in all its graphic detail. But I'll get there eventually.'

He looked at her, as if assessing something. 'I'm sorry.' His voice was quiet, as if he didn't know what else to say.

She looked him in the eye, noting the warmth of his gaze. 'It's fine. I don't want you to feel sorry for me. I'm not that person. It's something that happened to me; it doesn't define me.'

The tears came running down her cheeks, and that was when Nadeem pulled her close and cradled her against his chest. The gentle strength of his arms felt like a protective safety net. When she finally raised her head and drew away, he looked at her, concern for her written clearly on his face.

'You don't have to ask.' Jenny gave him a firm nod. 'I do feel better for that. A lot. So thanks.' She took a deep breath and let it out, feeling some of the tension drain away from her shoulders.

Nadeem shook his head. 'That wasn't what I was thinking. I was wondering if you might be ready for some lunch.' At the mention of food her stomach rumbled loudly and Nadeem laughed. 'I guess that's my answer.'

He got to his feet, pulling her up with him. 'I was going to have lunch here, but if you think you can wait another fifteen minutes, I'm going to take you somewhere special.'

'More special than this?' Jenny waved at the surroundings incredulously.

Nadeem shook his head. 'Not more impressive, definitely, but somewhere special to me.'

'OK.' Jenny was relieved that he hadn't turned her experience into a major issue, but as a medic he must have seen some fairly awful things. He was probably used to listening to people's stories. She smiled at him. 'Just lead the way.'

Chapter 5

They drove back up the road for a few miles and then Nadeem turned off onto a small single-track road which led up and away from the coast. Jenny couldn't help sneaking glances at him as he drove; he definitely knew the twisty tree-lined road well from the way he capably handled the car. She studied the stubborn angle of his chin and noticed that he had shaved again this morning. Was that for his parents, or had he made the effort for her? Her hand itched to reach out and touch his cheek, but she stopped herself. It wouldn't be good to distract him while he was driving.

He caught her looking at him and smiled, a warm smile that did funny things to her insides. She blushed, embarrassed that she had been caught staring.

It wasn't long before the trees thinned out and Jenny realised that the road ran along beside a wide river. A high peak rose on the other side, all browns and greens and purples with the heather. A bit further on the river widened out into a large lake.

Nadeem parked the car in a little lay-by, and turned to her. 'This is it.'

Jenny jumped down from the car. Nadeem opened the back and took out a wicker picnic basket.

'Gosh.' Jenny was impressed. 'Is that one of those ones with the proper plates and knives and forks and everything?'

'Yup.' Nadeem hefted it in one hand. 'Although don't expect champagne and strawberries.'

'You're driving anyway,' Jenny pointed out. 'And strawberries are out of season.'

Nadeem gave her an odd look, as if he couldn't quite make out whether she was joking or not. With his other hand, he reached back into the boot and took out a picnic blanket. 'Here you go, catch.'

He tossed it to her. Jenny caught it neatly and tucked it under one arm.

'Tell me we're not going to have our picnic in that field with those sheep.' She pointed to where a number of them were grazing on the other side of the fence. One of them lifted its head to regard them solemnly.

'No.' Nadeem sounded amused. 'Where we're going is down there.' He pointed down a grassy lane that had dry stone walls on both sides. They set off, and Jenny noticed that he deliberately slowed his long-legged stride so that she could keep up easily. It was another mark in his favour and she realised that she was really starting to like him.

The lane ended in a stile, and on the other side of it a short path led down to the lake. Loch, Jenny corrected herself mentally; it must be, they were in Scotland. The path ended suddenly in a small cliff, and she exclaimed in pleasure as she realised that below the drop was a beautiful gravel beach, completely hidden from the road. Nadeem jumped easily down and held out his hands for the blanket. She tossed it to him and then crouched on the edge, wondering if she dared jump down. It was almost as high as Nadeem's head.

Before she could think too long, she felt strong hands around her waist. 'I'll help you.' He started to lift her down, but somehow his hands slipped and she found herself sliding down his front. By the time he set her on her feet she was slightly flushed and when he withdrew she was sorry. But he had already turned away to spread out the blanket in the sheltered spot below the cliff.

Nadeem flung himself down full-length onto the blanket and patted the spot next to him invitingly. Jenny's stomach rumbled again; she really was very hungry. She settled herself down on the blanket, resting her back against the large log that someone had thoughtfully placed in just the right spot. Nadeem was already opening the basket where it sat between them. She was relieved to see that it at least had plastic plates in it; she didn't like the thought of real china out here on the rocks.

'This is a lovely spot.' She gazed out across the loch, which was lightly rippled by a soft breeze. On the far side a large cliff fell steeply into the water and somewhere high up above them a skylark sang. It seemed idyllic in the warm sunshine.

'I used to come up here all the time when I was younger.' Nadeem unpacked a foil-wrapped tray of sandwiches, all neatly arranged.

Jenny stared. 'Don't tell me you made those yourself.'

He had the grace to look slightly embarrassed. 'No, my mother sorted those out, she's very good at that kind of thing. I have no clue what's in them. Now you're going to tell me that you're vegetarian or something.'

Jenny couldn't help laughing at his face; he looked so serious. 'Nope, can't help you there.' She took one of the sandwiches and took a bite; it tasted like crab. 'Not bad at all. Congratulate her for me.'

Nadeem burst out laughing, and Jenny looked at him, surprised. He just shook his head. 'I'm so glad I met you. It's great to have someone so easy to talk to. And you're funny, too.' He took a sandwich from the tray.

Jenny frowned. 'You say that, but I seem to have been the one doing all the talking so far. If you don't mind, I want to hear your story too. With all its gory details.'

Nadeem shook his head. 'Trust me, you don't. I don't want to give you my bad memories on top of everything else you're dealing with at the moment.'

'Look, if you don't want to share things with me, don't. But don't use the excuse that I'm too fragile just to avoid talking about the difficult stuff.' She poked him in the ribs, trying to lighten the mood.

Nadeem ran a hand over the back of his hair. 'It's just – well – I'm not sure if I want to re-hash it all right now. It's kind of old news. You know the most of it anyway. I was enjoying just spending time with you, here, in one of my favourite places.'

Jenny knew a brush-off when she saw one, but she also didn't want to push him into it. Just because she had revealed personal things didn't mean he had to do the same. She turned to study the view. It was beautiful how the cliffs rose out of the loch, and the fluffy white clouds scudding across the sky made it look even more idyllic. They both sat there in silence for a while, munching away, enjoying the gentle lap of the water and the sunshine on their faces.

When all the sandwiches were gone, Jenny motioned towards the basket. 'Is there anything else in there?'

'Well...' Nadeem flipped the lid open with a smug smile and lifted two huge wedges of chocolate cake out onto plates. Another dip into the basket turned up a pot of cream, which he dolloped generously on top. He handed her one of the plates, and then rooted around in the bottom of the basket.

He came up looking a bit confused. 'She forgot to put any cutlery in.'

'Are you sure?' Jenny was puzzled too; it somehow didn't fit with the precision of the sandwiches. 'Don't worry, fingers will do.'

She carefully broke off a small section of the cake and put it in her mouth. 'Mm, this is amazing.' She licked her fingers slowly, then realised Nadeem was looking at her strangely.

Jenny scooped up a fingerful of cream and put it in her mouth. It was only when she saw Nadeem closely following her every move that she realised the effect she must be having on him. She couldn't help a laugh escaping her. 'So how is your cake?'

The corners of Nadeem's lips curled upwards. 'Erm...soft...sweet...luscious...' His smile was wicked now.

Jenny felt her heart flip over in her chest. Oh, he was attracted to her, and no mistake. Still, she tried to spin it out just a little longer, taking another bit of cake and chewing it slowly, savouring the sharp taste of the chocolate mixed with the sweetness of the filling. She was just about to lick the chocolate off her fingers when Nadeem pointed to them. 'May I?' His eyes glinted dangerously.

She hesitated fractionally, then nodded and relinquished her hand to his control. She was already turned on at thought of what he was going to do, but when he took her thumb into his mouth heat seared through her body and she bit her lip. His mouth was hot and wet, and his tongue flickered over her skin tantalisingly. He slowly sucked her fingers one by one, keeping his eyes on her all the while.

'Are you enjoying this?' Jenny tried to focus her thoughts.

He quirked one eyebrow. 'Mm-hm.' The vibrations sent a fresh wave of pleasure shooting through her body.

When he had removed the last trace of chocolate from her hand, he clasped it in his own and pulled her gently towards him, rescuing the basket from between them and placing it over to one side.

'You have a chocolate smear on your lip.' He gave a satisfied smile. 'I think I just have to help you with that one too.'

Jenny just closed her eyes and tilted her face up to meet his. He kissed her gently at first, curving one hand around the back of her neck. She opened her lips, welcoming him in as he took it deeper, her body aching for his caring touch. She could sense that he was still holding something back and she knew he was waiting to see if it was too much for her. Her heart swelled at the thought that even in the midst of his desire he might be so thoughtful about her, and in answer to his unspoken question she reached up and tangled her fingers in his hair, deepening the kiss until she lost all thought except the feeling of the contact between them. All she could think of was getting closer to him. She reached over and slipped a hand between his thighs.

He suddenly broke away and Jenny looked at him, confused. 'What's wrong?'

He cupped her cheek. 'Oh Jen, I want you so much - but not here, not like this. I want to take things slowly, especially given what's happened to you.'

It was true that this wasn't really the ideal place for an al fresco liaison. As if to make his point, at that moment a pair of ramblers appeared on the top of the cliff on the other side of the loch. Their shouts and waves broke the spell, and Jenny and Nadeem waved back half-heartedly.

Nadeem leaned back on the blanket and held out his arms to her, and she snuggled close, resting her cheek against his shoulder. He stroked her hair gently, twirling his fingers slowly through the curls.

'I think we may have to leave the rest of the chocolate cake.' His voice was regretful. 'You eating any more is going to cause me serious issues.'

Jenny lifted her head, looking him straight in the eye. 'I don't know. Maybe I could feed you?' A wicked smile curved across her lips.

He shrugged, pretending to look nonchalant. 'I don't mind giving it a try.'

It took quite a while for all the cake to disappear. When Jenny was once more snuggled up under Nadeem's arm, she suddenly spoke again. 'Your mother seems so organised. Do you think that she left the spoons out on purpose?'

Nadeem let out a short, sharp laugh, which startled Jenny into sitting up. 'You know, I wouldn't put it past her.' A wide smile crossed his face. 'She is a bit of a romantic.'

Jenny laid her head back on his chest, staring up at the sky, where white wisps of cloud floated against the brilliant blue. 'This is a lovely place. How did you find it?'

He curved one hand around her waist while the other played with her hair, disentangling the curls one by one. 'I used to come up here when I was about nine or ten, on my bike, with my friends. Mum and Dad met while they were both working in a hospital in Edinburgh. My dad's from up here, and when the local doctor retired he came back to Brora and brought my mother with him. They didn't mind if we came up here by ourselves as long as there were a few of us.' He smiled, remembering. 'I think I smoked my first cigarette here, and I definitely drank my first bottle of beer in this very spot.'

Jenny turned her head and looked up at him, surprised. 'Cigarettes? Beer? When you were nine or ten?'

'No!' He hastened to correct her far-out impressions of his childhood. 'When I was eleven I went down to school in Edinburgh. I stayed with an uncle, my mother's brother. But I still came up here in the holidays.' He laughed. 'The beer episode was funny. I think we were only about thirteen. My best friend Nate and I nicked a couple of bottles from my parents' stash and came up here with my cousin to try it out. Looking back, I think it must have been pretty strong stuff. We shared them between us and then fell asleep and missed dinner. There was a hell of a row that evening when we were late back. But they never found out about the beer.'

Jenny laughed too, picturing the scene. 'So you were a bit of a rebel. I'm kind of surprised that you decided to go into the Army then.'

'I wasn't that bad when I was a kid. But actually joining the Army was a bit of a rebellion in some ways. My parents were dead set on me studying medicine; they wanted me to become a surgeon. I stuck it out for a semester but as soon as I turned eighteen and got my freedom I packed it in and enlisted instead. Nate joined up too, he said he fancied travelling the world and seeing the sights. But I somehow couldn't get away from the medicine side of it; once they knew I'd been studying anatomy they persuaded me to become a combat medic and train up for that. I guess I'm glad really; it meant I had to shoot at fewer people.'

From the tone of his voice, he evidently had no regrets. She was enjoying the way his fingers played with her hair; it was almost lulling her to sleep.

'So what's Nate doing now?'

Nadeem's hand stilled suddenly on her head. 'He died.'

Jenny flushed, not knowing what to say. 'I'm sorry.' She closed her eyes fully so she had an excuse not to see Nadeem's face.

Nadeem stroked her hair softly. 'Don't be. It happens. Like you said, war is ugly. The good guys don't always win, and the heroes don't always come home safely.'

Jenny gently squeezed his hand. 'But you came home safely. Surely Nate would have wanted that.'

Nadeem was silent for a while. 'It all depends on what you call safe. There were times afterwards I thought I wouldn't make it. I think if it hadn't been for my family – especially my sisters and my cousin – I wouldn't be here today. I still cut myself up about some of the things I did at that point.'

'What kind of things?' Jenny leaned up on her elbow to look at him.

Nadeem sighed. 'I've lost track of the number of times one of them held my head after I threw up from drinking too much. When I think back to that, especially as Mia was only a kid back then, it makes me cringe.'

He grimaced. 'I think my lowest point was when I ended an argument with my mother by storming off in her car – completely over the limit of course – and totalled it into a dry-stone wall. I think that was what really gave me my wake-up call. The reason I crashed was because I was driving on the wrong side of the road and had to swerve to avoid a car coming in the opposite direction. I guess it was because I hadn't driven a car on the left for a good number of years, having been abroad for so long. They told me later it was a family with three kids and if we'd hit head on then we could have all been killed.'

Jenny looked up; the chill that she had felt sweeping over her was not just her imagination, or solely driven by the tone of the conversation. A big cloud had crept over the sun and she shivered; without the warmth it felt more like the September day that it was.

'So there you go, that's my embarrassing history revealed.' Nadeem wrapped a corner of the blanket around her. 'I'm glad the day's a bit chilly, because otherwise we'd be swarmed by midges by now. And, I wouldn't have an excuse to do this.' He gathered her close to him.

'What about your job now? What do you really do?' Jenny wanted to divert him away from his sombre mood.

He sighed a deep breath that made her head rise and fall against his chest, and Jenny wondered if she had chosen the wrong topic. 'I've just recently taken on a lot more responsibility at work, and I sometimes don't have a clue what I'm doing. Until about six months ago I was teaching first aid in Glasgow and I loved it. Now it seems that all I do is paperwork and entertaining potential clients.'

He clasped her free hand in his, and toyed with her fingers. 'These last six weeks I was in Tanzania, setting up the groundwork for a big building project. I loved my time over there, but I wouldn't have had that chance if someone else hadn't been ill at the last minute and I was the only one with the right skills to go.'

'Ah, so that's where you got that tan line on your wrist.' Jenny was glad to have made the connection. 'I thought you'd been on holiday in Spain or something.'

'Pah.' She felt his laugh through his chest. 'If you ever catch me on a Spanish beach you'll know for sure that I've gone soft.' He lifted his hand, looking at it with a smile. 'Amazing how you notice the little details. I wore a watch when I was away because I didn't want to flash a fancy phone about unnecessarily.'

'So what do you really want to do?' Jenny couldn't help asking.

Nadeem shifted restlessly, his fingers playing with the blanket. 'I don't know. More doing. Less managing. But I guess the higher up an organisation you get then the harder it is to do that.'

'So why don't you go lower?' Jenny rubbed her cheek against his chest, enjoying the smell of him and the feeling of being wrapped up safe and warm.

Nadeem blew out the breath he had been holding in. 'You make it sound so easy, you know that? But sometimes it's more complicated. There are other people I want to help, people who are important to me.'

'Sure, but in the end it's your life. You can love someone very much, but they might not want what's best for you.'

'Anything specific you have in mind when you say that?'

'My mother.' Jenny's frustration seeped into her voice.

Nadeem laughed. 'I've been very lucky with mine, I know.'

'It's not that. When my dad died she just tore my sister and I out of our existence without a thought for whether that was what we wanted or not, and took us away from all our friends.'

Jenny clearly remembered the day, just a couple of months after her father had died, when she had come home to find her mother packing.

'What's going on?' she had asked.

'We're going to live with your grandparents.' Her mother had been curt. 'Go and find Isabella and help her pack her things.'

'What, Grandpa? But he's really old.'

'No, not him. My parents, your grandfather and grandmother.'

Jenny had been puzzled. 'How come we've never seen them before?'

Her mother had turned on her with a terrible face. 'Just go.'

Jenny had gone into her bedroom, and found her seven year old sister trying to squash all her toys into her suitcase.

'No, not like that.' Jenny had grasped her arms gently. 'You'll need some clothes too. Let's pick out some nice ones, OK?'

Bella had looked up into her sister's eyes, lip wobbling. 'I'm scared, Jin-Jin.'

Jenny clearly remembered just sitting down on the suitcase and pulling her close.

All her fears had been realised that day, Jenny reflected. They had been stuck in a rambling house with a mother who flitted between depression and intense episodes of social partying. Her mother's parents had been kind enough, but seemingly incapable of giving her the love that she had craved. It was so different from the warm home full of laughter that she remembered from her early childhood. And then her stepfather had come onto the scene and things had gone from bad to worse.

Nadeem's voice interrupted her reflections. 'What makes you so sure that she didn't have those thoughts?'

Jenny rubbed her forehead. 'I was twelve. That's definitely old enough to have an opinion. She could have just asked.'

This was getting dangerously close to revealing things about her personal history that she didn't want to think about. Had her mother just moved back in with her parents because she didn't have any other option? Or was it just the easiest thing to do?

Jenny sat up and checked her phone; it was after five. Where had the afternoon gone? 'Shouldn't we be getting back? The sun will be going behind the hill soon anyway.'

Nadeem smiled lazily at her, a smile that made her want to kiss him again. So she did, carefully and thoroughly, and by the time they surfaced again the sun had indeed dropped below the hill opposite and there was a definite chill in the air. They gathered up the scattered plates and re-packed the picnic basket, and took a slow stroll back to the car. As they clambered into the front seats, he turned to her with a contented look on his face. 'I had a great day.'

She smiled back, the warmth of his gaze heating her all the way down to her toes. 'I did too. Thanks for taking me out.'

'I'd love to take you out tomorrow too, if you'd like. I don't want to monopolise your time, but I only have a few days up here, so I'd like to make the most of it.'

Was it her imagination, or did he look nervous? Was he expecting her to refuse? She nodded firmly. 'I'd like that too. I'm sure Alison and David won't mind.'

'Great, would about nine in the morning suit you? I know it's early, but I'd like to take you somewhere special.' He ran a hand through his hair.

'What, more special than this?' Her tone was teasing, remembering their earlier conversation at the castle.

Nadeem rolled his eyes. 'OK, not more special, just different special. You'll find out tomorrow. But bring some old clothes and if you have some wellies then that would be perfect.'

'Sure.' She'd be able to borrow some from Alison. 'I'll just check with them tonight that they haven't made any plans and let you know.'

He whistled as he turned the car and set a course for home and Jenny felt a rush of warmth for him. Nadeem was thoughtful and caring, and made her feel safe with him, which given her recent experiences seemed like a miracle. She was definitely going to make the most of every moment they had together.

Chapter 6

After dinner Alison lit the fire and made some tea, while David disappeared into the study.

'So.' Alison looked at Jenny meaningfully. 'How are you getting on with young Nadeem?'

'He's not that young.' Jenny couldn't help a smile. 'But you were right. He is nice.'

Jenny didn't want to mention exactly what had happened. If Alison found out about the second episode then she might insist on a visit to the therapist she'd mentioned, and as for all the good stuff? Well, that was a secret to hang on to for now. Although if the knowing smile on Alison's face was anything to go by, it probably wasn't a secret any more.

When the washing up was done, Jenny forced herself to take the laptop from Alison's desk and retreated to her room. There was no point waiting any longer to get things written down. She needed to work out how to let go of that fourteen-year-old girl she'd once been and gather her courage to fight this as a grown-up woman.

She spent a few minutes holding in her mind the anger on Nadeem's face when she had told him her story, and the way his arms had felt when they were wrapped around her. Then she imagined Alison in a Wonder Woman costume, battling the forces of evil with her bare hands. All that broke through her mental block enough that she could begin to type. As she wrote she found herself reliving the experience, but in some strange way it helped, being able to recall the events so clearly. After a few tweaks to the wording she was satisfied it was as good as it could be. And then she burst into tears.

Half an hour later she slipped downstairs to where Alison and David were watching a film. They looked up as she came in, and she held out the laptop to Alison. 'Could you read what I wrote, and let me know what you think?'

Alison flicked the remote to pause. 'Do you want it now, or can I do it tomorrow? My eyes are a bit tired for reading this time of night.'

A smile spread over Jenny's face as she realised how much of a relief it was just to have got it all down in words. 'Tomorrow will do. There's no rush.'

True to the forecast, the weather dawned fine and dry the following morning. Jenny was up and waiting outside by the time Nadeem drove up the drive. A pair of Alison's wellies was in one hand and her back-pack was slung over her shoulder. She noticed he had a small trailer attached to the back of the Landrover.

'Morning.' She called out cheerfully as he jumped down from the car. He was dressed the same as her in a pair of old jeans and a faded t-shirt. A navy-blue fleece kept off the morning chill.

He strode over and wrapped his arms around her in a big hug. She relaxed into his hold and then squeaked in surprise as he lifted her up and swung her deftly into the car, before taking his place behind the wheel.

'Wow, someone's in a hurry this morning.' She couldn't help a wide grin forming on her face. He just made her feel so happy. Myself, she suddenly thought. He makes me not afraid to be myself. And the realisation brought a lump to her throat.

Nadeem looked at her with an almost conspiratorial look and she realised that he felt the same bubble of excitement that was welling up inside her. She grabbed his shoulder and pulled him towards her, planting a firm kiss on his cheek.

He looked at her searchingly. 'What was that for?'

'For whatever is in that trailer. Somehow I know it's going to be good.' Her eyes sparkled.

Reversing with the trailer was something Nadeem hadn't done for a long time, and for one moment he wondered if he was going to make it. He tried to ignore the distraction that was sitting next to him, with the sexy curve of her thighs in those skinny jeans and the faint apricot scent that drifted across from where she was sitting.

Nadeem dragged his mind back to the manoeuvre he was making and in no time at all they were heading up the coast in the bright sunshine. He wondered if he'd be able to keep his hands off her today. Not that she seemed to mind, but the last thing he wanted to do was push her too far. They still knew so little about each other, and he was painfully aware that if he wasn't careful there was a big chance of him triggering her trauma responses. Still, he couldn't let that cast too big a shadow over their day. This was a chance to just spend time with someone who made him feel good. He would just have to relax, enjoy the moment, and when he went back home they could just say their goodbyes and call it a day.

'Are you going to tell me where we're going?' Jenny's voice disrupted his thoughts. He glanced over at her, marvelling again at how gorgeous she looked; soft pink skin and brown curls with her red mouth to set them off.

'Nope.' The corners of his mouth turned upwards wickedly.

She sat back in her seat, crossing her arms, pretending to pout. 'You want me to beg. But I'm not going to. I can wait.' A satisfied smile crept across her face.

'Don't worry, I'll have you begging before the day is out.' As he made the joke, an image suddenly flashed into his mind of Jenny naked in bed, asking him to make love to her. He hardened painfully at the thought, and glancing over, he saw from the flush at the base of her neck that she was probably having pretty much the same mental images.

This was such a minefield. He knew from his own painful experiences that one minute someone could be just fine, and the next, the trauma could make them into a completely different person. He vowed then and there that he wouldn't push her to do anything until she was completely ready. Yes, ready and begging him for it.

'Earth to Deem, Earth to Deem.' Jenny was laughing, and he realised that he had missed her last comment.

He dragged his thoughts back into the real world. 'What was that?'

She reached up a hand and rested it along the back of his neck, playing with the short fuzz at the base of his hair. 'I was just asking if we had another equally impressive picnic lunch for today.'

Nadeem turned towards her, putting a look of horror on his face. 'I thought you were bringing lunch.'

She swiped at the back of his head, laughing. 'Liar! We both know that you agreed to sort it out. I've brought a couple of apples so that's your lot.'

When they turned off the coast road and started climbing up through a valley, Jenny started eagerly looking around; this was new scenery for her. There were endless sweeps of hillside with heather. The road curved up and around and at one point they passed a tiny station which was little more than a platform and a notice board.

'A station? Out here? In the middle of nowhere?' Jenny was incredulous.

Nadeem laughed. 'For some reason they keep it going. But I've heard it's a request stop.'

Jenny couldn't believe it. This was so far from London with its bustling crowds that it seemed like another planet.

They finally pulled off onto a dirt road and after about half a mile it came to an end. The moorland stretched out ahead, with a rough track leading off into the distance. Nadeem parked the car carefully at the side of the road and put his wellies on, then jumped out to uncover the trailer. Underneath the tarpaulin was a quad bike.

'Wow,' Jenny was impressed. 'I've always wanted to have a go on one of those.'

Nadeem smiled, unfolding the end of the trailer and pulling out a couple of ramps. 'Sounds like you're my kind of girl.'

Jenny swapped shoes for her own wellies, while Nadeem carefully reversed the bike down the wheel ramps. He clambered into the back of the car, emerging with the same picnic basket and blanket as yesterday and also two helmets. They looked like the ones Jenny had seen on scooter riders in London.

'This is my mother's.' He held a maroon one out. 'She's about the same height as you, so I'm hoping it'll be a good fit.'

Jenny took the helmet and tried it on. It was slightly small, but it wasn't too bad.

Nadeem fastened the picnic basket to the back of the bike and then swung one leg over and patted the seat behind him invitingly. 'Here you go.'

'Hang on.' Jenny wasn't quite ready yet. 'I take it you have plenty of water with you?' When Nadeem nodded vigorously, she took just her purse and a tiny bottle of sun cream out of her backpack and added them to the basket. Nadeem gave her the keys so she could lock her bag in the car, and with that done she clambered up and sat behind him. Her legs hugged his and she wrapped her arms around his waist, making the most of the well-placed opportunity to run her hands over his stomach.

'Much as I'm loving what you're doing, you'll probably do better if you put your hands on my shoulders.' Nadeem's voice brought her back to reality. 'Once we get going it'll be a bit bumpy and I don't want to clash heads.'

She did as he instructed, and the feel of his muscles under her hands gave her a thrill.

'Oh, and once I turn the engine on it will be a bit noisy, so you'll have to shout. If you need me to stop or anything just give me a couple of taps on the shoulder.'

She nodded, and he put his own helmet on. The engine was pretty loud, but not too bad, and they zoomed over the cattle grid and set off up the hill. Once she got the hang of how the bike dipped and bumped over the rough track, she started to really enjoy herself. The bright sunshine beat down on her shoulders, and with the warmth of the engine underneath her she soon started to feel slightly overheated. Or was it something to do with the feel of Nadeem's well-toned bum between her thighs?

After about fifteen minutes Nadeem pulled the bike to a halt just in front of a small stream and hopped off, switching off the engine.

'Why are we stopping?' Jenny tilted her head to look up at him.

'I thought you might like to have a go.' He nodded towards the handlebars.

She made a face. 'You've got to be kidding.'

He shook his head. 'No, please do, it's really easy. I think my arms are long enough so that I can reach around you from behind if I need to rescue things. Plus, we've got to cross the stream and I thought you might like to drive through it as a bit of an adrenaline thrill.'

'You want me to be the one who gets wet, more like.' Too late, she realised the double meaning that could be read into her words and glanced over at him. The glint in Nadeem's eyes told her that he had noted it too, and they both dissolved into laughter.

Nadeem showed her how to start the ignition and which handle to turn to rev up the engine, then he jumped on the back behind her. His long legs curved around her hips and his arms cradled hers, supporting them. She could feel his warm breath on the back of her neck, and suddenly found it very hard to concentrate on driving. She tried hard not to lean back to meet his warmth, but found herself doing so almost unconsciously. Was it her imagination or did his thighs squeeze her tighter?

She shouted over the noise of the engine. 'I thought you said it wasn't good to get too close?'

'Oh yes, I forgot.' She could hear the smile in his voice.

He did pull away slightly as they splashed through the stream and bounced over the deep ruts in the track. Jenny was sorry but also glad; he was enough of a distraction just sitting behind her, without his entire body leaning against hers. Being on the quad bike was something like riding a strange type of horse; it actually took quite a bit of effort to steer and keep her balance at the same time.

When Nadeem pointed for her to leave the track and go straight up the hill, she stopped the bike and looked back at him questioningly. He nodded and shouted in her ear. 'There's an old cairn at the top of the hill. Best way to get there is straight up.'

Jenny squinted up the slope. It looked pretty bumpy, but she totally trusted Nadeem; if he said that was the way to go then it must be doable. She twisted round on the seat. 'You don't want to do it?'

He shook his head, grinning. 'You're doing great. Go for it. There aren't any major potholes on this bit, so we'll be fine.'

Heart in her mouth, Jenny started slowly up the hill.

By the time they got to the top and she killed the engine next to the cairn, her legs were trembling so much she didn't know if she'd be able to stand. To buy herself time she pulled off the helmet and shook out her hair; the cool breeze felt good. Nadeem hopped off and held out a hand. When she swung her leg over and jumped to the ground she almost fell and he had to catch her.

He smiled down at her. 'It does take a lot of concentration the first time you do it.'

Jenny looked up at him. 'Yeah, I thought that it would be almost like driving a car, but in fact the rough ground means there's a lot of muscles involved as it sways from side to side. I'm sure I'll feel it in my legs tomorrow.'

Nadeem looked at her tenderly, smoothing her curls with one palm. 'I'm sorry, sweetheart, but that helmet mark on your forehead looks so cute I might just have to kiss you.'

'Yes please,' she breathed, bringing her face up to meet his. His mouth was soft and tender and left her aching for more.

Suddenly she felt him laugh and he pulled away, looking down at her with a satisfied smile. 'I guess I should take it as a compliment that you haven't even looked at the view yet.'

Grasping her gently by the shoulders, he turned her around until she was facing the other way, and Jenny exclaimed in delight. The hill rolled gently down away from where they stood, and below that was the sparkling blue of the sea, with the narrow strip of brown sand that marked out the beach. Down to her right she could see the way they had come up, and to her left was another deserted valley where a small herd of deer was grazing. They were high enough up that she could see the wind turbines far out at sea and make out something that she thought must be an oil rig.

Nadeem's arms came over her shoulders from be-hind and wrapped around her, hugging her to him. She leaned against him briefly, enjoying the way it felt to have something solid behind her.

They sat down in the sunshine with their backs against the cairn. Jenny had expected it to just be a pile of rocks, but it was much more sculpted and provided the perfect place to sit.

Being with Nadeem just felt so healing, somehow. While his kisses were amazing, just sitting here in the sunshine, shoulder to shoulder, was something wonderful too. It was as if all his gentle tenderness and respect was slowly erasing the trauma of that awful day at work.

They were silent for a while, drinking in the view. Finally, Jenny spoke. 'You know, we could have walked up here, it's not that far.'

'True.' Nadeem shaded his eyes to look back down where they'd come from. 'But after this I want to take you on further. There's a stunningly beautiful valley which you can't really reach by car and it would take all day to get there on foot.'

'Fair enough. I just hope that we've got enough petrol; I wouldn't want to have to walk out if we get stuck.'

'Not going to happen; we've got a spare tank on this thing.' Nadeem pointed towards the bike. 'If we run out on the first one, the second one will give us enough to get back.' He pulled a face and pretended to look affronted. 'This is me you're taking about. I don't leave anything to chance.'

Jenny looked at him, and felt something melt inside. 'You know, I have to thank you.'

Nadeem looked puzzled. 'What for?'

Jenny shrugged. 'For this. For making my holiday so great.' She could feel her eyes getting moist, and swallowed, trying to get rid of the lump in her throat. 'Recently things have just been so horrible, and somehow I'd lost my faith in everything. But you, with your openness and honesty, it's just been so refreshing. I feel like I can really be myself again.'

Nadeem was silent; he seemed to be pondering something. Then he suddenly jumped up. 'I'll be back in a sec.' He dashed off without anther word. Jenny was puzzled; was it a sudden toilet break?

A few minutes passed, and she was just starting to get worried about him when he appeared from behind the cairn and flung himself down beside her, lying on one elbow. He had some greenery in his hands. 'Sorry about that, but it took me ages to find a white one, and that's especially important.'

She squinted at him suspiciously. 'Are you sure the sun hasn't touched your brain?'

He laughed. 'No, I think the damage was done long ago.'

Focussing on his fingers, she saw that he had exactly three sprigs of heather in his grasp. 'So what are those for?'

He handed her the first one. 'Well, purple, that's the easy one, that symbolises admiration. But I think you already realise how much I like you.'

The little sprig in her hands was indeed covered in tiny delicate purple flowers. She lifted it up, noticing how they all ran down one side of the stem like a miniature set of foxgloves.

Nadeem was already handing her the second. 'White, that's the one that took ages to find, that symbolises protection from danger. If you need me at any time, you just have to give me a call.' He handed her the third one. 'And pink, that's for good luck, which I have to say you'll need if you're spending time with me. I seem to always attract the worst sort of trouble.' He winked at her.

Jenny stared at him with her mouth open. 'I'm sorry, but did you just turn into some kind of Victorian etiquette book or something? How the hell do you know all that kind of stuff?'

Nadeem laughed again. 'I wish I could show you the look on your face right now, it's priceless.' He pointed down at the heather in her hands. 'Everyone thinks that being in the Army means endless days of slogging through mud and adrenaline-filled gunfights. But really, a huge part of it is just waiting around for things to happen, with not much diversion except the other guys and free internet if you're lucky. You'd be amazed at the useless garbage I've picked up.' He took a mock swipe at her, which she dodged neatly. 'Anyway. Here I am trying to be all romantic and you're just completely missing the point.'

Jenny's heart did funny things in her chest. 'I'm not.' She looked down at the three sprigs in her hands, so tiny and yet so symbolic. 'I'd love to keep them, but I don't have anywhere to put them.'

Nadeem pondered for a minute, then flipped open the lid of the picnic basket. 'I'm sure I put some serviettes in here.' He pulled one out and handed it over to her. 'You can press them properly in a book when you get back home.'

As they stowed the heather safely away in a side pocket so it wouldn't get damaged, Jenny found herself thinking about his comments about the Army. 'What happened to your friend Nate?'

She caught the look of anguish which he flashed at her and added quickly, 'You don't have to. I mean, I don't want to pry. Just ignore me. You've already told me so much.'

Nadeem looked at her for a long moment, eyes unreadable. Then he took a long deep breath and let it out slowly, leaning back against the cairn. 'God, Jen, what is it with you? Most other people would be happy with idle chit chat, yada yada yada, but no, you have me wanting to reveal the darkest parts of my soul before you've even asked how old I am.'

Jenny blushed uncomfortably. She looked down, toying with a bit of grass. 'I'm sorry. Just forget it.'

Nadeem reached out and gently coaxed Jenny's chin upwards, cradling her face with his palm. His eyes were very tender. 'It's not a criticism. In fact, that's one thing I found really hard to adjust to when I came back home; out there people are fighting for survival and back here all most people are concerned about is the price of petrol and whether the latest celebrity has had surgery on their bum.'

Jenny had to smile at that. He let go of her and lay down on his back, resting his head on one of her thighs, and was silent for a long while, staring up at the sky. Jenny kept quiet, looking out at the view. The sunlight sparkled off the sea. It really was a perfect day. In fact, in another few minutes she would have to get out the sun cream.

Nadeem lay still for such a long time that if it hadn't been for the fact that his eyes were open, she would have thought he had fallen asleep. She studied him as he lay there, his long legs stretched out across the grass. He had taken off his jacket at some point, and his faded blue t-shirt stretched over his body in a very pleasing way. A spike of hair was sticking straight up at the top of his head, and she couldn't help reaching out a hand to smooth it down. He twisted his head around, looking up at her.

'Sorry, didn't mean to disturb you.' She smiled at him.

He smiled back, the corners of his mouth tilting upwards in that way she loved so well. 'I was just wondering where to start. There's so many places to do it.'

She was confused for a moment, then realised he must be still talking about Nate. 'It's fine. I mean, you really don't have to.' She smoothed her hand over his hair again.

Nadeem yawned and stretched, enjoying the feeling the sun was giving his body. He felt so much more relaxed than he had done for weeks – months, actually, if he was completely honest about it. And, looking at Jenny as she sat there, with that cute rosebud mouth and a serious look in those gorgeous eyes, he realised he did want to tell her about it, which came as a surprise because it was the first time he had felt like that.

It was probably something to do with the fact that she would understand at least some of what he had gone through, even if the cause of her trauma was totally different. His family tried to understand, but it just wasn't the same as actually living it. He rolled over onto his side so that he could look at her face more easily.

'It's OK.' He unconsciously repeated her reassurance. 'I think I kind of want to. You see, it has pretty much defined my life for the past seven years.' He paused, making patterns with his finger in a patch of dirt.

'There's not much to tell, really. We were out at night and the guys in front of us ran into an IED. We all came under heavy fire. Nate got shot in the leg – I saw him go down – and I dragged him into an abandoned house for shelter. It was only once I got a good look at him that I realised they'd got him in a couple of other places and he was losing blood fast. I patched him up as best as I could, but somehow we'd got separated from the others and the comms weren't working.'

He paused to catch his breath. He could see the whole image in front of him as if it had been last night: Nate, his face filled with pain, still trying to joke with him as he frantically worked to try and stop the bleeding. 'I had to decide whether to leave him to try and get help, or to follow procedure and stay with him and hope that the other guys would come and find us before he bled out. I chose to leave and get help.'

Would he really have done anything differently if he had the chance to change it? Would the end result have been the same? His hand was making frantic patterns in the dirt. He stilled his movements, swallowed, and kept his voice purposely steady. 'I was only gone a few minutes, but by the time I got back they had got to him, the bastards. He had taken down two in the doorway, but the guy who was left had blown his head to smithereens.' *And I let him down big time*, he thought fiercely. Tears pricked at the back of his eyes. He looked up at Jenny again, locking his gaze with hers. She bit her lip nervously, but said nothing, obviously waiting for him to continue.

'At first I thought I was OK, but then I realised I wasn't, and that I needed to get out. But of course I pretended I was fine; I had another four months to go, and the last thing I wanted to do was "wimp out". By the time I got home I was a wreck. The nightmares, the flashbacks, the spiral into drinking and all the rest I've already told you about.' He closed his eyes, his voice taut. 'I often dream that I'm back there and no matter what choice I make it's always wrong.' His voice broke, and he cleared his throat hurriedly.

Nadeem felt a gentle hand on his hair, and another one settled on his shoulder. He expected her to speak, but she still didn't say anything, so he just lay there, listening to the peaceful sounds all around him, thankful for the feeling of being close to her. 'I just wish I'd got to say goodbye, that's all. If I'd only stayed with him...'

Jenny spoke from above him. 'I think, when you're very good friends with someone, you don't need to say goodbye.'

He thought about what she had said for a moment, debating if that was really true. Then another image sprang into his mind; of looking back at Nate just before ducking out of the doorway, and seeing him flash a grin and give a two-fingered salute. That had been their way of saying goodbye since they were very small; and he had no idea why he hadn't remembered it until now.

He opened his eyes, squinting against the sunlight, and pulled her gently down until she was also resting her head on his legs. He ran a hand through her curls, savouring how real she felt, with the heat of the sun in her hair. She had given him some hope of redemption in his own mind, and his heart was so full he didn't trust himself to speak. So he just lay there, pretending that this day could last forever.

Jenny had watched Nadeem's face go through a hundred emotions, but she realised as he finally smiled that he looked somehow younger. The cleft in his forehead was smoother now, and some of the signs of strain had gone from around his eyes.

She laughed, remembering something he had said earlier. 'So now we've got the tough stuff over, how old are you actually?'

Nadeem laughed too, a deep hearty sound which startled her. 'Guess.'

She shook her head. 'I never do. I always end up insulting people.'

He laughed again. 'Well, eighteen, plus six in the army, plus seven-ish after.'

'So thirty-one. Man, that's old,' she joked, wanting to lighten the mood.

'Don't I just know it.' He seemed glad to play along. 'You just wait until you're thirty-one, then you'll know how I feel.'

'What makes you think that I'm not?' There was a challenge in her voice.

He shook his head, mouth turned down. 'Nope, not buying it. There's no way you're older than twenty something.'

'You're right, of course. My twenty-sixth birthday is in a couple of months.'

Nadeem smirked, obviously pleased with himself, so she jabbed him in the arm. They ended up in a tussle on the ground, which she lost all thoughts of winning when he started kissing her.

It took a couple of minutes before she could bring herself to complain. 'Hey! You play dirty.'

'You know what they say, all's fair...' He sat up, grinning, then reached out a hand. 'You've smudged your mascara. Let me just sort it for you.'

He gently wiped it away from her cheek, then took her hands and pulled her to her feet. 'I think it's time we got a move on.' He gestured to the expanse of hills. 'The best is yet to come.'

As they wended their way back down to the car, Jenny couldn't help a sigh of contentment. The afternoon had been magical; there were a multitude of special images in her head now, stored away for future rainy days. Seeing a herd of deer up close had possibly been the most amazing. She and Nadeem had been lying in the heather taking a break and the deer had passed by almost on top of them.

She was very quiet during the drive back home along the coast.

'Everything OK?' Nadeem put a hand on her arm as he spoke.

Jenny turned sparkling eyes towards his. 'Oh yes. I'm just trying to take it all in. Actually, to *drink* it all in. It's been an amazing day.'

'Really?' Nadeem's voice was suddenly husky. 'Look, I really need to spend some time with my family to-morrow, otherwise they'll disown me. But I'm coming up again in a couple of weeks for the gala, and I could probably sort out a day or two beforehand to take you out again as well. Would you like that?'

She nodded enthusiastically and he flashed a quick smile at her, obviously happy at the prospect of seeing her again.

When Jenny came through the door Alison was in the kitchen, preparing the dinner.

'I've looked at that thing for you.' She waved her potato peeler. 'It was pretty good. I've just made a few minor suggestions.'

Jenny gave her a kiss on the cheek. 'Thanks. I'll take a look now if there's time before we eat?'

'Of course.' Alison nodded.

'You don't need any help with the dinner?'

'Shoo.' A tea towel was waved in her general direction. 'Go get it done and then you won't have to keep thinking about it.'

It didn't take long to transfer everything to the on-line form. As Jenny went to hit the final confirmation her hand halted, hovering over the mouse. There was no certainty over where this would lead her. But her lawyer had said that she could pull out at any time, if she didn't want to continue, so there was nothing to lose. It was totally the right thing to do. She took a deep breath and pressed the button.

Chapter 7

Jenny was walking with Nadeem along a beautiful beach with the warm sun shining down on them. Her toes dug into the soft white sand, while the cool sea swirled gently around her ankles. She looked up at him and caught him smiling down at her. It was only when she saw the palm tree that she blinked, confused, and found herself opening her eyes in bed as the remains of the dream faded away.

The light was creeping in around the curtains, which meant it was probably time to get up. Something felt different this morning, but she couldn't work out what it was. She yawned and stretched, luxuriating in the feeling of the soft sheets and the comfy pillow. Her body felt different too. Then she realised what it was; she couldn't recall a single nightmare from last night. She couldn't remember any of her dreams actually, apart from the one she had woken up with, which had been pretty special.

Whether that was because of Nadeem, or just being away from London, she didn't know. And she didn't really care. Hopefully it was a sign that she was coming to terms with everything that had happened and was ready to move on. Submitting the evidence that would start the process had felt like a weight off her chest yesterday.

Humming softly, she slipped out of bed and pulled on some clothes. Today was the day that David and Alison were going to take her up to Loch Ness. She couldn't wait to see the place and try to get a glimpse of the famous monster.

David had insisted that Jenny go in the front of the car so that she could see the view better, but in the end she spent most of the journey turned round backwards to talk to Alison, who filled her in on more history of the area.

'Oh, and don't forget to keep an eye out for the haggis,' David interrupted.

'Haggis?' Jenny was puzzled.

'They run around in the hills. That's why they have one leg shorter than the other.'

It took Jenny a moment to work out that he was joking. 'And tell me, pray, when is the hunting season?' She had to bite her lip to keep herself from laughing.

David's eyes were twinkling. 'Oh, all year round, we're not particular.'

By the time they got to their destination Jenny knew more facts about Loch Ness than she had read in the guidebook, and a lot about the monster of course.

They had a great day out, but Jenny couldn't help feeling that something was missing and she realised it was Nadeem. She missed the casual way he touched her body which made her feel cared for. She missed the way he made her laugh, especially when she was taking herself too seriously. And the thought that his absence could downgrade what should have been such a special day made her slightly worried. She couldn't afford to let anyone control her emotions to such an extent. Not again.

Jenny had to admit she was falling for him, and didn't know what to do about it, especially because they hadn't yet discussed what would happen to their relationship when she got back to London. She wondered what he was doing with his family. The thought that he was so close but so far away made her feel a bit unsettled.

'Are you alright?'

Jenny jerked herself out of her own thoughts to find Alison looking at her. That was both the upside and downside of being with Alison; she didn't miss anything. It was another reason she made such a good lawyer.

Jenny nodded, trying to look reassuring. 'Just thinking, that's all. Seems like I haven't had enough time for that recently.'

Alison nodded understandingly.

David winked at her. 'Just be careful. Too much thinking's dangerous.'

Jenny volunteered to go in the back of the car on the way home, and Alison and David chatted away in the front while she closed her eyes and pretended to sleep. The truth was that at the start she hadn't really thought about what would happen when Nadeem went home. She hadn't really minded. But now she found that she did really care, and she realised it was bugging her that she didn't know whether he was really taking things seriously or not. She would have to make sure she got things straight with him before she got back to London, but until then, surely, they could just take it one day at a time.

Her resolute attitude lasted all the way through dinner and up into her bedroom, when her resolve suddenly crumbled and she sagged on the bed, face in her hands. She had come up to Scotland to get away from everything, not to be thrust into another emotional whirlpool. She felt trapped between her nervousness about what might happen if they did take things further and what she knew would be disappointment if they didn't.

Jenny reached for her phone, fully intending to call Nadeem to tell him she couldn't see him again, and saw a message on the screen.

Had a gd day? N. x

She massaged her forehead. Was that bad timing, or good? She found herself replying. *Great thanks. U? x*

The reply came back so quickly she wondered how he had time to type it. *Gd thx. Seemed like sthg missing tho. Cant wait til I cu again :) xx*

And with that Jenny knew she was lost; she could no more call it off than she could have grown wings and flown back to London. She just had to ride out the rest of the holiday and deal with whatever happened.

Can't wait either, she typed back.

The response made her smile. *Sleep well, will b dreaming of u. x*

Same, she wrote.

She caught herself smiling again as she went to brush her teeth and decided to keep it that way. She would just have to trust that she could handle whatever life threw at her.

Nadeem picked up his mobile to make the call, then put it back down again on the bedside table. He wiped his damp palms on his sleeves, then laughed out loud at himself. He, who had dashed through gunfire to rescue wounded casualties and who was never normally at a loss for words, was scared witless at the thought of talking to a woman. But that was the problem, she wasn't just any woman. He had no idea why he felt this way, but he knew that meant she was something special.

He settled himself back against the headboard of the bed, took a deep breath, and dialled the number. One ring, two... and then he heard Jenny's voice on the other end.

'Hi.' He could hear the smile in her voice. She would have seen his number come up on the screen, he reminded himself.

'Hi.' He felt like a schoolkid on a first date. 'Sorry I couldn't call yesterday, something came up at work and I didn't get home until well past midnight.'

'I'm gutted. I'll never forgive you.'

For one awful moment he thought she was being serious, but then he had to laugh and just like that all his nerves were gone.

'Just give me a sec,' she said. He guessed she was moving to somewhere more private. A door opened and closed. 'All good now. So tell me. What's new in the, erm, 51 hours since I saw you last?'

He shrugged, forgetting that she couldn't see him. 'Nothing much, just work as usual.'

There was a pause on the other end of the phone and then she spoke again. 'Can I ask you what kept you so late yesterday, or is it top secret?'

He blinked, surprised that she wanted to know about his work. Or was it that she didn't believe him? 'It's a long story, I'll warn you now. Are you sure you want to hear it?'

'I'm lying on my bed right now.' Jenny sounded amused. 'If you hear a snore that means I've dropped off, otherwise I'm all good.'

Her comment about the bed brought a smile to his lips. 'Fully clothed?'

Jenny laughed, the deep rich sound that always slightly surprised him coming from someone of her small size. 'Yes. I could take some of it off, but it's bloody freezing in here.'

He could hear the tantalising curve of her lips in her voice, and it made him long to kiss her.

'Besides,' she added, 'phone sex is never as good as people make out. Pun intended.' She giggled childishly at her own joke.

He had to laugh then. 'And you being an expert on all things sexual?' he teased.

The silence down the phone cut through the mood like a knife, and he cursed himself for his choice of words. Not for the first time, he wondered if he could cope with the whole situation. He didn't want to mess up with someone who deserved better.

He needed a distraction. 'The story you wanted to hear. Well, it all started with a stray dog in Amsterdam...'

It was only when he put down the phone that he realised that they had been talking for over an hour. That had to be a record for him, and he had barely noticed the time passing. What's more, he couldn't wait to talk to her again. Elated, he undressed and stretched out in bed.

But sleep, when it came, was filled with the kind of nightmares worse than he'd had for a while. He dreamed of that night in the mountains, soaked to the skin with both rain and the blood of his best friend. He was used to that but this dream had a new twist; every time he thought he'd woken up it turned out he was still asleep and things replayed again. He finally awoke in his own bed, drenched in sweat and heart beating wildly.

With the light switched on, he stared stubbornly at the ceiling. What was happening to him? It had been a while since he'd had a nightmare as bad as that. Moving to Glasgow, spending time out in the hills with some good friends; all of this had helped. Maybe it was just the stress of trying to fill his parents' places at work.

He shrugged, trying to think rationally. Really, it was only natural that talking to Jenny about it all would bring things to the surface. He headed towards the bathroom. A quick shower would sort him out, and then he would try catch another few hours of shuteye.

Jenny caught herself singing while she hemmed the bottom of the dress, and smiled to herself. It had nothing to do with the fact that today was Wednesday and she would be seeing Nadeem in less than forty-eight hours. Of course it didn't. But every now and again she had to stop and hug herself at the thought. Or pinch herself to check that she wasn't dreaming. They had talked almost every day since he'd left, and she had to admit that the more she found out about him, the more she liked him.

Not only that, in the past two weeks her nightmares had gradually receded, as she'd hoped. She'd had a confirmation back from ACAS that they'd received the details of her complaint and would be in touch as soon as they could, so there was nothing more she could do there.

She lifted the smooth fabric and let it run through her fingers, smiling to herself. Alison had taken her on a shopping trip the previous day and had gifted her some shoes and a small handbag to match the dress. If she could just get all the sewing finished in time for the gala then it was going to look stunning.

Her phone rang, and her heart jumped when she saw the number. 'Hello you. Alison and David are taking me out for dinner tonight, so I don't have much time to chat.'

Nadeem's voice was a bit distant and it sounded as if he was driving. 'I know. But I still wanted to call and say hi. I'm on my way back from a meeting in Coventry and I've got to go out with clients this evening anyway.'

Jenny hugged herself. They talked for a few minutes, then she heard Alison shout from downstairs. 'That's my signal, I have to go. But listen, on Friday the weather is supposed to be a bit rubbish. Alison and David are going to a meeting in Inverness, so I was wondering if you wanted to come over for lunch. We could light the fire and snuggle up in front of it. What do you think?'

'God, Jen, don't distract me with thoughts like that. I almost swerved into the barrier. How can I possibly refuse that kind of offer?'

Jenny didn't know whether to be thrilled or horrified at how much she had managed to divert his brain. 'I'd better go then. I'll see you soon.' She hung up and got her thoughts in motion. A good leaf through all the cookbooks in the house and a visit to the local shop to buy some goodies was definitely on the cards. Friday was going to be as special as she could make it.

The day dawned just as the weather had forecast; cold, damp and rainy. The summer feel had gone and it was almost as if autumn had come in a day. Shortly after breakfast Alison and David gathered their things together and departed, taking Scotty with them, and Jenny was left to her own devices.

Jenny spent most of the morning cooking and baking. She knew it was overkill but she didn't care; in any case she needed something to steady her nerves. She breathed a sigh of relief when the cake came out of the Aga looking perfect.

By the time she heard Nadeem's car in the driveway she had iced the cake and lifted the bread from the oven. He rapped on the door and she flew to open it, wiping her hands on her apron. Her heart did a flip when she opened the door and saw him standing there, a bunch of roses in his hands. He was even more gorgeous than she remembered.

Nadeem took her by the waist and kissed her gently, then raised his head and sniffed appreciatively. 'Wow, this place smells amazing. I hope that's our lunch and not the neighbour's.'

Jenny giggled. The nearest neighbour was a good half a mile away. It was in that instant she realised just how much she had missed him.

Nadeem took off his jacket and boots, and Jenny drew him into the cosy kitchen. 'Sit down and I'll serve up.'

She smiled when he caught her gently by the wrist and pulled him on top of her where he sat. 'Lunch can wait a few minutes while I say a proper hello to the gorgeous girl in front of me.'

Sitting like this they were roughly of an even height. She looked into his eyes and lifted a hand to caress his cheek, feeling the softness of his skin. He kissed her gently on the nose.

'Is that all?' Jenny poked him gently in the ribs.

The sexy smile that she remembered curved the edge of his lips. 'That's not all I'd like to do, sweetheart, but if I really get started then I very much fear your nice lunch would be wasted.'

He tightened his arms around her and pulled her against his shoulder. She lay like that for a couple of minutes, feeling the soft wool of his jumper against her cheek and drinking in the fresh clean smell of his skin, feeling herself slowly relax. She looked up at him. 'I missed you.'

He kissed her again, on the lips this time. 'I missed you too.'

Jenny wriggled off his lap, jumping up to get the big blue casserole dish out of the oven. When she lifted the lid his eyebrows rose appreciatively. 'Wow. What's that?'

'A lamb tagine.' Her pride showed in her voice. 'It's a Moroccan recipe. I was trying to think about what would work well in the Aga.'

She sliced the rosemary bread, still warm under her fingers, and put it on the table. 'Go ahead, serve yourself.' She pulled up a chair next to him.

He took a generous helping and broke a piece of bread. Then he looked across at her and smiled, bending forward to give her a quick kiss. 'Thank you.'

Jenny blushed; the honest praise in his eyes was worth more than any spoken compliment. She busied herself with a helping of food. They didn't speak much while they ate, just savouring the flavours of the meat and the soft white bread dipped in the rich red sauce.

'Don't eat too much,' she warned, as he reached for a second helping. 'We have cake for dessert.'

His eyes sparkled wickedly. 'Chocolate cake?'

She shook her head, returning his smile with an equally mischievous one of her own. 'No, carrot cake. It does have icing though.'

He groaned. 'What a dilemma.' His hand still reached for the ladle. 'I'm sure I'll manage both.'

'I've lit the fire, we could have it in the sitting room.'

Nadeem leaned over and kissed her again, clearly delighted. 'You're a woman after my own heart. Cake in front of a roaring fire with a gorgeous woman beside me? Sold.'

She cleared the dishes away hurriedly, leaving the tagine to cool on the sideboard, and cut two large slices of cake. 'I have spoons this time. We can't risk messing up the furnishings I'm afraid.' Her voice held a note of regret.

He pulled off his sweater, exposing a crisp blue shirt with the sleeves rolled up, then took the plates from her to carry them through. They settled themselves at opposite ends of the sofa, legs intertwined while they slowly demolished the cake.

Jenny looked across at Nadeem while she ate. It felt strangely natural, sitting here with him, watching the play of the flames in the fireplace and listening to the swish of the rain against the windows. She could almost imagine that it was their house and that this was something more permanent, and she felt an ache of longing in her chest.

Nadeem spoke around a mouthful of cake. 'So when are you going back to do the rest of your course?'

She blinked, trying to collect her thoughts. 'When I can save up the money. But I really need to find another job to do that. I've got about half of what I need, but I still need a good deal more. As soon as I get back to London I'll start looking. And if I can't find something straight away I might just have to go back to my old supermarket job.'

'What does your family think of your chosen career?'

'Why do you keep asking about my family? I've told you that we don't keep in touch.'

Nadeem's foot rubbed her thigh in what she knew was meant to be a reassuring manner, but it set off a slow burn inside her. 'That must be hard.'

She shrugged. 'I've got used to it. I have a couple of really good friends down in London and we all look after each other. And Alison and David too, although I don't see them as often as I would like. Sometimes adopted family are more precious than the real ones.'

'Maybe you just need to talk to your mother more.'

Jenny raised her eyebrows. 'You don't think I've tried? I don't blame her for the issues she has. But she never seems to face up to what she needs to do, and it drives me up the wall.'

'Maybe she just needs you to give her some support. Look where I would have been without the support of my family.'

Jenny suddenly found that she didn't want her last mouthful of cake, and set the plate on the coffee table. She pushed herself up and went to stand by the window, staring at how the rain drizzled slowly down the glass. She hated the way how his comments had raised the old feelings of guilt that maybe she could have done more.

'Look, Nadeem, it must be so easy for you, with your oh-so-perfect family. You can't understand what I went through. I tried to help her. I tried so hard. But when someone has dug themselves such a deep hole that you risk falling into it yourself when you try to help, that's when you have to get out. And it hurts like crazy to make that decision, so don't try to tell me what I should or shouldn't do.' She realised her hands were trembling, and she angrily twisted them together. 'Also, you have to realise that repeatedly pushing me on this is not good either. I know you're just trying to help, but I've told you I don't want to talk about it and you should respect that.'

Nadeem was silent, and when she turned back towards him his face was flushed with embarrassment. He held out a hand to her and she wordlessly sat down beside him as he wrapped an arm around her comfortingly.

Jenny shook her head. 'You know, I sometimes wonder what the hell I'm doing. I'm sitting here desperately wanting you to make love to me, and yet scared witless that I'll totally freak out when you do. I swing between confidence in my talents and abilities, and utter despair of ever doing anything right.' She could feel her eyes start to prickle, and angrily swallowed the tears away.

Nadeem put a hand up to her face and cradled her cheek in his palm. 'I'm sorry. I shouldn't have tried to tell you what to do with your family. I am very lucky to have mine, and I do try very hard not to take it for granted.'

He softly smoothed a curl behind her ear, and Jenny felt the tightness in her chest ease at his words. He pulled her down until they were both lying in the same direction, wrapping his arms around her in a huge bear hug. She could feel the heat of the fire on her back, and the warmth of his body from the front. For a few moments she just lay there, grateful for the feeling of being in his arms.

Nadeem kissed the top of her head. 'I know you'll get through this. Because you're an amazing woman. I don't think I've really ever met someone as strong and resourceful as you. You'll find a way.'

Jenny's heart fluttered at his words, and she bent her head into his chest to hide the flush that warmed her cheeks. She rubbed her nose in the hollow of his neck, left bare by the open buttons at the top of his shirt, and his arms tightened around her. He raised one hand to run it through her hair, massaging her scalp gently as he did so, and she felt the tension slide out of her body. She could feel his heartbeat strong and steady as her head lay cradled on his shoulder. He dropped a kiss lightly on her forehead, and then continued slowly down her cheek and nibbled gently on her ear. Jenny felt another kind of warmth creep through her. Daringly, she raised her head and ran her tongue lightly along his neck. Nadeem sucked in a sharp breath, and she felt the reaction in his body.

He grasped her shoulder with one hand and looked directly at her; his eyes were dark and the way he looked at her made her want him even more. 'Jen, babe, are you sure this is really what you want? Because you know we can stop any time you need to.'

In answer to his question, she bent her head forward and kissed him, first gently, then tentatively deepening the kiss. He groaned, and pulled her on top of him until she straddled him, running his hands through her hair. The heat of his lips set off sparks in her brain, and an urgent need inside her. Breaking off,

Jenny trailed kisses down his throat, undoing his shirt buttons one by one until she exposed the full length of his chest. She ran a hand down across his stomach. 'That's quite a six-pack you've got there, Army guy.'

Was that a blush she saw on his face? No, she must have imagined it. He smiled lazily. 'I'm surprised I don't look three months pregnant with all that food I've had. But then, I do my best to please the ladies.'

Her resolve wobbled for just a second. 'I'm...I'm not a lady. Not that kind of lady anyway.'

That sexy smile again. 'No. You're just you. And I want to make sure I treat you right.'

He touched a hand to her cheek, trying to smooth away the worry from her face. 'Jen. You have to understand that I would never willingly hurt you. You're the one calling the shots. If I do anything that you're not comfortable with, all you have to do is tell me. Or just tap my shoulder if you find you can't speak.'

When she nodded, he reached up to pull her closer to him, taking her mouth with his again. There was only gentleness in his touch. His hands slipped inside her blouse and made fire run along her skin. It was only when he started to tug her sweater up over her head that Jenny suddenly remembered where they were. In the living room, with a full-on view for anyone who turned up in the driveway. She pulled away, getting to her feet before Nadeem could stop her.

'Not here.' She pointed with a finger. 'Upstairs.'

Nadeem pulled her to a halt as they went up. He took her face in his hands and kissed her slowly and deliberately. She shivered.

'Cold?' He wrapped his arms around her.

Jenny laughed. 'Do you have any idea exactly what you're doing to me right now?'

Nadeem smiled wickedly. 'Some.' He bent his head to kiss her again.

They stumbled up the rest of the stairs, mouths and hands everywhere, driven by a blinding need for the other's touch and the feel of skin against skin. Nadeem slammed the bedroom door and peeled off her sweater and blouse in one movement. Jenny did the same with the rest of his shirt, and as she ran her fingers under the waistband of his jeans he gasped in pleasure. His mouth went to her neck while his fingers gently teased under the lacy fabric of her bra. He curved his hands around her backside and pushed her back against the door.

Jenny was lost in a haze of desire. Nadeem's hands were so gentle and his lips so tender that all of her fears had disappeared, to be replaced only with a sense of trust and belonging that made her sigh with relief. Not only that, but the other feelings he awakened in her, the need that she felt for him, made her long to just take him to bed and never let him go. Then he pushed her back against the door and trapped her body with his. Her breath caught. Trapped. Yes, trapped. She was suddenly back in the office. Watching as the scene replayed. *She couldn't move, she couldn't breathe, she was frozen as his mouth crushed down on hers...*

As the memory dissolved, she crumpled to the floor in a torrent of tears, hugging her knees to her chest.

Chapter 8

Nadeem swore with a mixture of frustration and anger as Jenny dropped to the floor and he realised what he had done. He sat down beside her, wishing he could erase all the hurt and pain. 'Jen. It's me. Can I put my arms around you?'

She nodded once, tears still streaming down her face, and that was all the signal he needed to pull her into his arms. He held her close and stroked her hair gently until her sobs finally subsided.

She mumbled something against his chest and he bent his head down to hers. 'What was that?'

'I said I'm sorry.' Jenny's voice was barely audible.

Feeling an odd ache in his heart, he wrapped her even tighter against him. 'Oh sweetheart, don't be, it's not your fault. Anything but that.'

'But I disappointed you. And I disappointed myself too. Damn it! Why can't I just do this like a normal person!' She smashed a fist onto her thigh.

He put a finger under her chin, and lifted her face to meet his. 'Disappointed? You could never disappoint me. It's far more important to me that you're alright; and if you need to stop then stop. Never worry about disappointing me.'

She sniffled, and he dragged his handkerchief out of his back pocket. 'Here you go, blow.'

She stared at it as if she had never seen one before. 'A real handkerchief? I thought no-one used these any more.' He saw her smile through her tears, and it eased some of the worry in his chest.

'You have no idea how useful these can be. It's not just snotty noses, but one of these makes a great triangular bandage too.'

Another smile; he was doing well. She took the handkerchief and blew obediently, then balled it in her right hand. He stood, pulling her up with him, and led her over to the bed.

'What are you going to do?' Her voice betrayed her nervousness.

'We, sweetheart, are going to get into bed, and I am going to put my arms around you, and that's all. Would that be alright?'

She nodded gratefully.

'Jump in then.' He held open the covers for her, then snuggled in behind her. He wrapped his arms around her, feeling the delicious curve of her backside against his front, and breathed in the scent of her, trying to ignore the desire that was never far below the surface. 'OK?'

'Yes.' Her voice was very quiet.

They lay like that for a long time. Just when he thought that she might have fallen asleep, she twisted around to face him, her head cradled on his arm. 'How long did it take you to get over your PTSD?'

The question caught him by surprise, and for a moment he didn't want to answer. But he owed it to this woman to tell her the truth, no matter how painful. 'I'm not sure it ever really goes away. I went through a real turning point after a couple of years of therapy. But things definitely faded with time. I haven't had proper flashback in a long while, although I still have nightmares sometimes.'

'Didn't it scare you, not being in control of your emotions like that?'

He was silent for a while, thinking. This, and other similar questions, were things he didn't really want to consider. 'Maybe. But life moves on, you know? I've learned to accept the impact my experiences have on me, find ways to cope with it, and keep moving forward. It has to be like that.'

She was silent for a while, then looked up directly into his eyes, fiddling with the button at the waistband of his jeans. 'I'm scared. I'm scared that I'll never be able to have sex again, even with someone as drop-dead gorgeous as you.' There was a tremor in her voice which cut through his heart like a knife.

Nadeem raised his hand and cupped Jenny's cheek gently, brushing the chestnut curls away from her face, then bit his lip, trying to think of the right question to ask. This was getting dangerously close to a therapy session, but if they were going to work this out, he had to be open with her. 'What is it about it that scares you?'

He watched her face screw up as she thought. And when the answer came, it was so quiet he could hardly hear her, even though their faces were just inches away.

'It was...' She hesitated, as if she was searching for the words, while her eyes darted around nervously. 'Not being in control. When you pushed me up against the door like that...'

He let out the breath he had been holding, while at the same time mentally berating himself for not thinking of that before he'd done it. Although if he was honest with himself, he hadn't been thinking very much at that point at all.

Maybe there was a way they could rescue this. He raised one eyebrow, trying to keep his tone light. 'Oh, that's an easy one to solve.'

Jenny looked puzzled. 'What do you mean?'

'Well, you'll just have to be the one on top; then you get to call the shots.'

He held his breath, praying for a positive response, and was rewarded by a small upturn of her lips.

'You know, I think I might like that idea.'

Smiling, he leaned over and kissed her gently on the cheek, and then softly on the mouth. She responded hesitantly, then as she realised he was holding himself back, she tentatively deepened the kiss. He felt her trembling, and pulled himself away to look into her eyes.

'Sweetheart, we really don't have to do this.' He smoothed one hand across her hair.

She looked back at him, her expression unreadable, then suddenly made an exasperated sound. 'I know, I know. But I just feel that if I don't do this, then that bastard has won somehow.' Her fists curled up angrily.

Nadeem tightened his arms around her and nestled his chin in her hair. 'It's not about winning or losing. He's a tosser, you're amazing. In fact, he doesn't even deserve to be in the same sentence as you. Bad Deem. Bad.' He slapped himself twice on the side of the head. Humour was the only way that he had been able to survive his darkest days; maybe it would help her too.

'It's not funny.' Her voice was muffled against his neck.

He stopped himself just in time from sighing. She had to go through this at her own speed. He damped down his frustration, remembering what it had been like for him in his first few months.

'I wasn't laughing at you, Jen. I guess what I'm trying to say is that you can't push these things. When the time is right, it'll be right. I don't want to have sex with you just because you feel you ought to. I want you to really want this, and for it to be something special.'

He moved his fingers across her back in small circles, gradually easing lower as he felt her body begin to relax. 'Come on. Just flip. Let's do some more spooning. Sex can wait.'

She nestled into him. 'More talking too?'

'If you like. It will take my mind off the way I'm wanting you like crazy right now. Any particular topic in mind?'

She did laugh then. 'Since when have we chosen a topic for our conversations?'

'Well, you know, I'm thinking we could choose something light. Like favourite films, maybe. Or tell me more about your next dress design.'

Jenny thought about her best-loved films, relieved to have some distraction from what had just happened. 'Well, I think there are too many to really have a favourite. But Dirty Dancing, of course.'

When Nadeem made fake vomiting noises, she elbowed him gently in the chest. 'Not because of the romance, you idiot. It's a real coming-of-age story. And I like the way the heroine defies her parents to do what she thinks is right. It's the same with something like

Legally Blonde. She proves everyone wrong by becoming a damn good lawyer. And she wins the case because she's a girl, and knows something that blokes just wouldn't.'

'About the hair thingy, wasn't it?'

'You watched it?' Jenny was surprised.

She could almost feel Nadeem rolling his eyes behind her as he spoke. 'Oh come on, I've got two sisters and one of them is only a year younger than me. They pretty much forced me to watch those kind of films. But I have to admit I kind of liked it too.' Nadeem tightened his arms around her. 'Was that the inspiration for your choice of career?'

Jenny considered. 'Well, maybe a little bit. Alison's been a big inspiration too.'

Then she thought about her own sister, and felt a wave of loneliness sweep over her. 'Look, Nadeem, there's something I really need to tell you about my family. About some stuff that happened when I was younger.'

'Actually, there's something I should tell you about my family too.' Nadeem's voice sounded a bit strange.

Just then Jenny heard the sounds of a car in the drive and she sat up, pulling the covers with her. 'It'll have to wait. That's Alison and David! They're back early. Shit!'

Nadeem pulled her back down again. 'Chill. We're grown-ups; they'll understand. In fact, if I know Alison at all, she'll actually be pleased.'

He was probably right. Still, she reached for her clothes anyway. 'We'll still need to go down and talk to them.'

Nadeem pushed back the covers and scooped up his shirt, shivering as the chill air caught his skin. They could already hear the front door opening downstairs. Jenny pulled on her blouse and sweater. 'It feels like the time I got caught smoking at school.' Her voice was a whisper.

Nadeem looked at her in surprise. 'You used to smoke?'

Jenny waggled her eyebrows. 'Oh, I had my rebellious teenage period, just like you.'

She opened the door and they stole down the stairs. Alison poked her head out of the kitchen. 'Hello Jenny. Oh, hi Nadeem. Won't you stay for a cup of tea?'

She didn't seem at all surprised to see him, but then his car was in the driveway and his shoes were by the door.

Nadeem shook his head. 'Sorry to disappoint you, but I really must be going. My parents will be expecting me home for dinner.'

Alison nodded. 'I bumped into your mother yesterday in the village and she was telling me about your father's heart attack and how you've stepped up as managing director. I'm sorry to hear he's not been well.'

'What is she talking about?' Jenny looked at Nadeem, confused.

He returned her gaze uncomfortably. 'It's a long story.'

Alison glanced from Nadeem back to Jenny. 'Oh dear, I seem to have put my foot in it. I thought you would have known already.'

'No, I didn't. He somehow left that one out.' Jenny couldn't help being puzzled.

Nadeem shrugged. 'My parents own the company I work for. It's a small multi-national that specialises in medical logistics. We do a lot of work for NGOs and we just won a massive contract for the military which is going to kick things up a notch once we really get going. I took over running the company when my dad had a heart attack about six months ago.'

Everything suddenly fell into place. The designer clothes, the Landrover. The things he had said about taking on more responsibility. Even though he had told her some things about his family and his job, he had somehow avoided specific details which might give the game away. She started to laugh out loud.

Nadeem stared at her as if she was going mad, but Alison knew exactly what was in her mind and smiled. 'I think, my dears, that you both need to clear some things up between you. It's stopped raining now, and there's a lovely light across the hills. Why don't the two of you take yourselves off for a walk? I'll have dinner ready at six.'

When Nadeem opened his mouth to protest, she held up a hand. 'It's fine. Like I said, I'd love to catch up on all your news.'

Neither of them spoke until they reached the shore path, when Jenny finally stopped and turned to Nadeem. 'Just when were you going to tell me?'

He ran a hand through his hair. 'I was going to tell you. Just now, when we got interrupted.'

She shook her head. 'Just now? Your family is mega-rich and you've waited all this time to tell me?'

At the top of a small rise she found a large flat stone and sat down, gazing out to sea. The late afternoon light was truly beautiful, with white tufts of spray on the waves in the sea.

Nadeem spoke next to her. 'We're not mega-rich. Just kind of well off.'

When no reaction was forthcoming, he tried again. 'Look, I'm really sorry I kept it from you. But I really, really wanted, just once, for someone to like me for who I actually was, not who I might seem to be on the surface. I've learned that the hard way.' He sat beside her on the rock and laced his hands together nervously. 'I didn't tell you on the plane because there didn't seem any point, and after that the longer I kept it from you the harder it was to tell you. It's not an excuse, I know.'

Jenny just looked up at him and smiled, swinging one leg across his so she could turn to face him. 'You know what? It's absolutely fine. In fact, the reason why I laughed earlier was because I've been doing the same thing.'

Nadeem looked puzzled. 'The same thing? Are you telling me you've got money too?'

Jenny scuffed the grass with the toe of her shoe. 'Not any more. My mother is from a family who can trace their origins right back. Balls and parties were the norm when I was a teenager. But then I gave it all up.'

'When you walked away.'

Jenny nodded. 'Yes. It didn't make the decision any easier. To give up a comfortable life where you can buy whatever you want, for unemployment and uncertainty?'

'So you left because your mother was dragging you down?'

She could see Nadeem was really trying to understand. 'It wasn't just her. I was only twelve when my dad died. He had a small garage in Peterborough. We lived a pretty normal life until that point; a semi-detached, the local school, that sort of thing. He'd teach me how to fix cars on a Saturday. But after that my mother just ripped my sister and myself away from all that and went back to live with her parents.'

Jenny sighed. 'It was like something out of a fairy tale. I'd never even known they existed, because they'd cut her off when she married my dad, but suddenly we had people to do everything and as many dresses as money could buy. I went to a posh private school. It was fine. I can't complain. But when my stepfather arrived on the scene, it all started to go downhill. I knew right from the start that he was only after my mother's money. And the ink was barely dry on the marriage certificate before he started terrorising all three of us.' She shivered as some of the memories came back to her. 'I didn't abandon my family. I escaped.'

She rested her head on Nadeem's shoulder, suddenly feeling exhausted. 'My stepfather controlled everything. What we wore, who we talked to, who came to the house. Every single thing. The only thing I could control in that situation was whether I stayed or left. So I left.'

'Was it really that bad?' Nadeem's voice was low.

Jenny considered for a moment. 'You ever watch an old black and white film called Gaslight?'

'The one where the husband convinces his wife that she's going mad? Yeah. It was totally creepy.' Nadeem grimaced.

'It was that kind of emotional manipulation. When you start to doubt your own judgement. You give up on your friends because they're telling you things that your fake reality thinks just can't be true.' It surprised Jenny how casual her voice sounded. 'Alison wrote to me when I turned eighteen. They were very good friends of my dad, and apparently when he died they'd invited us to Switzerland to see them for a while, just to get away from things. But for some reason my mother had told her and David not to contact us again. It was strange; when my mother went back to her old life then it was almost like she wanted to scrub out any memory of my dad.'

She gave a wry smile. 'Not so strange if I really think about it; her and my dad were madly in love so I can't imagine what losing him must have been like for her. Alison was the one who helped me sort everything out. She and David gave me a place to stay while I figured out what to do with my life.'

'And you left your family just like that?' She could hear the surprise in his voice.

Jenny dropped her eyes. 'Not just like that. It took me ages to make the choice. But it got to the point where I was willing to do anything to get away, even if it meant working in a dead-end job for a pittance. It was when my stepfather realised that I was really serious about leaving that he gave me an ultimatum; if I did then he would stop me from ever seeing my sister again. I think he just said it because he thought it would make me stay.'

'But you didn't.' It wasn't a question.

'No. I couldn't. It was awful. He had my mother wrapped around his finger. Whenever he was nice to her, she was on cloud nine. And when he was cruel to her she was practically suicidal. I tried to avoid getting sucked into it all, and to support her as much as I could. But when I lost my best friend because of the lies he was telling, that was it for me. That night I packed a bag and walked out of the house and they couldn't do anything because I was already an adult.'

She found her hands were clenched into tight fists and she rubbed them against each other, trying to release some of the tension.

'I'm sorry.' Nadeem's gaze had softened. 'For all those comments I made about you leaving your family. I should have known better. I should have trusted your judgement.'

Jenny looked across at Nadeem searchingly. 'You said you learned about people the hard way? Are you saying someone screwed you over?'

Nadeem rubbed a palm across his face. 'Not exactly that, but it wasn't really a great experience.'

Jenny took one of his hands and cradled her own around it. 'What happened?'

He looked straight at her. 'You really want to know? It's not a story I really enjoy telling.'

Jenny let out a short burst of laughter. 'You really think that talking about my family was a walk in the park?'

'OK, you got me there.' Nadeem smiled wryly and looked away again, staring out to sea. 'My dad originally set up the logistics business from home as a way to make a bit of extra cash. I remember the house always being full of boxes when I came home on leave. I was twenty-four when things finally took off and he won a big contract which meant he could finally hire some real staff and start a proper business. I'd just got out of the Army, with what seemed like a huge amount of money they'd given me for what I'd done. Soon I was out every night on the social circuit in Edinburgh, living off the inflated stories I told about my family's success and the savings I'd accumulated.'

He shifted his gaze down to his feet. 'This was all alongside the mental health problems I was in denial about, so you can imagine what a mess I was in. Anyway, that was when things all started with Elaine. Our families know each other up here and one day she contacted me and said she'd moved down to Edinburgh and did I want to meet up. Things just went from there really. She was beautiful and I was so over my head that I never noticed it was always me who paid for things.' He turned to look at Jenny, eyes unreadable. 'It was while I was dating her that I started realising things were getting out of hand - I had the car crash I told you about - and decided to give up drinking. I think that being with her also made me understand there were other things to live for.'

'Did you love her?' Jenny couldn't help asking.

Nadeem considered the question for a few moments, staring down at his feet. 'I thought I did then, but when I look back now, I just don't know. My emotions were all over the shop and she was just in the right place at the right time. My memories of that period of my life are a bit screwed up anyway.'

He rubbed his forehead, frowning. 'Where was I? Oh yeah. Giving up drinking helped a lot; after about a week of terrifying withdrawal symptoms I started sleeping a bit better and feeling less paranoid. But Elaine kept complaining that I was no fun any more, that I never wanted to go out anywhere. After a month or so she just left me.'

He laughed humourlessly. 'After losing Nate it was just the last straw. It was my sister and my cousin who rescued me that night and I've never forgotten it. And since then I've always been careful about who I get close to. For ages my family were the only ones I would trust with the real me.'

He paused, swallowed. 'That's why I was so reluctant to share the details with you about my background. I didn't want to jinx things. Because I think I'm starting to really like you.' The last part was almost a mumble, hidden in the collar of his coat. Jenny tightened her arm around him and felt him hug her closer in response.

Nadeem continued. 'Anyway, I decided after that I'd have to get a proper job and stop swanning around. I moved to Glasgow and took a job training people in first aid. I loved it. Found some great friends. But when my dad had his heart attack back in February, he needed someone he could trust to run the company. And lately I'm finding that my heart's just not in it.'

'I don't see why you can't find a way to give it up.' Jenny still couldn't work it out. 'I mean, I know it's your family, but isn't your own happiness more important?'

Nadeem made a strangled sound which could have been frustration. 'It's just not that simple. My dad's been told to rest and take things easy. My mum wants to stay with him; they've always been really close. And taking on his work was the only way I could get him to actually take a break. Other family members have been helping out with our charity work, but me and my cousin are the only people Dad would trust with the business side of things.'

He stretched, a smile creeping across his face. 'Working with my cousin has been fun actually. He'll be there tomorrow and I can't wait for you to meet him, he's a great guy.'

'I still think it's sad that you have to fill in for your dad when you don't really want to.' Jenny frowned. 'There must be plenty of good people who are perfectly capable of running things for him. Why does it have to be you? Why should you have to sacrifice your dreams to satisfy him?'

The crease was back between his eyebrows now, and he stared out to sea, not looking at her. 'Just because you left your family behind, don't expect me to do the same. I need to do this. For him. For my mother. And for the rest of my family.' He shrugged. 'Anyway, it's not so bad. I try to enjoy what little free time I get. I've got this great canal boat which I've been renovating since I moved to London and I love living on the water down in Hackney. There's a real sense of community among the boat owners.' He brightened visibly, and Jenny could tell that this was something he really did feel passionate about. That would explain the callouses on his hands too.

Jenny found she was holding her breath and let it out slowly. She scuffed the ground with her shoe again. 'I'm sorry for being so hard on you. You're right, it is your life to do what you want with. Alison said that you were a good one, that I should trust you.'

Nadeem laughed. 'She's an interfering individual, but her heart's in the right place.' He smiled down at Jenny, and she felt a thrill of anticipation as she knew that he was going to kiss her, and that she was going to kiss him right back. Suddenly the day seemed even brighter.

Nadeem cupped her cheek with his other hand. 'You're a very special woman, Jen.'

Jenny deflated a little. 'I may be special, but after what happened this afternoon I think I really need to get some help. I'd already asked for a mental health referral after what happened at work, but these flashbacks are really worrying. I know it's a perfectly normal response, but still, I don't want to be like this for the rest of my life. I can't let that tosser ruin what should be an amazing time with you.'

'You just do what you need to do. I'm happy to take this slowly.' Nadeem ran a hand gently over her hair. 'I've got my own issues with relationships after everything that's happened, and it's going to take me time to work through them too. But I did mean it when I said I really like you. And if a night with you means just holding you in my arms until all this goes away, then that's totally fine with me.'

Jenny felt her tension disappear as she took his words in and her heart swelled with happiness. He really was serious about her. 'You mentioned issues. Is that your PTSD?'

'Not really. As I said, I think I've put a lot of that behind me now.' She saw his chest rise and fall in a sigh. 'It's more just issues of trust. In myself, if I'm honest. I screwed up once with Nate and I'm terrified I might do it again.'

'We'll work it out. I know we will.' Jenny gave his thigh a squeeze, and he looked at her gratefully.

Nadeem checked his watch. 'I feel bad, but I really can't stay for dinner. There's still so much to do for the gala tomorrow night, and I promised my parents I'd help. I can't let them down.'

'Don't worry, Alison won't really mind.' Jenny looked back towards the house. 'I'll tell her why you had to go.'

Her tone was wistful, thinking of her own family. For the first time she wondered if she had made the right decision about leaving them. Maybe she should have tried harder instead of running away. Still, what was done was done and it was too late for regrets now. Nadeem was right, the only way to go was forward.

Chapter 9

The two of them were mainly silent on the way back to the croft, just enjoying the early evening light and the sound of the sea, hands intertwined as they walked along. As they reached his car, Nadeem looked down at Jenny. 'You will be there tomorrow, won't you?'

She couldn't help her doubts creeping through. 'Isn't it a bit soon to be meeting your family? I thought this was just a holiday fling.'

He frowned. 'You know it's more than that, so don't try to pretend. Anyway, don't forget Mia asked me to invite you before we even really knew each other.'

Jenny hesitated. 'I'm not sure. All those people... won't they wonder who I am?'

Nadeem rolled his eyes. 'Come on, I'm sure you'll ace the social scene. Besides, you'll have Alison and David with you. They bought their tickets months ago.'

She considered for a few seconds. 'OK. What time does it start?'

'I'll pick you up about seven. And I'd really like it if you stayed over.'

Her body heated at the thought of spending a proper night with him, even if it was just spent lying in his arms as he had promised. The kiss he gave her as he left made her wish it wasn't going to be almost twenty-four hours before she saw him again. She just prayed that her mind would finally stop messing with her and let her enjoy what they had together.

It was late Saturday afternoon by the time Jenny finally finished the last touches on her dress. It was floor length, with a modestly daring neckline but a breathtaking scoop cut out at the back. The grey fabric had a slight silver shimmer and as she walked it molded to her body like a lover's touch and swished softly around her ankles. She knew no-one would guess that she had made it; this was her masterpiece and it had taken hours and hours of planning over many weeks to get it just right.

She paired it up with some simple silver jewellery; a twisted chain necklace and some pear-drop earrings, and the bag and shoes that Alison had bought her. She did her make-up and nails with care, and tamed her unruly curls slightly with generous amounts of hairspray. Fifteen minutes ahead of time she was ready in her coat, with a change of clothes packed into her little blue rucksack.

Alison and David came down the stairs, David dressed in his blue and green kilt, and Alison in a sleek black dress with a spray of the same tartan thrown over her shoulder.

'Isn't that the one I made while I was staying with you in Geneva?' Jenny was surprised.

'Yes, it's still good.' Alison smoothed her hand absently over the skirt. 'And even better, I still fit into it.' Her eyes sparkled wickedly.

Jenny flopped down on the living room sofa. 'I don't know if I can do this if it's going to be all posh toffs and la-di-da. And what if his family doesn't like me?'

'Oh, don't be ridiculous.' Alison waved a hand dismissively. 'There's bound to be some interesting people there. I've heard half of the area's been invited, even some of the plebs.' There was a note of laughter in her voice.

Jenny made a sound of exasperation, but she couldn't stop herself smiling.

Just then a knock sounded on the door. Jenny jumped up. 'Here's our ride.'

Alison shook her head. 'We're going in our car, darling. From what Nadeem told me, there won't be room in his.'

'The Landrover? What do you mean, won't be room?'

David gave Jenny a wink. 'From what I've heard, he's borrowed something a bit more special for tonight.'

'We'll see you there.' Alison turned back to David, adjusting his tie.

Jenny opened the door and what she saw on the other side nearly took her breath away. Nadeem stood there in a dark grey suit, with a crisp white shirt which was unbuttoned at the neck.

'Oi.' His voice interrupted her thoughts. 'When you've quite finished ogling me?'

Jenny couldn't help smiling. 'You'll have to excuse me. I just never expected a James Bond lookalike to come and pick me up.'

She moved closer, needing to touch him, and slid her hands around him. He bent his head to kiss her, and she returned the favour enthusiastically. She broke off the contact, feeling flushed, and stepped away from him.

He turned, and that was when she saw the car. Instead of the usual wreck there stood a sleek silver sports car, its paintwork gleaming in the evening light. Jenny murmured appreciatively.

'I begged my mother for the use of her only toy.' Was Nadeem blushing in the shadows?

Jenny pursed her lips and pretended to simper at him. 'Oh darling, you shouldn't have. How did you know it would go with my dress?'

Nadeem's shout of laughter startled her, it was so sudden. 'You, my dear, are one in a million.' He dropped a kiss on her forehead, holding open the door for her as she slid into the low-slung seat.

Jenny really enjoyed the ride, even though she was itching to try out the car herself. She was almost disappointed when they rolled up into a large courtyard. Noticing the look on her face, Nadeem just nodded. 'I know. I'll take you out for a longer spin tomorrow, I promise.'

Nadeem made sure he gave Jenny a hand to help her out of the car and as she stood he wrapped an arm around her, curving his hand around her hips. When they entered the hallway, both his mother and Mia were there, helping to relieve the guests of their coats. He turned to Jenny to help her with hers but she had already shrugged it off, and what he saw underneath drove all other thoughts from his mind. Her dress was made of some silver material that accented the soft tones of her skin. But it was the shape that made him glad of the length of his jacket to hide the evidence of what it did to him. Sheer and smooth, it skimmed over her breasts and bum, accentuating all her curves, tempting him to mold his hands around them. It made him seriously want to skip the whole party and just take her to bed right then and there.

'Nadeem?' His mother's voice broke into his thoughts and he looked at her questioningly. 'Aren't you going to introduce us to your guest?'

He collected himself hastily, motioning towards Jenny. 'Mum, Mia, this is Jenny. Jenny, this is my mother, Anita, and my sister Mia.'

Jenny put out her hand. 'Pleased to meet you.'

His mother drew Jenny in for a kiss on the cheek. 'I'm so glad you could come. Mia here will introduce you to some people while Nadeem helps me with the coats, won't you Mia?'

Mia grabbed Jenny's hand. 'Sure thing. Come with me. I'll make sure I steer you away from all the boring old fogeys.'

Completely ignoring her mother's warning frown, Mia looped a friendly arm around Jenny's shoulders and took her off for a tour.

His mother watched the two women as they left. 'She seems nice.'

'Mum, how can you tell?' Nadeem had to stop himself from rolling his eyes like a teenager. 'You barely saw her for a minute.'

His mother laughed. 'You're right. I don't really have a clue. But she does have nice manners, and you obviously like her, so that means a lot.'

She suddenly turned away from him and switched into her hostess mode. 'Oh, Chris and Lorna! So good to see you. I'm glad you could actually make it. How's your ankle doing?'

Nadeem found his arms laden with more coats, and he grabbed a couple of hangers from the rack. By the time he had them neatly stowed they were alone again.

'Have I ever told you how good you are at this?' He looked at his mother with a smile. 'This hostess thing, I mean.'

She looked up at him in surprise. 'You think? I do try. I'm always worried I'll forget someone's name and they'll be upset.'

'Yeah, Mum. You're the best. I know how much effort you've put into arranging all this.' Nadeem put an arm around her shoulders.

She shrugged. 'I wanted to do something at least. I do feel a bit guilty letting you and Derek shoulder such a big responsibility, although you seem to be doing really well and I'm proud of you both.' She frowned at him. 'But I can see the signs of stress in your face and worry that it's all a bit too much.'

Nadeem was saved from having to reply by more people arriving, and filing the coats away gave him time to think about how honest he wanted to be with his answer. 'It is stressful. But what other choice do I have?'

His mother smiled at him. 'There are always choices.' She reached up and touched his hair gently. 'I just want you to be happy. It's the most important thing in life. That's why I'm so glad you've met Jenny. I can see how happy she makes you.'

He wasn't ready to share his feelings on that front, so he just put his arms around her and kissed the top of her head. 'Thanks, Mum. I love you.'

She rested her head on his chest for a brief moment. 'I love you too.'

As they wended their way into the party Jenny felt glad she had worn the silver dress, as the clothes most people were wearing were definitely on the posher side. Nadeem's mother had been in a dusky red floor-length gown that contrasted perfectly with her greying black hair, while Mia's was a green that perfectly set off her skin tone.

A marquee had been erected at the back of the house, with a proper wooden floor inside. Comfy sofas were dotted around the edge of the room, although many people had chosen to stand. Mia led her slowly through the crowds, stopping frequently as people congratulated her on her recent birthday and made jokes about alcohol and freedom.

'There's a temporary toilet block out the back.' Mia stooped to murmur into Jenny's ear. 'It's pretty swanky though. Looks almost like a proper one.'

Bella would be about the same age as Mia by now, Jenny suddenly realised. Just slightly older. The thought of her sister as a young woman made her catch her breath for a moment. Barely twenty. At university by now probably. And able to make her own decisions. But what would she think of her big sister? Would she ever forgive her for leaving?

The last time Jenny had tried to get in touch, Bella had been sixteen, the typical angsty teenager, and it hadn't gone well at all. Which was totally unsurprising; they had both been young, and Jenny had lacked the finesse with words to explain exactly how she felt.

They finally reached the bar, which had been set up back in the main house, in a small room that looked as if it normally served as a dining room. A tall lanky young man was mixing cocktails, and smiled broadly when he saw Mia. 'Ah, first proper party when you're legal, eh? Come to make the most of it?'

He had an attractive soft Scottish burr. He handed off two large glasses to a couple who were waiting, then turned towards them.

Mia rolled her eyes. 'Oh, not you as well. That must be the thousandth time I've heard that this evening. Just make us some cocktails, please Jamie.' She settled herself on a tall stool by the bar and Jenny did the same.

Jamie winked at Jenny, pushing the printed cocktail menu over to them both. He had warm brown eyes, she noted, and a pleasing face, and he looked like a nice person, as far as she could tell.

Mia waved the menu away. 'Jamie, you pick. You always make good choices.'

He pretended to eye them up speculatively, then turned away to the bar and began picking up bottles. She noticed how skilfully he poured and mixed, without any of the usual twiddling bottles nonsense that barmen usually did to impress.

He set a cocktail glass on the bar in front of Jenny and placed a twist of lemon peel in the glass. It was vague pinky-red colour and looked very pretty.

'What is it?'

'A Silver Cocktail.' He gave her another wink. 'In honour of that stunning dress you're wearing. Gin, vermouth, maraschino, orange bitters. Careful, it has a fair kick.'

She took a cautious sip. It had a complex blend of flavours that lingered behind on her tongue. She nodded. 'Nice. Thank you.'

Jamie turned back to the bar. Two more minutes, and he placed another cocktail glass in front of Mia. Jenny looked at it curiously. It looked like it was full of coffee.

'A Screaming Orgasm.' Jamie gave a big grin. 'If you've got your freedom, you may as well go all the way.'

Mia pretended to hit him, while he theatrically took cover behind the bar. 'You bad boy, Jamie, and after you promised to be on your best behaviour, too.' It was clear that these two had some sort of friendship that meant Jamie was more than just an employee.

Mia leaned on the bar. 'So Jamie, how are you getting on with doing up the old house? Have you finished the new kitchen yet?'

He shook his head. 'Not quite. Although Nadeem gave me a fine hand today. There's only a few things left to do.'

'Mum and Dad gave Jamie our old house down in Brora when they moved in here.' Mia was quick to explain. 'He's been doing it up.' At Jenny's enquiring look, she clarified. 'Jamie's my foster brother; Mum and Dad took him in when his parents died. He's only behind the bar tonight because he loves doing cocktails.'

Mia slid off her stool. 'Come on, let's leave this good-for-nothing to his work. I want to introduce you to Dina.'

They took their drinks and left, and Mia made her way towards a dark-haired woman sitting on one of the sofas, holding a champagne glass. Jenny's initial nervousness soon evaporated as Dina admired her choice of study and asked where she had bought her dress. When Jenny shyly confided about her creation, Dina went into ecstasies of delight, and said that if she ever decided that law wasn't for her she would be able to make a fortune as a dress designer.

'I had real problems finding nice clothes while I was pregnant.' Dina rolled her eyes. 'They all seem to be either disgustingly expensive, or expect that you don't mind walking around looking like a frump all day.'

She waggled her champagne glass. 'It's fizzy water, in case you were wondering. Saves me a lot of questions.'

'Who's looking after the baby?' Jenny wanted to know.

'Oh, Mo, that's my husband, he hates these kind of things. He's in a back room somewhere catching up on medical journals, while Kami's asleep. He'll come and get me when it's time for a feed.'

Mia put a hand on Jenny's shoulder, drawing her attention. 'You are dating Deem, right? Because it's obvious how much he likes you.'

Jenny shouldn't have been surprised that Mia had been so direct, but it still made her blush. 'Kind of. We're just seeing how things go.'

'I think that's the best way to do it.' Dina shot a look at her sister, but what was contained in it, Jenny couldn't tell. 'There's no point rushing things.'

'Nadeem told me he used to be in the Army.' Jenny couldn't help mentioning it.

Dina nodded. 'Tell you what, give me your number and I'll send you some pictures. I've got some embarrassing kiddie ones I can send you too.'

They spent some time laughing over the photos and Jenny decided that she really quite liked the sisters. At some point Mia was dragged away by further well-wishers, and Jenny was left with Dina. It turned out that

Dina worked as a dentist in Edinburgh, although she was currently on maternity leave.

'I'm afraid medical careers seem to run in the family.' Dina sighed. 'It's all our parents' fault; they met while they were working in a hospital together. Oh, and Mo and I met in the same surgery in Edinburgh. All because one of his colleagues was ill.'

'Let me just go to the bar to get some more drinks, then you can tell me the whole story.' Jenny got up. She nodded at Dina. 'More fizzy water?'

'Are you sure? I sort of feel like you're a guest.' Dina looked worried.

Jenny nodded firmly. 'It's no problem, really.' She suddenly caught sight of Nadeem across the room with a stunningly beautiful tall blonde woman. It was clear from their body language that they knew each other well. She felt a sudden stab of jealousy as he bent his head close to listen to something that was said.

'Who's that girl with Nadeem right now?' She tried to sound casual.

Dina craned her neck to have a look. 'Oh, that's Elaine. She's the daughter of some family friends. Some people seem to think that there's something going on between them, but there's no chance of that. They've been there and Deem will never go back.'

So that was Elaine. Jenny felt another twinge of jealousy, then a pang of guilt. Nadeem's relatives were really doing their best to be nice to her. If they knew how she had just walked away from her own family, would they be so kind?

Jenny made her way back to the bar, where Jamie was waiting.

'Back so soon?' His eyes sparkled. 'What will it be this time?'

She put her order in for a gin and tonic and a champagne glass of fizzy water, and sat watching him mix up the drink. When he passed her the glasses his hand brushed hers, and she looked up into his eyes, startled.

'Are you flirting with me?' She was surprised at her own forthrightness.

Jamie shook his head, voice tinged with a note of sadness. 'Nah. I can tell when a lass is taken, like.'

Jenny looked at him in surprise. 'What makes you think that?'

Jamie smiled, and leaned close to murmur in her ear. 'It's the look in your eyes. And the way you keep glancing around, as if you're looking for someone, makes me think that he's either here, or you're expecting him.' He straightened up, a glint in his eye. 'Nah, I'm just messing with you. Truth is, Nadeem wouldn't stop blethering on about you while we were working together today, and there's no way I'd tread on his patch. Besides, I'm spoken for too.'

'Oh.' Jenny wasn't surprised at that. 'Is she here tonight?'

To her amazement Jamie looked uncomfortable. Comprehension suddenly dawned on Jenny. 'It's Mia, isn't it!'

'Hush.' A dusky red started to creep up the back of Jamie's neck. 'She doesn't know.'

'Don't worry, I never would have guessed if you hadn't brought it up.' Jenny leaned over the bar, beckoning him closer. 'Don't leave it too long. Take her out under the stars and give her a first kiss to remember.' Then she just laughed and gathered the glasses, giving him a wink of her own as she turned away.

As Jenny reached the door she yelped as someone touched her on the shoulder, surprise almost making her drop one of the drinks. She turned, the irritation on her face fading as she realised it was Nadeem, and smiled up at him. 'Hello, you.'

Nadeem took the champagne glass from her, slipping his other arm around her shoulders. His breath tickled her ear, and made her tingle all the way down to her toes. 'I can't wait to strip this gorgeous dress off you and see if you have underwear to match.'

She looked up at him innocently. 'What happens if there isn't any at all?'

He groaned. 'That's dangerous talk. I've half a mind to carry you off and find out right now.'

She skipped out of his grasp. 'Not now, we have a drinks delivery to make.'

They made it back to Dina, who took the glass grate-fully. 'Thanks. It's not long now before the dancing starts.'

'Will it be Scottish dancing?' Jenny was curious.

'Of course.' Dina smiled. 'Have you done it before?'

'Not at all. Is it difficult?'

'Oh, not really. If you have a good partner it's really easy. We'll give you the Deemster, he'll keep you on the right track. He's actually really good, although he'd never admit it. Would spoil his manly image, you see.' Dina hid a smirk behind her hand as Nadeem pretended to look affronted.

They had just finished their drinks when the band started up a few chords and a compère with a microphone announced the Gay Gordons. The centre of the room emptied suddenly, and Jenny noticed that everyone was pairing up. It was generally men with women, but there didn't seem to be any hard and fast rule. Nadeem took Jenny's hand and led her onto the dance floor. She looked at him worriedly.

'Dinna fash, lass.' His accent was pure Scots and took her by surprise. He grinned at the look on her face, and said in his normal voice, 'It means, don't worry. There's enough people here who are new to this that they'll call out the steps, and I'll keep you right.'

Sure enough, the first dance was easy to get the hang of, and Jenny relaxed and began to enjoy the lilt of the music and the feel of Nadeem's strong arms around her. He was always there for her, guiding her in the right direction, and she began to see why this had been the traditional way for couples to meet and get to know each other before committing to a life of marriage. For what better metaphor was there than a dance for life's twists and turns?

Jenny was sorry when the dance came to an end, and Nadeem bowed theatrically to her. She was abruptly taken back to that first day they had met on the beach, and suddenly wished that the two of them were alone together. The evening was fun, but she loved spending time just with him.

Her breath caught as she considered the word. Love? Was this really love? Was it possible to love someone after only a couple of weeks? But she had no time to take all this in, as the compère announced the second dance and she found herself swept up into a group of six with Nadeem and his two sisters and two rather portly gentlemen who still managed to exercise quite considerable skill on the dance floor.

They called a break half-way through the dancing and Jenny found herself sitting next to Nadeem's mother. Nadeem had gone off 'to circulate', as he put it, and Dina was getting more drinks. Mia was nowhere to be seen. Jenny hoped that meant that Jamie had taken heed of her words.

Anita smiled encouragingly. 'Alison tells me you're planning to be a lawyer. I imagine that's pretty challenging. So much to remember!'

'It can't be any harder than studying to be a doctor.' Jenny suddenly remembered what Dina had said about how her parents had met and plucked up the courage to ask.

Anita laughed, a lovely sound which made Jenny smile too. 'Oh, she told you about that?' She draped an arm over the back of the sofa. 'There's not much to tell. The children always seem to think it was romantic, but it's a bit sad really. I had just lost my first patient and was beating myself up about it and Alan was very kind to me. What started off as a friendship soon developed into something more and now look at us.'

She laughed again. 'All the best relationships start that way I think. If you want a long-lasting relationship my advice is to be friends first and lovers second. Although a dash of mutual attraction never goes amiss.'

Jenny winced inwardly. She felt like a bit of a fraud, sitting next to his mother without telling her what was going on. Should she come clean about them both? Then she realised that Nadeem would have had that conversation already, when arranging for her to stay over. There was no need to worry so much.

Alison and David arrived and Jenny could see from David's flushed face and Alison's untidy hair that they had been enjoying the dancing too. They perched themselves on the sofa.

'So glad we found you.' Alison used her hands to smooth down her hair. 'We were wondering where you'd got to.'

'Lovely party, Anita,' David remarked. 'I can't help thinking though that you must have...well...subsidised the entrance fee somewhat.'

Anita smiled. 'I didn't want to make it too expensive for the locals. Don't tell anyone, but some of the attendees are paying rather more than others.' A wicked look crept into her eyes.

Jenny decided then and there that she rather liked this woman. She was so different from her own mother; so warm and open. *Like Mum used to be before Dad died.* She froze in shock at the realisation. What had really happened to her mother? How could someone go so quickly from normal to messed up?

The others were still talking around her, but Jenny didn't hear them. She suddenly realised that she really wanted to know. Had her mother been depressed all her life, and relied on her dad for support? Or was it something brought on by his death?

What's the point of knowing anyway, a small mean voice inside her asked. Why care for her if she never cared for you? But it was as if everything she had built her foundations on was crumbling. What if her mother had only moved back in with her parents because she couldn't find another way to support herself?

'Jenny?' Alison's voice permeated into her thoughts.

'Sorry. I was miles away.' Jenny blushed.

'I was just saying that you should go with Nadeem for the next dance.' It was Anita who spoke. 'I've been trying to find him a nice girl for ages. Don't mess it up now.' She waggled her eyebrows suggestively.

Jenny looked at her. Had the lack of spoons in the picnic indeed been deliberate? She decided to play it safe and grabbed David by the arm, hauling him to his feet. 'I'm going to have the next dance with the only eligible man for me. Alison, you can take Nadeem. And give him my apologies.' She smiled at Anita, who just laughed again as they disappeared in the direction of the dance floor.

It was almost eleven by the time the dancing finally stopped, and Jenny threw herself raggedly onto a sofa. A few seconds later Mia plopped down beside her, also breathing heavily.

Jenny wiped her forehead with the back of her hand. 'Wow. I never thought I would survive this long.'

'You're really good at it, you know. I would never guess that you'd never done it before.' Mia smiled happily, fanning herself with a napkin.

'Well, as you say, it does help if you have a good partner.' She smiled over at Nadeem, who had been snagged by yet another woman. She saw from his pained glance in her direction that she had nothing to worry about, so she leaned back, settling herself into the cushions.

'Oh, nonsense.' Mia waved a hand. 'I can see that you're a really good dancer.'

Jenny couldn't help herself. 'Talking about partners, what about Jamie?'

A blush crept into Mia's cheeks. 'What about Jamie?'

'It's obvious that he's crazy about you.'

'Yeah.' Mia's eyes sparkled. 'But I didn't know just how much until tonight.'

It was all the confirmation that Jenny needed of her earlier suspicions. She sighed happily. 'Isn't it great when you find someone who makes you feel good?'

Mia nodded vigorously, then jumped up. 'I'm parched, and you must be too. You stay here and I'll get you another drink.'

'Just water, please.' Jenny wiped her face again. 'I think I'll shrivel up if I don't replace some liquids soon.'

A couple of minutes later Alison and David came looking for her.

'We're off home.' Alison kissed her warmly on the cheek. 'We're just going to find Anita to say thank you and goodbye.'

Jenny gave her a hug. 'Drive safely. I'll see you to-morrow. I've got my key so you don't have to worry about staying in.'

'Have a great time.' Alison's eyes twinkled know-ingly at her, and Jenny blushed again as they headed off.

When Nadeem saw his cousin standing on the other side of the room, he politely disengaged from the per-son he was talking to and made his way towards him. 'Derek! I was thinking you'd got stuck in London.'

'Well, here I am.' Derek gave a big smile. 'I almost did, but then I found out that George was flying up this way and he offered to take me. He dropped me at Rovie Farm and from there it was easy.'

'That's what a posh school does for you! Useful con-nections to people in the know.' It was a long-stand-ing joke between them that the place where Derek's father worked had included a contribution towards a private school, while Nadeem had just gone to an ordi-nary one.

Derek just grimaced. 'Yeah. Connections. They're useful, but it always feels a little bit awkward. Anyway, I've spent the last couple of hours discussing the new cabinet appointments with your dad in his study. I to-tally lost track of time.'

Nadeem felt a rush of warmth for the other man; his cousin had obviously done that on purpose to stop his father from getting involved in the dancing.

'Thanks, DK.' He squeezed the other guy's shoulder.

Derek shrugged. 'It was the least I could do. Besides, it was an interesting conversation. I've left him chatting to my parents now, so he's in good hands.'

He leaned closer. 'He's really proud of you, you know. And grateful, too. He says he wouldn't have been able to trust anyone else besides the two of us to take over.'

Does he care that I almost lost my sanity in the process? The words slipped unbidden to Nadeem's mind. Had he said them out loud? He didn't think so. He breathed a sigh of relief. Although he almost wished that he had. He desperately longed for someone to take this crushing weight of responsibility away from him, if only just for a short while.

'Are you alright?' Derek had a look of concern on his face.

Nadeem forced a smile which he hoped was convincing. 'Fine, just a bit tired. All the stresses of the last few months have been taking their toll. I'm going to go and sit for a while.' He would go and find Jenny. It would be good to spend some time with her.

'I need to go and circulate.' Derek rolled his eyes. 'There's a couple of potential big donors here who I think could be persuaded to give some money to the Foundation.'

'Sounds good. But before you do that, there's some-one I want you to meet.' Nadeem scanned the crowd quickly, and saw Jenny perched on the arm of a sofa. He made her way towards her, Derek behind him.

'Derek, this is Jenny. Jenny, I want you to meet Derek. He's the cousin I've been telling you about.'

Chapter 10

Jenny had thought there was something familiar about the man Nadeem was chatting to, but with just the back of his head visible, there hadn't been much to go on. It was only when he turned around to look at her that she froze in horror.

It was the guy who had assaulted her in the office. What was he doing here? For a few moments she thought her eyes were playing tricks on her again and she blinked furiously, trying to clear away the unwanted vision.

As the two men came towards her, all she could do was stare at them. She was willing her legs to move, to turn and run, but once again they seemed frozen in place.

The bastard stuck out his hand as Nadeem made the introductions, and as she shook it automatically she cringed at the touch of his palm and swallowed, suddenly wanting to throw up.

'Pleased to meet you.' His voice was smooth and polite. Nadeem was smiling at them both and looked totally unaware of what was happening.

That creep himself. Here. At a party a million miles away from London. And he was Nadeem's cousin. Was this all just a cruel joke?

The realisation hit her that Derek didn't recognise her. Her new hair must have confused him, which just made her all the more angry. He had cost her a job and he didn't even care enough to remember her face.

A casual observer would never have dreamed the two were related, but with them both side by side she could see the similarities. True, Derek's light hair, blue eyes and fair skin were nothing like the darker tones that Nadeem had obviously picked up from his mother, but they were pretty much the same height. There were certain mannerisms that she recalled. And they both had similar ways of speaking.

She shuddered. No wonder Nadeem had been such a trigger for her flashbacks. She had to get away from him. For her own self-respect she couldn't make a scene, but it was all she could do not to spit in Derek's face and kick him where it would hurt the most.

'Are you OK?' Nadeem's concerned voice dragged her attention back to him.

Jenny had to swallow a couple of times before she spoke. 'I think it's just the heat, I'm going to go get some fresh air.'

Blindly seeking a way out, she turned and started away through the crowd. When someone touched her arm she whirled around, expecting it to be one of the two men, but it was only Mia, holding out a large glass of water. Jenny took it gratefully and took two deep gulps, trying to slow down and think rationally.

Mia saw her face and frowned, looking concerned. 'Are you alright?'

Jenny nodded, twisting her hands around the glass so Mia wouldn't see them trembling. She couldn't stay here. This was all just so humiliating. 'I'm fine. Just the heat, I think. I'm going to go and use the toilet.'

Mia pointed off to her right. 'Just use the private family ones if you're not feeling well, they're through that little door and down the corridor. Dina should be down there somewhere; I think she went off to feed the baby. There's a small sitting room where you can sit for a while if you want. Do you want me to come with you?'

'Thanks, but I just need a moment to myself.' Jenny turned and made her escape.

As soon as she closed the door, she sagged against the back of it, all strength gone in her legs. She pressed a hand to her mouth as her stomach heaved. To find out that the man who had caused all this was Nadeem's beloved cousin was just too much to bear.

But what to do now? There was no way she could go back in there. She cursed Nadeem for not telling her who his cousin was, and then had to laugh bitterly at herself. Somehow, in all their conversations, Nadeem had never mentioned the name of the company he worked for. And neither had she. The two men didn't even have the same last name. What a farce.

She racked her brains, trying to remember if Nadeem had ever been mentioned in the office, but those first days had been such a whirl of information and new faces that she doubted she would have remembered someone who was just a name on paper. Now that she thought of it, the reference to Tanzania did sound somehow familiar. It was always easier to join up the dots when you had the whole picture.

Jenny noticed a door open on her left, which seemed to lead off to the room Mia had mentioned. She stumbled along the corridor and sank down gratefully in one of the comfy red chairs which sat on either side of the hearth. A fire burned in the grate, and she held out her hands to it, thankful now for the warmth. She raised her head to find Dina staring at her from across the room, and let out a small shriek.

'Shh!' Dina put a finger to her lips. 'I've only just got her back to sleep.'

She motioned to the carry cot which was lying on a nearby table and crossed over to sit opposite Jenny, her face registering concern. 'Are you alright?'

Jenny nodded automatically, then realised what she was doing and shook her head. 'I'm sorry. I just don't feel well.'

She found she was still clutching the empty glass. Dina gently prised it out of her hands and poured out some water from a jug on the sideboard. 'Here, drink this.'

Jenny sipped at it gratefully and gazed numbly into the flames in the hearth.

Dina knelt in front of her and took her other hand. 'Your fingers are like ice!' She pulled a soft knitted blanket off the back of the sofa and wrapped it around Jenny's shoulders like a shawl. The shivering slowly ceased as the warmth of the fire began to seep in.

Jenny smiled gratefully at Dina. 'I just need to go home.'

'There's no way you're going home in this state.' The other woman's voice was firm. 'I'll take you upstairs to your room instead. Mum can come and look at you if you don't feel well.'

Jenny shook her head. 'No, you don't understand. I need to leave. And now.'

The door burst open, banging back against the wall.

'For goodness sake, the baby!' Dina spun round, putting a finger to her lips. Faint murmurs started to come from the cot and she hurried over to give some reassurance.

Jenny steeled herself for both men, but it was only Nadeem. He took in the situation in an instant and came to sit beside Jenny, his forehead creased in a worried frown.

'What's the matter? Are you alright?' His voice was quiet but she could hear the concern underneath it, and it made her want to cry. He had been so lovely to her. But if he heard what she had to say he would hate her forever.

'I'm fine. I just need to go home.' She started to get up but he tugged her back down gently.

'You're not going anywhere in this state. What's going on? As soon as you saw Derek you went so pale I thought I was going to have to do some serious mouth to mouth to resuscitate you.'

She knew he was joking on purpose, but her hands were trembling so badly her only thought was to put her glass down so she didn't drop it. 'I'm really sorry to cause you all this hassle. It's just I never expected to see him here.'

A horrible thought struck her. Did Nadeem know what Derek got up to? Or was he just as clueless as so many other men seemed to be in these sorts of situations?

'You've met him before?' Surprise showed on Nadeem's face.

Anger burst through her and out into her words. 'He's the bastard that lost me my job.'

Nadeem looked at her disbelievingly. 'Derek? No way. He would never do something like that.'

Jenny just shook her head, not trusting herself to speak. And her heart sank just a little further; why would Nadeem believe her when the person she was talking about was obviously his best friend?

Nadeem was shaking his head, clearly still trying to take things in. 'Are you saying that you used to work for us? That's just weird.'

Jenny nodded, her fingers curling tightly around the blanket. 'I didn't realise it. Honestly. You never told me the name of the company you worked for, so how could I know?'

He shook his head again, as if he couldn't quite believe it. 'And we met by accident on the plane. So weird.'

A sudden suspicion crept into her mind, and the words came out of her mouth before she had time to think. 'Are you sure you didn't arrange all this? The meeting on the plane, I mean? Is this all part of some twisted plan by the two of you to totally ruin my life?'

He stared at her, eyes wide. 'God, Jenny, no. I swear. How could you think something like that?'

'I'm sorry.' She buried her head in her hands as the memories threatened to overwhelm her. 'I'm really sorry, Nadeem. I should have told you. If I had any idea about any of this, I would have done. I'm so sorry.' She was close to tears as she looked back up at him.

Nadeem rubbed his forehead with his fingers, a frown on his face. She could tell he was still trying to process the news. 'So let me get this straight. You're trying to say that my cousin assaulted you? That's impossible. I've known him all my life and he would never do something like that.'

He shook his head, this time decisively, then his eyes narrowed. 'Wait. Did you set all of this up? Follow me up here just to get some sort of revenge?'

Anger mingled with the hurt she was feeling and she leapt to her feet, her eyes blazing. 'Why would I do that?' Her fingers itched to slap him. 'You're not thinking straight, Nadeem. You told me yourself that you switched planes at the last minute. How would I have managed that?'

Nadeem suddenly looked less certain, doubt beginning to show in his face. 'You're right. I don't know. But this can't just all be a coincidence. Maybe meeting on the plane was an accident, but are you really telling me you didn't recognise who I was back then? If you worked for our company, you must have known who I was.'

She could tell that he was really struggling. It seemed like he wanted to believe her, but was torn by his loyalty to a man he'd known all his life.

'I think you should at least listen to what she's saying, Deem.' Dina's quiet voice broke the silence. They had both forgotten that she was there.

Nadeem glared at Dina. 'Why are you taking her side, sis?'

Dina shrugged. 'This always happens in these type of situations. No-one ever believes the woman because "oh, he's such a nice man".' The venom in her voice made Jenny wonder if she had personal experience of such a situation.

Nadeem's mouth flattened, then suddenly his shoulders slumped. 'No. It's true. You're right.'

As Jenny sank gratefully back onto the sofa, he paced up and down, running his hands through his hair. 'But I still can't believe it. Not Derek. I've known him forever. He's my best friend, for goodness sake.'

He stopped suddenly in front of her, looking down with exasperation. 'Why didn't you report it?'

Jenny laughed humourlessly. 'I did. Your HR department were the ones who fired me.'

'Melissa fired you? She's one of the kindest people I know.' Nadeem resumed his pacing. 'I just can't take all this in. It seems so unbelievable.'

To Jenny's horror she found herself crying, loud sobs which she quickly tried to stifle for fear of waking the baby.

Nadeem sat down beside her. He tried to put his arm around her but when she flinched, pulling away from him, he held up his hands. 'Look. Don't cry. Please. We can deal with this tomorrow, sort things out then. Let's go outside. Get some fresh air and forget about all this for now.'

Jenny suddenly found herself too weary to fight any more. After all, it wasn't Nadeem's fault who he was related to. Could she really hold it against him when he obviously didn't know what kind of man Derek was? That was a question she didn't feel like she had the brain power to answer right now.

She wiped her eyes with the back of her hand. 'OK. I could do with some fresh air.'

Nadeem nodded at Dina, who nodded back. Some unspoken communication passed between them which Jenny couldn't read and it only made her feel more guilty. If she had actually stayed with her family, she might have had that kind of relationship with her own sister.

Nadeem led Jenny out of a side door into the gardens. The windows in the marquee were casting long strips of light onto the perfectly manicured garden, and he guided her to sit on a small wooden bench. The DJ was playing eighties disco sounds and the party was getting pretty lively, but outside the weather was beautifully still and clear.

'I have to say that my nose is dripping in a most unladylike fashion right now.' Jenny sniffled. 'I don't suppose you have another handkerchief?'

He pulled the one out of his jacket pocket and handed it to her. 'Blow away.'

She did as instructed and then Nadeem shoved the handkerchief in his trousers. 'I think you're amazing, sweetheart. You're such a strong person. Look at all the things you've been through, and yet you come out fighting.'

Jenny sighed. 'That's what I keep telling myself. But sometimes it just doesn't feel like it.'

They were both silent for a few more minutes, watching the stars.

'You do realise this thing between me and your cousin isn't just a misunderstanding, don't you?' Jenny couldn't help herself; they both had to accept that this wasn't just going to go away. 'You know that I've already submitted my claim to ACAS. That means you and I are going to be on opposite sides of the table when all this goes to mediation.'

Nadeem turned to face her, placing his hands on her shoulders. 'Don't. Just don't.'

'Don't what?' Jenny's tone was bitter. 'Be myself? Tell the truth? You need to face up to this, Nadeem. Your cousin assaulted me. He's the one who needs to hear the word "don't".'

Nadeem was just about to reply when he heard a noise from the darkness just off to the left. It was unmistakeably a gunshot. He pulled Jenny close and tried to scan the darkness, automatically reaching for the weapon that wasn't there. If only he had some night vision right now...

There was no sign that anyone inside had heard anything, but with the level of the music as it was then it was hardly a surprise.

'What is it?' Jenny's voice was muffled against his shirt.

'Gunshot.' He murmured very quietly. 'Ten o clock.'

'Shit.' Jenny swore softly and froze.

The strips of light made it impossible for him to adjust his eyes to the darkness, and as he frowned, trying to focus, the memories crowded in of that stormy night in Afghanistan.

The lightning flashed, screwing his night vision to hell. He ripped off his goggles as he ran back towards the place where he had left Nate, praying that his own eyes would guide him in the darkness. Using a torch would mean instant death for both himself and the three men following him. The MERT would be landing in ten minutes, and they had to get Nate out to the rendezvous point before then. It would be a full flight with all the hits the men had taken. This whole night had been a complete Charlie Foxtrot.

He heard the shots when he was only twenty yards away and froze, flattening himself against the wall. Nate's weapon, he thought, with equal parts of terror and relief. Because that meant that he was under attack, but fighting back.

He was running for the door when he heard the sounds of an unfamiliar rifle ring out, and cursed. After that everything seemed to go in slow motion. The man in the doorway, falling to the ground as bullets smashed into him. Jumping over him into the room, fumbling for the torch, looking down at the bloody mess which was all that was left of his best friend...

'Stay here.' Jenny felt herself roughly pushed back down into the bench, and then Nadeem catapulted off, running across the garden in the direction of the sound. His speed was pretty impressive.

She curled up tightly on the bench, hoping to keep herself as invisible as possible. Or would it be safer to go inside?

'Such a stunning dress you have there.' Jenny jumped at the voice, then froze as she realised who it was. An opponent far more threatening than a shadow with a gun.

As Derek materialised out of the darkness Jenny felt a surge of adrenaline and wrapped her hands tighter in the blanket to keep them from shaking. Or from punching him, she realised; the last thing she needed was for him to sue her for assault.

She stood up. It seemed better to face him head on.

'Good evening, Derek.' She kept her tone cordial, although she didn't expect him to be fooled. 'What a surprise to meet you here.'

'Likewise.' Her opponent inclined his head. 'I thought something was familiar about you when I saw you first. How the hell did you get an invite?'

Jenny was damned if she would tell him about her relationship with Alison and David. The less he knew about her real life the better.

'Oh, you know. Connections.' She waved a hand dismissively.

'Well, I see that Nadeem is quite smitten with you.'

Jenny hoped the dim light hid the rush of panic in her eyes. She shouldn't be surprised he had picked that up. It was pretty clear for anyone to see.

'What do you want from me?' She lifted her chin.

'Nothing. I just wanted to make sure you weren't causing any more trouble.' His words were mild enough, but somehow his tone sent a shiver down her spine. He leaned in closer, and she shuddered, but stood her ground.

His voice was soft. 'You need to leave. Now. And if you ever tell anyone what happened between us, then I will make sure that you never work in legal circles again.'

The threat was so similar to some kind of mafia warning from a film that she almost laughed out loud. Derek would find out sooner or later that she had filed her claim. She was surprised that he hadn't been notified already. There must be a backlog in the admin.

'I'm not interfering with your family, Derek.' She kept her tone polite, even though her fingers itched to hit him. 'If I'd known you were related to Nadeem, I would have run the other way as fast as I could.'

She drew herself up to her full height, gathering her courage like the blanket she still clutched around her. 'If you don't mind, I have better things to do than stand around talking to you.'

Jenny pushed past him and made her way back into the house. She barely managed to get as far as the toilet before she threw up. Afterwards she rested her head against the wall, grateful for the coolness of the tiles.

A vision of his face made her retch again. She had to get out of here. The idea that she could somehow hang on to Nadeem without having to deal with Derek suddenly seemed very naive.

Splashing water on her face, she planned her escape route into the main corridor, where she could retrieve her bag and get away.

Chapter 11

Nadeem closed his eyes, trying to calm his rapidly beating pulse. There was no time to think about what had just happened; Jenny would be waiting for him, and worried. He rushed back to the bench. 'It's alright, someone just-'

She wasn't there. She must have got cold and gone back inside. He marched back into the family lounge, only to find Mo and Dina sitting next to each other by the fire.

'Where's Jenny?' The memories of Nate that had been stirred up made him unusually curt.

Dina shrugged. 'She's not been in here since you went outside. I thought she was with you.'

'She was. But some tosser thought it would be a good idea to bring their shotgun with them and try it out in the garden after a few drinks. By the time I sorted it out she'd disappeared.'

Mo frowned. 'Maybe she went upstairs.'

Nadeem collected himself. 'Probably. I'll go and have a look.'

Dina got up. 'I'll come with you.'

They went upstairs together, but there was no sign of Jenny. They did spot Derek, heading towards his room.

'Have you seen Jenny at all?' Nadeem couldn't help asking.

Derek shrugged. 'Disappeared, has she? No idea. Is she always that unreliable?' He nodded to Dina and continued on down the corridor.

Nadeem stopped and looked at Dina. 'She wouldn't just go off like that, without saying a word. I need to find her. Especially after everything that went down tonight.'

Dina nodded. 'You take the back of the house, I'll take the front. Then we can both take torches and look in the garden. If she's slipped and fallen somewhere...'

Nadeem shook his head. He didn't even want to consider the thought.

It was almost half an hour later, after a thorough search and a few calls that went through to Jenny's voicemail, that Nadeem finally had to concede that Jenny was nowhere in the house or garden. They had found the blanket in one of the toilets, but Jenny herself seemed to have totally vanished. A sudden thought occurred to him; would the Campbells know where she was? He didn't want to get them worried, but maybe Jenny had said something to them before she left.

He couldn't find them, but he and Dina soon ran into his mother, who was helping the catering staff start their behind the scenes clean up. 'Oh yes.' She nodded. 'They went home already. I can't remember exactly when they left. So many people; the night's a bit of a blur.'

So maybe Jenny had changed her mind about staying over. But why would she do that without saying goodbye? Was she that angry at him? If she wasn't picking up her calls now he'd have to try again tomorrow. Or go and see her on his way to the airport.

'Do you want a hand with the clean-up?' Habit made him offer.

His mother shook her head, drawing him in for a kiss. 'Don't worry. You get yourself to bed. You look tired.'

He left her to it, making his way towards the stairs. He needed to be by himself for a while. The bombshell that Jenny had dropped on him lay heavily on his mind. With a pang he realised that he really cared for her, in spite of the fact that they had only known each other for such a short time. Had it only been two weeks since they had met? All the things that they had shared made it seem much longer than that.

Up in his room, he dimmed the lights, counting the slow rise and fall of his breath to calm his inner mind.

This story about Derek, it was pretty fantastical. For sure, Derek was no saint; he'd always been on a bit of a short fuse where his temper was concerned, but Nadeem had never seen him act with anything but respect towards women. Why would Jenny lie? Unless it was just a ruse to get some attention? Or some money?

He shook his head. They'd only known each other for a short time, but if he had anything to say about Jenny, she wasn't an attention-seeker. Which just left the possibility that she was maybe telling the truth. But that would mean that he had to revise everything he knew about Derek, which was just impossible. So he was back to square one, meaning Jenny had to be lying, which he also couldn't believe.

Nadeem balled up his fists and shoved them into his eyes. It was all just too much to think about right now. Seeing Nate again had just been exhausting. And concerning, too. He had been so sure that his flashbacks were a thing of the past. Somehow dealing with Jenny's trauma was making him re-hash his own.

Jenny had managed to successfully leave the house without running into anyone she knew. The walk home wasn't as bad as she had imagined. It took her almost an hour, but the night was fine and the cold air cleared her head. Scotty greeted her at the front door as she let herself in, and she hugged him to her, grateful for his warmth.

When she finally calmed down enough to dig her phone out of her bag there were missed calls from Nadeem, so she sent a message to let him know that she was safely home, explaining that she couldn't possibly see him again, and then firmly switched her phone off with a sigh. She was going to stick to her resolve no matter how hard it was; if he was related to that man then there was no space in her life for him.

Not only related, but good friends as well. The thought made her shiver. It was time to sleep. Tomorrow was another day, and she would cope with it when it came.

Daylight was creeping through the curtains when Jenny finally awoke. She smiled; she hadn't remembered to close her bedroom door and Scotty was sleeping on her feet. But then the rest of the evening hit her and her stomach instantly knotted.

What had woken her? She reached for her phone which was charging by the bed and switched it on. Eight am. She had several more missed calls and just as she was about to unlock the phone it rang again. She looked at it, hope blossoming in her mind when she saw Nadeem's number. If he was calling then maybe he believed her.

'Hey.' She tried to keep her voice level.

'You left without warning last night. I was worried sick. And then you dumped me with a message.' She could hear the frustration in his voice. 'How could you do that, after everything we've shared?'

Jenny shrugged, trying to muster up a dismissive tone, although she could feel her heart thudding in her throat as the confrontation with Derek flashed into her mind. 'What is there to talk about? You clearly don't believe me about your cousin at all, despite "everything we've shared". I just didn't see the point in staying.'

'It's not that I don't trust you. It's just that's it's such an unlikely story. That man has been like a brother to me. Are you really sure it's not just your mind playing tricks on you?'

Jenny couldn't believe it. 'My mind? You're trying to say that I might have dreamed all this up with my screwy brain?' She wanted to strangle him. 'So much for your ridiculous sprig of white heather. I really needed you last night and you failed me at the crucial moment, and I had to deal with it all by myself. Like I always do. So it's fine. I can do without you too.'

She heard his indrawn breath and instantly regretted her words, but it was too late to take them back.

'Don't be ridiculous.' Nadeem's voice was tight. 'What's important is that you're basically asking me to trust your word against my judgment, and my family's too. And Derek is one of my closest friends. I've only known you for two weeks. Surely you can understand where I'm coming from?'

Jenny felt like a hand was constricting her chest. She couldn't deal with this now. She had to stop this conversation, before she became a gibbering wreck. 'I totally understand. That's why I'm not asking you to do it. I completely agree with you; why should you trust my word over theirs? So I'm removing myself from the equation. Have a nice life.' She cut the call and then reached for the heather she had placed carefully on the bureau. A few swift movements had it torn in pieces and thrown out the window.

Her anger suddenly subsided and tears began to fall down her face. How could he have chosen his family over her? She couldn't imagine feeling the same about her family. But the more she thought about it, the more she realised how much she still felt for them. She missed them so much, even her mother with all her failings. And how was that even possible?

Nadeem paced furiously back and forth in his room, his body burning with anger. He lifted one of the ornaments from the windowsill, ready to smash it on the floor, but stopped himself just in time.

Damn it! How could Jenny just go off, as if all the things they had shared together meant nothing to her? And now she was going to sue the company and fleece them for everything they had too.

Numbly, he sank down onto the bed. He had no idea how long he had been there when he heard a gentle tap on the door.

'Go away.' His voice was a growl.

Dina stuck her head around the door. He threw a pillow, which she dodged neatly. 'I heard you shouting at yourself. What happened?'

Nadeem was all set to shout at her too, but then he deflated. 'I don't know. I was going to have it all out with Derek this morning and ask for his side of the story, but Jenny's gone and dumped me. Why would she just run off like that?'

Dina came in and sat on the end of the bed. 'I don't know her like you do, so I can't say. I think you just have to trust your instinct on this.'

He rubbed his hands across his face. 'My instinct has gone haywire. You know why. I used to trust it, but ever since the night I lost Nate, it's failed me.'

Dina looked at him with a frown. 'You never told me exactly what happened that night. You said I wouldn't want to know the details.' She shifted over so they were lying shoulder to shoulder. 'I think now might be a good time.'

He told her, missing nothing out. The memories came back clearly after the previous night's episode and he told her about that too. When he had finished he looked across at her, not knowing what he would find in her face.

She took his hand and grasped it firmly, her shorter fingers curling around his, and the silence stretched out as she absorbed the information. He saw the tears brimming in her eyes. 'I loved him too, you know.' Her hand squeezed his.

'You mean...?' He couldn't finish the thought out loud.

She saw where his mind was going. 'No. Not like that. Well, maybe now that you make me think of it, it's possible. But when you love someone that much it's hard to tell.'

She shifted, laying her head on his shoulder. 'From what you say though, that night, it seems like you had a no-win situation. If you'd stayed with him he probably would have died. Leave him? At least there might have been some chance of getting help. So I think your instinct was right. You chose the one that was the better of the two situations. You took some action. Even if it meant going against what you'd been trained to do.'

'Maybe.' It was hard for him to accept her summary, after carrying his guilt around for so long. 'But now I'm in another no-win situation. Choose one way, I'll lose Derek. Choose the other, I'll lose Jenny. And I can't just give up on Derek like that. I won't lose another friend.'

'Then I suggest you talk to him. And take things one step at a time.'

She slid off the bed. 'Just make sure you take care of yourself, OK? I've been a bit worried about you lately, with the stress of taking over from Mum and Dad. You've not been yourself these last few months.'

'I'm fine.' The reassurance was out of his mouth before he even had time to think about it.

'I trust your judgment.' He didn't miss her pointed reference. 'But just make sure you take care of yourself too.' She kissed him gently on the cheek. 'I'm going to get some breakfast. I'll leave you to think about what you're going to do.'

'Dina?'

Her hand was already on the door. 'Yes?'

'Don't tell Mum and Dad about any of this, will you? I don't want to worry them.'

She wrinkled her forehead, but then nodded. 'OK.' Her concern for their father stood out clearly on her face and he almost called her back, but by the time the thought crystallised she was gone.

Nadeem lay on the bed, kneading the crisp white duvet with his fingers. He threw another one of the pillows across the room where it bounced off the wall and landed on the floor. It didn't make him feel any better. It didn't matter what he should have done, Jenny was gone and that was that.

But this thing with Derek, what was he to do?

Trust his instinct, Dina had said. He'd known Derek all his life and Jenny just two weeks. There was no competition. She could take her lies and be damned.

He'd need to talk to Derek and sort out a strategy for winning this case. His heart would repair itself in time.

That's the last time I believe a woman who says she cares for me.

His head finally clear, he packed his bag and left for the airport.

Nadeem's first action on stepping off the plane was to call Derek. 'Where did you get to? I thought you were flying back down with me.'

'That was the plan. But I met an old friend at the party and we ended going back to his. We're just in the middle of a round of golf.'

Derek seemed to move in totally different circles these days. Nadeem thought about his friends back in Glasgow and their walking trips to the hills, and sighed. He should try to make time for a visit. And soon.

He was getting distracted from his real purpose. 'Did you know that Jenny had filed a harassment claim against us?' The thought of it made his hand tighten around the phone, and the other clench into a fist.

'No. But I'm not surprised.' Derek's tone was dry. 'We fired her because she was spreading bullshit about me, clearly in the hope of doing just that. I'm sorry, Deem. I could tell how much you liked her.'

Nadeem hesitated. Derek had always been honest with him and yet he couldn't help asking, just to be totally certain. 'And you're sure there's nothing that might have happened between you? Nothing she might have misinterpreted?' He bit his lip, unsure what he would do if Derek said yes.

'Never.' Derek sounded a hundred percent sincere, and Nadeem breathed a sigh of relief. 'I wouldn't go near the scheming little bitch. I was nice to her, that was all. Because she was new.'

So Jenny had worked for them. At least that part of her story was true. Her words about trying to save money for her legal studies came back to him. Clearly she had just seen their company as an easy way to make the money she needed to further her own interests.

A woman threw a worried glance at him and Nadeem realised he was stomping down the corridor, swinging his free hand wildly, a scowl on his face. He forced himself to stop, lean against the wall and relax his shoulders, rolling his neck to ease the tension.

What he really couldn't work out was if Jenny honestly hadn't known who he was, or had realised from the start and decided to cosy up to him to make him more likely to believe her story. Anyway, it didn't matter now. No-one messed with his family like this.

'You still there?' Derek's voice came through the phone.

He put it back to his ear again. 'Yeah. Yeah. I'm here. We'll have to talk when you get back in the office tomorrow. We need a strategy for dealing with this. We can't let her shit us around.'

'Sure. I'll see you then. But we should get some help too. Get Legal and HR involved.' Derek's advice, as always, was totally sound.

'Will do. We'll sort this out. Enjoy the golf. Oh, and whatever you do, don't tell Dad. I don't want him knowing anything about this, he'll just worry too much. Which means you can't tell Mum either. You know how they talk.'

He paused, thinking. 'Just don't tell anyone. Dina knows, but she's the only one.'

'No worries.' Derek sounded cheerful. 'My lips are sealed. I'll see you tomorrow. We've got this.'

'Colin's just coming.' Melissa strode into Nadeem's office and sat down. 'He asked what it was about, but I didn't want to tell him in the open plan office.'

Nadeem just nodded, his mouth set in a thin line. With Melissa to give him HR advice and Colin on the legal side they could handle this. He just had to ignore the personal and focus on the practical.

Colin popped his head around the door. 'Everything alright?'

'Thanks for coming. Take a seat.' Nadeem motioned to an empty chair. 'We need your help on something serious.'

He quickly explained the situation. 'So as our legal counsel, Derek and I need your advice on how best to proceed.'

Colin looked towards Derek, a small crease in his forehead. 'And are you maintaining that nothing actually happened between you?'

Derek nodded emphatically. A few moments of silence stretched out.

'I'm not sure I'm the best person to advise you on this.' Colin had a worried expression on his face as he spoke. 'You see, as her manager Ms Lang came to me first, on the day that the alleged incident happened. Before she left, I advised her, as was my duty, on her legal rights in this matter, and her options, should she feel her dismissal was unjustified.' His discomfort with the situation was obvious and he was clearly choosing his words very carefully. 'But more importantly, beyond the basic regulations, this is not my area of expertise; as you know I specialise in commercial contract law. So if there are details that Melissa's knowledge doesn't cover, I would seriously recommend hiring in an external party.'

Nadeem groaned inwardly. Lawyers, he knew, cost a fortune. 'Is there anyone you would recommend?'

A faint colour appeared on Colin's cheeks. 'I do have a personal contact, but unfortunately, I also recommended this source to Ms Lang without thinking about the implications for our company, and if what you say is true, I would imagine she has contracted his services.'

'You bastard.' Derek started to get to his feet, but Nadeem clamped a firm hand on his shoulder and forced him back down.

'Leave him be, Derek. He's only being honest with us. Besides, the more we can show that we've followed proper procedure in this, the more likely we are to win our case.'

He turned to Melissa. 'We did follow the proper procedure, right?'

She nodded. 'The law states that there has to be a proper investigation. I investigated with Derek and found that there were no grounds for complaint. Jennifer could, of course, have involved the police, since this is an accusation of sexual harassment, but she has clearly not done so, which I think strengthens our case.'

Colin pushed back his chair abruptly. 'I think it may be better if I leave you to it. Melissa knows my views on this matter, and she can relay them to you if she feels it is appropriate.' He closed the door behind him gently, but they could hear him stomping back to his desk.

Nadeem frowned. 'What was all that about?'

'Colin believes her story. Such a soft-hearted idiot.' Melissa shook her head disapprovingly. 'You've got to be really careful of these manipulative types. My husband had his career ruined by a situation exactly like this where the woman was totally lying about it. Cost him his job, and now no-one will touch him with a bargepole.'

For a moment her face flickered with emotion and Nadeem saw a vulnerability in her that he had never seen before. Then she squared her shoulders and leaned her arms on the table. 'Right. This is what we're going to do.'

Chapter 12

All Saturday morning Jenny had expected Nadeem to turn up at her door, demanding that she change her mind. But when two o'clock came and went, she knew he was on his flight back down to London and that was when she finally realised it was over.

After two days of moping around in bed she could tell that Alison was getting worried about her, so she dragged herself downstairs to sit in the living room by the fire. Scotty climbed up on the sofa and came to lie beside her, pushing his cold nose under her hand. It was this friendly contact which finally made her break down. Alison quietly placed a box of tissues beside her and piece by piece got the whole story out of her, holding Jenny close and stroking her hair.

'How could I be so wrong?' Jenny sniffled, blowing her nose. 'I thought I could trust him. But he didn't trust me.'

Alison shook her head. 'I feel angry with myself that I didn't connect up the dots after reading through your legal submission, but then the company name doesn't have any connection with their family name, so why would I have done? I was racking my brains to try and remember if Anita mentioned it when she told me about her husband on Friday, but I honestly don't think she did, and all the fanfare on Saturday night was about the Grayson Foundation and not the company. What a mess.' She sighed. 'Being abroad for so long has taken me right out of the loop on local news.'

'You can't blame yourself.' Jenny reached over and touched Alison's arm gently. 'I've been thinking the same. But I realised Saturday night that it's always easier to connect up the dots when you have the whole picture.'

Alison handed her another tissue. 'It must be hard for Nadeem though, if he really didn't know what Derek gets up to. How would you react if someone told you that I had murdered someone?'

Jenny blew out a breath. 'I know, you've got a point there.' She fiddled with a curl. 'But really, it doesn't matter now. He's gone and in some ways it's a relief too. Having a relationship with him would just be too complicated. Even if he did apologise, there's still the fact that Derek's his cousin and that's never going to change.'

She dried her eyes and blew her nose again. 'Let's not let it ruin the rest of my holiday. I still have another two weeks and we should make the most of it.'

Jenny felt strange waiting for Katie at the airport, as if she lived in the area. She briefly wondered what Katie would be wearing; high heels and posh dresses just wouldn't work up here. Her mouth opened when Katie waltzed out in sturdy shoes and a waterproof jacket. It was of course a very stylish jacket, but still it was quite a shock and Jenny said so.

'Well, darling, I did have to buy them specially, but I just couldn't ruin any other shoes in all that mud. And one does have to blend in with the locals.' Jenny knew by the airy tone that the last part was a joke. That was the thing about Katie; most people thought all she cared about was fancy clothes and London's social scene, but underneath all that there was a heart of gold, and someone who spent a lot of her free time fundraising for a local women's shelter.

Katie loved the little croft house, and was delighted to be sharing the attic room with Jenny. She was eager to see all the things that Jenny had told her about, and of course wanted to know all about what had happened with Nadeem. Jenny hadn't been comfortable talking about everything over the phone, so she filled her in on the first night, as they lay snuggled in their beds in the dark.

Katie's reaction was totally predictable. 'I still can't believe that his cousin is that creep. How disgusting.'

Jenny nodded, then realised that Katie wouldn't see her. 'Yes. And there's no way he was going to believe my word against his.'

She shivered. 'It *was* creepy, him coming across me in the garden like that. It took me right back to what had happened. But also to how my stepfather used to manipulate me. And I realised, Katie, that this whole thing isn't about what Derek tried to do to me. It isn't about sexual intimacy. It's about being in a situation that I can't control. And the worry of people doubting me. My stepfather twisted things around so much that I even ended up doubting myself.'

There was a rustle of blankets, and then Jenny felt Katie climbing in beside her. They lay side by side for a few minutes.

'You'll get through this, JJ. You're strong. One of the strongest people I know.'

'That's what Nadeem said actually.' Jenny sighed.

Katie laughed at that. 'Darling, I wouldn't give up on him just yet. It's probably just a lot for him to take in. Wouldn't you feel the same if someone came to you and said I was actually a first-class bitch?'

'Funnily enough, that's what Alison said too. Only she's a murderer apparently.' Jenny couldn't help a faint smile.

'Oooh! I'll have to be careful.' Katie wriggled under the covers, searching for a more comfortable position in the single bed.

Jenny shook her head. 'Really, I just have to move on. Get the tribunal over with and then put it all behind me. I can't wait around for other people to sort out my life.'

She felt tears prickle at the corner of her eyes. 'I'm just so tired of being strong, Katie. I want to be weak sometimes. For someone else to take the strain.'

An arm crept around her, hugging her close. 'You've got me. I can be strong for you, just like you are for me. I mean, for goodness sake, I would have never survived all that shit with Tony if you hadn't been there for me.'

'Yeah, mega judgment fail on that one.' Jenny couldn't help laughing. 'How did you not see that one coming? I knew he was a tosser the first time I saw him.'

'But he was soooo gorgeous.' Katie protested as she slipped back into her own bed. It wasn't the first time they'd had this exchange. 'And he wasn't nearly as bad as that guy who tried to ask Reena to marry him when they'd only been dating three weeks.'

'Oh, the one who opened his proposal by complimenting her on her childbearing hips?' Jenny went off into a fit of giggles at the memory. Soon they were swapping stories and laughing until they finally fell asleep.

'Alison's organised some amazing trips for us,' Jenny said happily as they sat around the breakfast table the following morning.

'Can't wait.' Katie grinned as she munched a mouthful of toast. 'What's the plan?'

Alison buttered her own slice. 'I've booked two nights in Orkney. The bird life is spectacular, and I've arranged a boat trip around the island so that you get a better view.'

'Any fit farmers up there?' Katie gave a suggestive wink and Jenny kicked her under the table. 'Ouch! I was just asking.'

'Also, there's a woollen mill up the coast and, given the love both of you have for clothes, I thought you might like to have a look. I've been waiting to take Jenny until you arrived.'

'Awesome.' Katie gave a thumbs up.

Alison continued. 'There's not much else up here in terms of fashion, just a couple of nice vintage shops in Inverness which Jenny's already been to. I can take you both on the way to the airport. So it's mainly going to be outdoor sights. Jenny, I know you've already seen the castle, but it's so impressive I hope you won't mind going again.'

Jenny swallowed. 'No, of course.' Much as she didn't really want to go back there, it would be good to overwrite her memories of Nadeem with some other ones. 'It is pretty spectacular.'

She reached for her phone to check if there were any important messages. At her intake of breath the other three all looked up, concerned.

'I've got a date. It's in three weeks.'

None of them had to ask what she was talking about. Katie reached over and squeezed her hand and David folded his newspaper.

Alison got up from the table. 'That's good. Means at least you know what you're doing now. You should call that lawyer of yours and tell him.'

'It's him that sent me the email. I asked that all correspondence could go via him.' She scrolled with a thumb. 'But you're right, he has said I should call him.' She checked her watch. 'I'll go and do that now. Get it sorted before I forget.'

Her stomach felt slightly strange as she dialled the number, but the cheerful voice on the other end of the line made her relax. The guy obviously had faith in her, otherwise he wouldn't have agreed to represent her on a no-win-no-fee arrangement. She was totally doing the right thing. She took heart from the fact that his most important instruction was for her to enjoy the rest of her holiday, because they could sort everything out when she got back to London.

The next ten days were such a whirl of activity that Jenny barely had the chance to think about Nadeem during the day. Jenny could almost imagine that Alison and David were her parents, and Katie a glamorous sister.

But it was the nights that were difficult. For it was then that Jenny's thoughts were left to wander back to the way that Nadeem's arms had felt wrapped around her in the same bed that she was lying in. Just for a short time she had felt safe, as if nothing could ever hurt her again. She missed his laugh, and the way he made her laugh too. And now everything was all screwed up.

'Get a grip, woman.' She had a stern word with herself one evening as she lay sleepless in her bed, listening to Katie's soft breathing from the other side of the room. 'You're better off out of that situation, and that's that.' But even as she stiffened her resolve she knew it would be a long time before she could forget him.

The day they went to the woollen mill there was beautiful sunshine and the girls caught their mood from the weather, swapping funny stories in the back of the car until Alison pleaded with them to stop so she could concentrate on the driving. After that they just sat back and admired the view, exchanging glances with each other from time to time and breaking out into giggles for no reason at all.

The place was a good hour's drive away, up past Wick and round the coast. Jenny and Katie were amazed to find it ran on water, powered by the same stream that had run under the building for more than a century. Jenny thought the machines themselves were impressive, clacking away individually, and it was fascinating watching the patterns build up line by line, as the bobbins swished back and forth. But when Jenny stepped into the warehouse shop her breath caught. She had been expecting a typical storage area with basic shelving and a concrete floor, but this looked more like someone's living room.

A stove burned brightly in one corner, and a couple of plush sofas sat in front of it, covered in tweed of course. Samples of woollen cloth were draped tastefully around the sides of the room, and bolts of fabric were arranged on sturdy shelves along one wall.

The tour guide smiled at Jenny's expression. 'We get a lot of bespoke orders, so we want somewhere comfortable where we can discuss designs and so on.'

Jenny spied a dressmaker's dummy in one corner. 'Do you also make clothes?'

'Not really.' The woman shook her head. 'It's more just there for a bit of ambience, although some people do use it to see how the fabrics fold and drape.'

Katie had been examining the rolls of material. 'Wow, look at this one.' She fingered the smooth purple folds gently. 'It's so thin!'

The guide smiled. 'You have good taste. That's one of our most expensive fabrics. Very tricky to make, because of how fine the thread is.'

Jenny had a look at it. It was beautiful, even if it wasn't quite the colour she would pick for herself. She perused the shelves, running her fingers over the bolts of cloth. A quick check of some of the price tags confirmed her suspicions; these were all far out of her affordable range. But she couldn't resist looking anyway.

Buried away on a bottom shelf, a quick flash of colour caught her eye. She pulled out a small roll and studied it. It was red, but also so much more than that. Differing shades swirled in seemingly random gradations through the fabric. It was a perfect accompaniment to some material she had sitting in her cupboard at home. Her mind flexed through all the possibilities. Bolero? Jacket? Wrap? Wrap, she decided. It would fit with the style of the evening gown she had in mind. She searched for a price tag but couldn't find one.

The tour guide seemed surprised to see what she had pulled out. 'Oh! I didn't think we had any of that left. It's a good few years old. Before my time anyway.'

Jenny turned to her. 'There's no price tag. Do you know how much it might cost?'

The woman shook her head. 'I'll have to go and ask in the office.'

She was back a couple of minutes later with a smile. 'They say that we'd normally sell this for ninety-five pounds a metre, but because there's only just over two metres and it's so old you can have the lot for a hundred.'

Jenny sucked in a breath and considered. Still pricey, but it was just so tempting. It would make the perfect partner to the next dress she was planning. Those colours...

It was at that precise moment Jenny realised that she wanted a workshop of her own, just like this. And to have people sitting on her couches talking to her about her designs.

'I'll take it.' She meant the material, but also her revelation. Screw the law career. Or maybe she could make it work side by side. Somehow. She had to, because she knew she would never be happy if she didn't.

The image of the cosy little workshop stayed with her during the drive back. 'You're very quiet,' David commented, after half an hour had gone by without Jenny saying a word.

'She's building castles in the air.' Katie smiled at her. 'I can tell by the look in her eyes.'

Jenny didn't reply, still lost in her own thoughts. Something to dream of for the future. Maybe she could start things off alongside her career, and if she was successful then she could go it alone. She would just have to manage it somehow.

'I have to go for it.' Jenny blurted the words out as they were getting ready for bed. 'My own business, I mean. Not now, necessarily, but eventually I will.'

'What about your dreams of being a solicitor?' Katie raised her eyebrows.

Jenny sat on the bed and pulled her knees up to her chest. 'It's a good career, and I'm planning on doing it for a good few years at least. After all, I'll have to save up money if I want to start my own business. But this is really where my heart is. This is really what I want to do. Although the idea of actually doing it scares the shit out of me.'

Katie reached over and gave her a quick hug. 'Go for it, girl. I can tell you're right from the way your eyes are shining.'

Jenny blushed. 'It's an amazing feeling. I just feel like everything has clicked into place.'

'Sleepy time, career woman.' Katie jumped into bed. 'You've got a big future ahead of you.'

'And what about you?' Jenny couldn't help asking, as they lay there with the light off. 'Are you still happy in your job?'

'I love event planning.' Katie's reply was quick. 'I always thought about doing it for the fashion industry, given how much I like clothes, but it's really not my scene. I love doing events that seem more worthwhile. Like this medical conference that's just been. Knowing that they wouldn't be able to exchange important ideas without my work behind the scenes feels really great.'

'I don't know how you keep track of things, to be honest.' Jenny shuddered at the thought of talking to so many people on a regular basis.

Katie laughed. 'Loads of technology. And a gift for winging it when things go wrong.'

When they finally dropped the two women off at the airport, Alison hugged Jenny tightly and David dropped a quick kiss on her cheek.

'Are you sure you're going to be OK?' Alison's voice was concerned.

'Oh yes.' Jenny was cheerful. 'I've got a new job to find, and I've got the inklings of another dress design in my head. It's going to be great to have some free time to work on it until then. And I've got to prepare for the battle ahead.'

Alison hugged her again, looking slightly less worried. 'Good. Just keep in touch and let me know if you need anything. It was lovely to have you here, we really enjoyed it. Come again soon. And you, Katie.' She hugged the other girl too.

As the plane lifted into the sky Jenny leaned her head back on the seat with a contented sigh. 'Thanks for coming up. I've had a great time.'

'So have I!' Katie squeezed her hand. 'Thanks for inviting me.'

Jenny could feel her friend looking at her, and she swung her head round to meet Katie's gaze. 'What?'

'I was just wondering how you feel about going back to London.' Katie spoke more quietly this time, and the concern in her voice was evident.

Jenny considered the question for a few moments. 'Mixed, I think. I'm steeling myself for this legal battle, which I know isn't going to be pretty. And I also need to find another job, which with all this hanging over me won't be easy either. But in some ways I'm really happy to be going back. As much as Scotland is beautiful, I love living in London. And I love living with you. It's where I really want to be.'

'If you really loved living with me that much, you wouldn't constantly gripe about my hair being in the bathroom plughole.' Katie was joking, but Jenny could see how much the compliment had touched her from the slightly misty look in her eyes.

'Constant griping, is it? How many times did I actually mention it? Twice?' Jenny shook her head in a mock despairing manner, struggling to keep a straight face.

'Shush now.' Katie put a finger to her lips. 'Any more of this and the people behind us are going to think we're a married couple.'

'Oh Katie. I've missed you.' Jenny couldn't help a fond smile. 'I'm so glad we're going home.'

Chapter 13

Jenny looked up from the design she was sketching, easing out her cramped back. The red dress was almost how she wanted it, but something about it just wasn't right. She checked the time; late morning. If she took the tube down to South Kensington she could wander around the Victoria & Albert museum for some inspiration and then have some lunch. It was also a long time since she had been in Harrods and she was about due for a visit. It would be packed with tourists of course, as always, but she loved looking at all the elegant designer displays. She tossed her sketchpad in her bag in case she got some sudden inspiration and pulled on her coat.

There was a small exhibition in the V&A of dresses from the twenties. It was one of Jenny's favourite periods for fashion, and she ended up sitting in front of a gorgeous pink number with an elegant beaded design. The twenties was when hemlines had first gone up to the knee. When women had dared to cut their hair. When they'd had the vote. But one hundred years later, had anything really changed? Were women really respected?

She remembered her boss's frustration when she had been fired, and the anger on Nadeem's face when she had first told him about her experiences. That was progress. Anger about these things was good. It meant that they weren't as normalised as they had been in the past. So there was hope for the future, even if things weren't as good as they should be.

She rubbed a hand across her forehead. Screw Derek. She may not be able to control her nightmares, but there was no way she was going to let him infect her thoughts.

By three o'clock Jenny was feeling pretty happy. She had treated herself to a gorgeous sandwich at a posh café and the dress design was already starting to come together. If she just tweaked the skirt a bit and adjusted the waist like that other dress she had seen, it would be something really special.

It was time to go home and get on with her life. She would visit the local supermarket on the way to see if she could have her old job back. For now. It would tide her over while she looked for a proper opportunity.

The Underground was pretty crowded by the time she got down onto the platform. As she squeezed herself into the carriage, she felt a hand brush against her from behind. She froze, anxiety building, and then anger took over all her other emotions. Yes, there was a guy behind her and he had just casually groped her. As the train started off, she turned and opened her mouth. 'You tosser, you just groped my arse!'

Her voice was much louder than she had intended, and a number of the heads in the carriage swivelled towards her. Some looked shocked, some angry, and others just smirked.

The man now standing right in front of her blushed bright pink and shook his head. 'I'm sorry. I didn't mean to, honest.' He rubbed the back of his neck. 'It's so crowded in here...' His voice trailed off and by now his face looked so red that she could have swapped him for a radish and barely noticed the difference.

'It's my fault.' A woman standing just behind him spoke up. The noise of the train in the tunnel meant she had to speak loudly and Jenny could tell that everyone was pretending not to watch, fascinated to see how this mini-drama would play out. 'I stumbled when I was getting on and pushed him.'

Now it was Jenny's turn to go bright red, as she realised what she had done. She was so embarrassed she got off at the next station, not wanting to stay in the same carriage with all the people who had witnessed her humiliation. Her chest felt tight, and the warm muggy air in the station was no help at all.

Sitting on a platform bench she struggled to regain her composure. This was bad. Really bad. Her face burned every time she thought of what she had done to that poor guy, and her panic rose at how easily she had been triggered.

Trains came in and out and people walked past her without so much as a second glance. Finally, a staff member in a high-vis orange waistcoat came up to her.

'You alright, love?' His voice was kind.

She raised her head. He would be worried that she was sick, or suicidal probably. 'I'm fine.' She stood up to reassure him. 'Honestly, I am.'

But she walked the rest of the way home.

Jenny felt as if the meeting room walls were closing in on her. Her stomach twisted again, threatening to empty the contents all over the floor.

She focused on counting breaths.

By the time she reached thirty both her nausea and panic had receded somewhat. Lifting her head, she focused on the other two people in the room. 'I feel like I'm going to throw up. I honestly don't know if I can see him again. Can we not just call this whole mediation thing off and do it another time?' Her plea was only half-hearted though; she knew it was far better to get it over and done with.

Katie squeezed the hand she was already holding. 'I'll be waiting for you when you get out. And Clive will be by your side the whole way. Those tossers won't be able to get anywhere near you.'

Jenny gave a faint smile. 'Thanks for taking the morning off to be here. And thanks, Clive, for taking a chance on me.'

'No worries.' Her lawyer repeated the phase he'd used every time she'd thanked him over the last half hour. 'You just leave the talking to me.'

Jenny put a hand to her mouth as her stomach twisted again. 'Let's do this then. Just make sure I've got something to throw up in when I get out. I refuse to give them the satisfaction of doing it in front of them.'

Katie held up a red plastic waste bin. 'I wouldn't say that's what they designed it for, but it will probably do you.' She made a good attempt at a cheeky grin, even though the rest of her face was drawn with worry.

Jenny looked from her friend to the bin and back again, and suddenly found herself laughing. Slightly hysterical laughter, but it went some way towards easing the knots in her stomach and shoulders.

There was a discreet tap on the door and it opened slightly. The woman from the mediation service poked her head in and nodded at them. 'We're ready for you now.'

This random office building near London Bridge was considered neutral ground for both parties. Nadeem had offered their premises, but Jenny knew she couldn't step through the doorway of the office again, so Clive had made alternative arrangements. When she had worried about the cost, he had told her there wouldn't be any, but had refused to tell her how. She suspected he had called in a favour, and the kindness had only hardened her resolve to proceed.

Clive hadn't been anything like she expected; he wore the regulation suit, but sported a gold stud in his left ear and when he had rolled up his shirt sleeves at their first meeting she had seen a lot of tattoos. She actually really liked him. His sensitive and thoughtful approach had boosted her confidence, and he seemed to really know his stuff.

Even with all that on her side, there was still a lot of uncertainty about how the negotiations would go. The three of them had discussed a host of possible scenarios, but until they were actually in the room there was no way of knowing exactly what the other side would suggest.

The other side. Nadeem would count among that definition now, which still felt very strange. Jenny took another breath and stood up, motioning Clive to go first.

The mediator led them across the corridor to another meeting room. Jenny racked her brains for the woman's name, but she had been so close to panic when they were introduced it had completely slipped through her mind.

As she reached the doorway Jenny paused; her skin crawled and an overwhelming urge to run away sped through her. Another deep breath helped to focus her mind. She was here to fight, not cower in a corner. Clenching her hands, she stepped forward.

The details of the room stood out starkly in her vision. The big wooden boardroom-style table. The black leather chairs. A picture of the Eiffel tower on the far wall. And the three men sitting on the other side of the table. Derek and Nadeem had another man just to their right. Their lawyer, she supposed. It wasn't usual to bring lawyers to this type of meeting, but Jenny had refused to go in without Clive, so she wasn't surprised that they had responded in kind.

She slid into the chair, folding her hands in her lap. Her anger rose and she let it, knowing it would help her courage. Just as long as she could keep her composure. She could do this.

All three men were wearing suits and it was the first time she had seen Nadeem wearing a tie. He looked uncomfortable in it, as if he didn't wear one very often. Or maybe he just felt uncomfortable about the whole situation. He refused to meet her eyes, focusing his gaze instead on the mediator.

Once the basic formalities had been exchanged, the mediator turned to Nadeem's side of the table. 'I know that you have studied all of the documents. Are there any further details you wish to clarify?'

All three men shook their heads and their lawyer spoke. 'There are no further details we require. However, may I speak briefly?'

On receiving a nod he leaned forward and rested his clasped hands on the table. 'My clients have reviewed the situation, and flatly refute any suggestion that Ms Lang's story is true. However, we are also aware that proceeding to a public tribunal will have a costly impact on the reputation of our business, whatever the outcome. With this in mind, we would like to offer Ms Lang a single payment of one year's salary, so thirty thousand pounds, providing she agrees to retract her accusation and sign a non-disclosure agreement which prohibits her from any mention of anything to do with this case.'

Jenny glanced at Clive. This was one possibility they had discussed, but she hadn't thought that the opposition would fold so quickly.

'You are aware that a number of people already have detailed knowledge of the accusations, including various close friends of Ms Lang, and, I believe, Mr Grayson's own sister?' Clive's voice was calm and considered.

The other man nodded. 'We are aware of that. The Grayson family have no interest in spreading details of these false accusations, and the terms of the NDA we have drawn up make it clear that we expect Ms Lang to be responsible for the actions of any friends of hers.'

Jenny wanted to lean across the table and smash the man in the mouth. He was sitting there so calmly, accusing her of lying. Thank goodness she had Clive to fight her corner.

The man across the table continued. 'Added to that, this offer is only valid at this current time. If the offer is not accepted by the conclusion of this meeting then it shall be rescinded and I will be advising my clients to proceed to tribunal.'

Jenny sucked in a breath. Out of all the scenarios they had considered, a time-limited one was not among them.

The silence stretched out.

Clive gave no outward sign of what he was thinking when he finally replied. His composure was impressive; she could take a few lessons from him for her future career. 'You will appreciate, I am sure, that this offer is unexpected. Might I request a fifteen-minute break for me to discuss this with my client?'

The other lawyer looked at Nadeem and Derek, and Nadeem nodded.

'Very well. But no more than fifteen minutes; my clients are busy men and they have work to be getting on with. I would also like to remind you that it is in your best interests to accept our offer. I am sure you are aware that proceeding to a public tribunal can be very costly and very damaging for the reputation of both parties involved.'

That last statement did almost have Jenny reaching across the table. Only the knowledge that it had been carefully crafted to insult her made her keep her cool. The implication that their time was more valuable than hers. That they had more important things to do than deciding on her future. And the veiled threat to drag her name through the mud was just the icing on the cake.

Jenny paced up and down in the small meeting room, swinging her fists. 'Those bastards. They're asking me to trade off money for my reputation.'

'So don't do it.' Katie was sitting in one of the low chairs, and she shrugged. 'Take them to court.'

Jenny came and sat down beside her. 'It's not as easy as that. Thirty grand? It's a huge amount of money. That could almost pay for my studies, even once Clive has taken his cut. Think of all the other people's cases I could fight once I qualify. Might it not be worth it?'

She turned to Clive. 'What do you think I should do?'

He frowned. 'I'm afraid in a tricky situation like this I can't really recommend a definitive course of action; you're right that it's a trade-off and not a perfect solution. Taking this forward to tribunal could go either way, unfortunately, since it's only your word against his, especially as they've made it clear they'll create a hostile situation. I'd like to think that it's probable you would win, but there's no guarantee.'

'Shit.' Jenny ran her fingers through her hair and resumed her pacing. 'Talk about life-changing decisions.'

She had to ask herself, what did she really want? Was the whole purpose of this to prove a point? Or should she just take the money and move on with her life?

The sight of Nadeem on the other side of that table had affected her more than she cared to admit. The thought of him not believing her was bad enough, but him seeing her as just another business transaction hurt even more. She had hoped he could have at least given her the benefit of the doubt. But no. He hadn't even had the courtesy to do that.

'You don't have to take their offer as it is.' Clive's voice broke into her thoughts. 'You could ask them to raise it.'

Jenny sat down opposite him. 'Interesting thought.' She ran her fingers through her hair again, trying to think rationally. 'If I did that, I'd have enough to finish my studies and even put some aside to start up my own business when the time comes.'

She looked at Katie, as an idea came to her. 'And, I could donate some of it to the women's shelter. That would be amazing. And one in the eye for both of those bastards.'

'Don't be ridiculous. You don't have to do that.' Katie's tone was dismissive. 'This is all yours. You deserve it.'

Jenny shook her head firmly. 'Don't you see? If I do this, if I take this money, then I have to make the most of it. If I'm signing that NDA and can't tell anyone else what really happened, it has to have the maximum positive benefit.'

There were only a few minutes left. It was decision time and her future hung in the balance. Take the money and put it all behind her? Or see this through so that the world would know exactly what had happened? She felt like someone had asked her to choose which one of her friends to throw over a cliff.

She turned to Clive. 'How much do you think they might be willing to pay?'

Nadeem watched the second hand of the clock on the wall tick around to the top for the twelfth time. Would she take the money, or fight it out? He couldn't tell. The woman he thought he knew didn't exist, and he now found himself on unfamiliar terrain. Still, if they weren't back in three minutes, then it was only going one way.

He sighed. With everything else that was going on the company didn't have the time or resources to prepare for a tribunal. Plus a case like this, if it went public, could totally destroy their reputation. That was why he had reluctantly agreed to this plan. If she took it, the problem would go away forever, and he could just focus on doing his job.

They desperately needed more employees at the moment with this big contract starting up, but it was so hard to find good people, and all this happening had made him incredibly wary now of taking anyone else on. Still, he had to do something about their understaffing problem. He would make it his top priority when he got back to the office.

The door opened and he dragged his gaze from the clock. They were back.

He found his heartbeat speeding up. Much as he pretended this was all just work, he deeply cared about the success of the family business. Almost eighty people were relying on him for a job, and he couldn't screw that up.

He still cared about Jenny too, in spite of his best efforts not to. When she had first entered the room he had noticed she looked thinner than the last time he saw her. Dark circles smudged her eyes, much like when he'd first met her. All that was his fault. God knows what this must be doing to her.

He pushed down his guilt. She was doing it to herself. If she hadn't started all this, they wouldn't be here. He had noticed the theatrical way she had paused in the doorway, just trying to draw attention to herself. She didn't deserve a second thought.

When they were all sat down her lawyer spoke. 'We have carefully considered your proposal. Ms Lang is willing to accept, provided you raise the sum you are offering to sixty thousand pounds. We feel that this is an acceptable amount to compensate her for the distress that has been caused.'

Nadeem hadn't felt true rage for a long time, but it hit him now. His instincts had been right; she was just out to fleece the company for all she could get.

Fine. Let her have the money. He wanted her out of his life and away from him. And then they could all move on. His lawyer started to speak, but Nadeem cut across him. 'Done.'

The man looked at him in surprise. 'Are you sure?'

Nadeem stood up. 'Give Ms Lang the amount she wants. But make sure that agreement is bloody watertight. I'll leave you to finish off in here. My cousin and I have better things to do with our time.'

He straightened his jacket and left the room, Derek directly behind him.

Jenny looked after them with disbelief, her elation at getting what she had asked for and relief at Derek's disappearance overwritten by the anger in Nadeem's voice. Sure, she hadn't expected him to be happy, but that scornful look he had flashed her as he stood up had her face burning. Because all that money would be amazing, would help in so many ways, but it wasn't really what she wanted. What she really needed was for him to believe her, but it seemed like that would never happen.

So that was it. She would take the opportunity that life had dropped into her lap and move on. Finish her studies. Start giving something back. The thought that she could now do all this left her feeling surprisingly calm.

When the paperwork was finally all done Jenny stood up, reaching a hand out to the mediator. 'Many thanks for your time.' She extended a hand across to the other lawyer, who looked vaguely surprised, but she couldn't hold a grudge, not when he was just doing his job. Some day that could be her in a tough situation, although she hoped life would never put her on that particular side of the table.

Clive followed her out. 'If you need some work experience at any point just let me know.'

She shook his hand too. 'Thanks for the offer, I really appreciate it.' Jenny stood a moment longer, suddenly realising that this might be the last time she saw him. 'Thanks, Clive. For everything you've done. I couldn't have done it without you. You were amazing in there.'

He ducked his head, obviously unused to such compliments. 'It's my job.'

She smiled at him, motioning towards the door. 'So go and enjoy your generous fee. You deserve it.'

Katie was waiting in the lobby with Jenny's bag, pacing in front of a grey leather sofa. Her eyes held a question, and Jenny just responded with a brief nod.

Katie grabbed her in a tight hug and then handed Jenny her things. 'I've got to get back to work. Unless you really need me. Are you sure you're going to be OK?'

'Yes. I'll be fine.' Jenny nodded again. Everything seemed a bit unreal and she knew it would all hit her later, but she couldn't keep Katie from her job. She would just have to handle this by herself.

As she made her way home, she could feel her anger building, even though she tried to tamp it down.

'Stupid man. With his stupid cousin.' She spoke out loud, ignoring the passers-by who looked at her curiously as she stomped along the pavement. 'Blah blah blah. *Better things to do with our time.* Bastard. Damn him. Damn them both.'

Her anger lasted all the way up into her bedroom, and then as soon as she slammed the door she burst into tears and flung herself onto the bed. How could she have misjudged him so badly? She had thought he would be the one to believe in her no matter what, and he had let her down yet again.

She tried to console herself with the thought that at least it was all over now, but the truth was that it was far from over. Even just thinking about what had happened that morning triggered her back into the memory of the original incident, and that in turn pushed her back to memories of her childhood. Before she knew where she was, she was having a full-blown panic attack, with sweating, chest pains, and uncontrollable shaking.

Just breathe. You'll get through this. You are not going to die. There was no way she was going to let this beat her down. They were not going to ruin her life. She focused on counting her breaths, trying to make sure they were as even as possible. She lost track of the numbers several times but kept on going, and eventually her panic slowly began to subside.

That was the problem with a whirlwind romance, she reflected some time later, when she was a lot calmer. The trap was that you thought you knew a person intimately, but they could always surprise you. In good, or in this case, in very bad ways. And if she was really honest, she could kind of understand Nadeem's position, but it didn't make his lack of trust sting any less.

Jenny suddenly felt very alone. She envied Nadeem his good relationships with his family, his easy banter with his sisters, and the way they always looked out for each other. She had built that up with a few close friends, but it wasn't the same. Family was family, with all its flaws and pitfalls. If only she had that with her sister and her mother.

It could be, she told herself, with just a little effort, it could be.

A lot of effort, the cynical part of her said wryly. Her mother never seemed to really care for her, and Bella had seemed more concerned about what her friends thought about her, than the things Jenny really cared about. Still, they had all been close once. When her dad was alive. She missed him, even now. He seemed to be the glue that had held the whole family together.

On a whim, she reached for her mobile and looked up her sister's number. She hadn't used it in a long time; there was only one way to know if it was still working or not. She pressed the button to call.

It was answered almost straight away. 'Hello?'

Jenny realised Bella wouldn't recognise her new number and she found herself unable to speak. All the things she had wanted to say for so many years clustered in her throat and completely blocked it off.

'Hello?' Her sister's voice spoke again.

Jenny hung up. She had no right dragging Bella back into her life just because of what had happened today. Maybe some day, when the time was right, but not right now. It would just be one more thing to cope with on top of everything else. It was time to close the door on the past and work out how to live her future the way she really wanted. But what did she really want? To reach for her dreams and take some chances? Or play it safe and give something back to society?

Chapter 14

Nadeem shifted in his chair, stretching his neck and shoulders. He should be gone already, but it was the only time he'd been able to catch up with Derek, who was in their New York office all week.

He had just hung up when his finance director put her head around the door. 'Nadeem, could I have a word?'

'I didn't realise you were still here.' He turned away from his laptop with a sigh of relief. 'Sure, what's up?'

Germaine sank gratefully into the seat on the other side of the desk. Nadeem noticed that even at this late hour her impeccably styled hair was not a millimetre out of place, and her trademark trouser suit was still unwrinkled. It was the outward sign of her carefully ordered and brilliant mind, which he couldn't have done without this last nine months, and especially over the last few weeks.

He had to admit that the team his father had built up was top-class in all respects; this gave him a weird mixture of reassurance that they could actually make this thing work, and a slight inferiority complex about his own abilities.

'I feel bad that you're here in the office so late instead of spending time with your family.' He spoke without thinking.

Her face creased into a faint smile. 'To be honest, I'm not the one my kids want to spend time with these days. You know what teenagers are like.'

Germaine crossed her legs and leaned back in the chair, her face serious. 'Nadeem, I've been going through the accounts, just to get things prepared for the year end closure, and I found a strange payment of sixty thousand pounds. So I asked Melissa if she knew why we'd paid money direct to Jennifer Lang last month and she told me the story.'

'Fair enough.' He probably should have told Germaine anyway. If his finance director didn't know about the incomings and outgoings in the company then she couldn't do her job. 'So what's on your mind?'

'Thing is.' Germaine leaned forward. 'Melissa may not be aware of this, but in this office, among the women, Derek is well-known for being someone to avoid.' She smiled wryly. 'He's never tried anything with me, but then I would hardly say I'm in his target demographic. Neither is Melissa, so that's probably why she hasn't realised.'

Nadeem frowned. 'She never mentioned anything like this.'

Germaine shrugged, palms up. 'Melissa doesn't smoke. Things get shared outside that back door that people aren't willing to talk about in the office.'

This was news to Nadeem too. 'So how come none of them have raised a complaint?'

She shrugged again. 'It's a tricky situation. Word gets around, the women avoid him, he can't do anything, so they have no concrete cause for complaint. I can only assume that Jennifer was either too naive or too polite to do the same thing. And besides, he's the nephew of the owner. It's not exactly an easy complaint to bring up.'

Nadeem shifted some papers randomly around on his desk, trying to think. He was still unwilling to believe what he was hearing. 'So you think she might have been telling the truth?'

Germaine shifted in her chair. 'Who knows. Maybe, maybe not. Based on what I've heard, it's totally possible.'

His head was whirling, still trying to process the implications of what he was hearing. 'Excuse me for asking this, but why you haven't come to me before now?'

Germaine frowned. 'Until I spoke to Melissa, I assumed that everyone knew. I'd been trying to work out what to do about it, given that you obviously didn't seem to care that it was happening.'

Nadeem drew in a breath. 'You thought I knew? And didn't care? Wow.' It stung that she would think so little of him. 'You should have come straight to me as soon as you found out.'

She shifted in her chair, looking slightly embarrassed. 'I suppose if I'm really honest with you then I was kind of hoping it would just go away. You'd said originally he'd only be here temporarily while you went to Tanzania, so I was thinking he'd be gone after that. I know that's no excuse, but there's only so much one woman can do to change the world.'

A weary sigh escaped her lips, and Nadeem was reminded of how late it was. 'This is pretty important information. Could you leave it with me to think about for a while?'

'Do that.' She got up to go. 'You make a good manager, Nadeem. A little green around the edges, maybe, but I've seen how much you care for your people, and it makes me glad. I've watched too many family businesses go to pot because the next generation just isn't up to the job, and that's why I wanted to tell you about this. So that you can come to your own conclusions and make the best decision.'

Nadeem found himself growing warm at the unexpected compliment. 'Thanks, Germaine. I'll always rely on you to tell me how it is.'

Germaine just smiled at him as she left.

Nadeem sank his head into his hands as the door closed. How had he missed all of this going on? *You were busy trying to keep the company afloat*, he reminded himself. *And then you were a few thousand miles away.*

Almost as a reflex action, he called his mother. She would be able to give him a solid opinion. He greeted her with his usual opener. 'How are you doing?'

'I'm well, darling. Alan was out playing golf today so I took the chance to catch up on some admin. I want to get everything in order before we head off to Italy for the proper sunshine.'

She lowered her voice. 'He's still not doing that well; he managed a couple of hours and then Roger said they spent the rest of the afternoon in the club house. He's already gone to bed.'

'You're going to Sicily soon, right?' Nadeem managed to remember.

'Yes, dear. We're staying with some friends. Anyway, love, it's rather late. Was there anything specific you needed?'

Nadeem forced himself to calm his pounding heart. He cleared his throat. 'About Derek, Mum. What do you really think of him?' There was a silence on the other end of the line for a few moments. 'Mum?'

'I'm not sure exactly what you mean.' Her voice sounded slightly puzzled.

'There's been rumours here that he's been a bit too pushy with some of the women. Perhaps even more than pushy. I thought you might know something about that if it was true.'

Her response was quick. 'He's never been anything less than a gentleman with me and your sisters. So no, I wouldn't be able to tell you anything about that. But then, we are family.' There was a pause. 'Wait a minute. Now that you mention it, there was a bit of unpleasantness last year with Leyla, you know, the girl who comes in to clean for us sometimes? I thought it was just a misunderstanding between them so I didn't think much of it at the time. She basically said the same thing. That he kept asking her to go out for dinner with him and wouldn't take no for an answer. I had to have a word with him and tell him to stop bothering her. But then, he's always been one to go after what he wants. It's just his character.'

'And what do you think of him?' Nadeem couldn't help asking.

He could tell she was thinking before she spoke. 'If I'm really honest, darling? I feel like I barely know him these days. With him down in London these last ten years I've hardly seen him.'

'Thanks, Mum, that's really helpful. I won't keep you any longer. Love you. Give my love to Dad too.'

Nadeem hung up, his palms sweating. The reality of what he had done was starting to hit him. If all these stories were real, it seemed quite possible that Jenny had actually been telling the truth all along.

He dropped his head into his hands with a groan. That would be a nightmare, if it was the case. More than a nightmare. It would blow his world apart. If it was true, he would have to call Jenny and apologise. No, more than apologise. He would need to grovel. Do some A-grade grovelling. If she would ever speak to him again.

He shut off that train of thought. He had to have it out with Derek first. Nadeem leaned back in his chair, considering the situation. If he was so wrong, how could he have been mistaken? Sure, Derek talked about women a lot, but then didn't most guys?

He tried to think rationally and push aside the sense of betrayal that threatened to engulf him. Hadn't he heard about these kind of situations, where people acted in one way with some people and in another way with others? It was just possible that Derek kept the two sides of his personality separate. It would explain why he himself had totally missed the signs. Although that would do nothing to lessen his sense of guilt, if all this was true. Sexual harassment happening in this company, in this very building?

He banged his fist on the desk. Yes. He would leave it to confront Derek until his cousin got back tomorrow. Because if all this was true, Derek wouldn't be able to get out of this place with his face intact.

Reign it in. The more mature side of him put an imaginary warning hand on his shoulder. He needed to listen to that side of himself; it had kept him out of trouble numerous times.

OK. But a verbal ass-kicking at the very least. He would make that promise.

He looked at his watch. Security would come and close up the office building in a few minutes and he didn't want to be locked in. It was time to go home.

A bad night's sleep meant that it was after nine when Nadeem finally got to the office. He poked his head around Derek's door; his cousin must have come straight from the airport because he was already there, dressed in casual trousers and a slightly crumpled shirt.

Nadeem was almost about to commence the piece he had carefully rehearsed when he realised two things; firstly, that everyone in the office would be able to hear him, and also, if he wanted to seize the advantage it would be better to corner Derek on home ground.

'How was your journey?' He hoped the other man didn't hear the frustration in his voice.

'It was fine.' Derek looked up. 'Although I'm as jet-lagged as hell. I might go home in a bit, if you don't mind.'

'Sure, but could you come to my office first? There's something I need to discuss with you.' He tried to speak casually, so as not to give the game away.

'Of course.' Derek seemed unperturbed. 'I need to discuss the latest staffing plans for this new contract with you anyway. A couple of countries are proving to be a bit tricky.'

Nadeem settled himself in the comfy chair behind his desk and motioned for Derek to sit down. He realised he was starting to think of the room as his own office and not his father's. Did that mean something? Was he finally starting to hack it all?

'Some things have come up which are pretty serious and I really need to talk to you about.' He tried to keep his voice calm, and he realised that a large part of him still hoped that it was all a mistake. Some horrible misunderstanding.

Across the table he saw his cousin's face crease into a worried frown. 'What's going on? Don't tell me our supplies haven't come through or something.'

Nadeem shook his head. Derek's total commitment to the business was what made all this so hard for him to believe. 'There's a few women who've said that you acted inappropriately towards them. We can't have that kind of behaviour in the office. You're getting yourself a bit of a reputation, and not a good one.'

'Hey.' Derek spread his hands out and shrugged. 'There's no crime in asking a beautiful woman out to dinner. All they have to do is say no.'

'That's not exactly the sort of thing I'm talking about.' Nadeem pressed on.

Derek stood up and leaned over the desk. 'Have you been talking to that bitch again? What kind of lies has she been pouring into your ears?' He stepped back and folded his arms. 'Don't say you believe her. After all the work I've put in for this company that hurts. It really hurts, Nadeem. I've put my own career on the back burner here, just to help you out.'

Nadeem shifted in his chair. 'Yeah, that may be true, but that doesn't make these other things acceptable.'

Derek made a dismissive sound. 'All I can say is, seems mighty funny that all these women are only bringing it up now. There's no proof. No evidence. And if there is, I say bring it on.' He spun around and headed for the door. 'When you're ready to discuss real business and not just fairy tales, I'll be in my office.'

As the other man stalked out Nadeem just placed his head in his hands. What was he going to do now? Who was he supposed to believe?

Trust your instinct, Dina had said. Regardless of that though, with no proof, where could he go? He should probably start a proper formal investigation, but Melissa, who would normally be able to help him with that, was clearly biased, based on recent events.

Germaine had made her thoughts clear and was in the other camp. His parents would be biased too, because it was Derek. So who could he turn to?

He was deep in his thoughts when a knock on the open door made him look up, half-expecting to see Derek again, but it was someone else.

'Yes, Reena?' He tried to put some warmth into his tone so she didn't think his anger was aimed at her.

'We're all waiting for you in the conference room.' When he just stared at her blankly, she added, 'Ops meeting?'

He had totally forgotten about it. 'Oh yes.'

Gathering his pad and pen, he stood up. This would have to be parked for now, but not for long. He would have to get to the bottom of all this, and soon, before anything else happened. And he needed to call Jenny. If she would still speak to him.

Jenny's phone rang. She ignored it; she was just about to slide her scissors into the red silk that was draped over the kitchen table. It was a special experience cutting into an untouched piece of cloth, and she needed all her concentration to get it just right. Added to that, Katie would be back in about an hour and then they were going out for her birthday, so the window of opportunity was small.

By the time she finally picked up her phone there were three missed calls showing on the screen. The bottom of her stomach dropped out. Nadeem. But why was he calling her at all?

At that precise moment a key turned in the door. Katie took one look at Jenny's face and frowned. 'What's up?'

Jenny showed her the phone. 'It's Nadeem.'

She saw the conflict on her friend's face between excitement and outrage. 'Are you going to call him back?'

Jenny's mouth twisted. 'I don't know. What could he possibly want?'

'Maybe he changed his mind.'

'Peh.' Jenny scoffed. 'Maybe he wants his money back.'

Katie just looked at her, one eyebrow raised.

'No, seriously.' Jenny crossed her arms. 'You're really suggesting I talk to him? After everything that went down?'

'Oh, don't get me wrong.' Katie crossed the room quickly and caught her up in a hug. 'He's the one person in the world who I'd like to strangle most right now. Well, apart from maybe one of my clients who keeps constantly changing their mind about conference room layouts.' She rolled her eyes. 'But are you not just a little bit curious to see what he wants?'

Katie was right, although Jenny hated to admit it. 'Maybe. But it still hurts a whole load more.' She crossed her arms.

Katie perched on the back of the sofa. 'Of course it hurts. And that's why I'd go for the strangling option. But this is up to you. It's your decision. How much do you like him, and how much are you willing to forgive?'

'I liked him a lot. But what he's done is something I can't forgive.' Jenny shook her head. 'I never want to see him again. He can go fuck himself.'

'Sheesh. Strong words coming from you. You never drop the f-bomb.' Katie looked at her appraisingly.

Jenny just shrugged, struggling to maintain her composure. 'He's the last person I want to think about on my birthday.' Gathering up the folds of material, she placed them carefully on a shelf. 'Let's go out and forget about him. Come on.'

'Where are we actually going?' Jenny asked the question for the tenth time as they walked along Islington High Street.

'Shush! It's a secret!' Katie cried as Reena opened her mouth. 'That's all I'm telling you. First to a bar, and then you'll see.'

Jenny just smiled good-naturedly as Reena rolled her eyes. She linked arms with both of them. 'I can't tell you how glad I am to have the two of you around. Especially you, Reena, I haven't seen you in ages.'

Reena wrinkled her brow, and her lovely face clouded. 'To be honest, I was kind of trying to keep a bit of distance. After all, I was the one who helped you get that job. I was a bit worried I might just remind you of things you don't want to think about.' She grimaced. 'And on top of that I'm still working there, which is even worse. I've been trying to find another job, but it's just impossible at the moment.'

'Rubbish!' Jenny squeezed her arm. 'You're the one who saved me from that creep. If you hadn't knocked on the door exactly when you did, who knows what would have happened. I'm grateful for that every day of my life. And it's fine. With all the money I can afford to finish my studies now. So maybe I should thank him for funding that!'

As Reena looked relieved, Jenny laughed. She suddenly realised that yes, she had just made a joke about it, and the thought that she could sent a tiny burst of warmth floating through her. She hugged her friends' arms close once again.

Katie pulled them to a stop in front of a brightly-lit window. Jenny just looked at her and smiled. 'I should have guessed you'd bring me to Alfie's. This is turning out to be a bit of a tradition.'

'Well, we did meet here, darling.' Katie turned to her. 'Only this time, I got us a booth.'

'Whoop!' Jenny gave her a high five and pushed open the door.

The inside was just as she remembered. It always reminded her a bit of a French bistro. Scrubbed wooden tables stood on a tiled floor, and black and white photos of film stars littered the walls. But the casual atmosphere was misleading; every single photograph was signed personally by someone who had visited the place.

As the manager ushered them towards the back of the room, Jenny saw two other people sitting at the big round table in the corner. She blinked. Was it really? It couldn't be.

'Jenny!' A tall Black woman in a beautiful sea blue dress unwrapped herself from her seat and exploded across to give her a huge hug. Jenny couldn't believe her eyes. This was Evie, and the shorter White woman was Hayley. They had been inseparable while she was on her study year in the States but Jenny hadn't seen them since she left. Evie was now working in San Francisco, and Hayley had gone to teach English in Delhi, after falling in love with an Indian man in her final year at university.

Jenny shook her head again. 'I just can't believe you're here.' She couldn't help a huge grin splitting her face. 'How did you manage it?'

She turned to Katie. 'Even more importantly, how the hell did you manage to keep Hayley from spilling the beans?'

It was a well-known fact between the three of them that Hayley could keep a confidence to the grave, but when it came to good news she just couldn't hang onto it.

'Hey.' Hayley elbowed Jenny in the ribs. 'That's my reputation you're talking about.'

Jenny laughed, and hugged them both once again, and Reena and Katie as well, just because she was so happy. 'So tell me, how long are you going to be here for?'

'I'm afraid it's just tonight.' Regret laced Evie's voice. 'I'm on my way to a conference in Barcelona, and Hayley's going home to the States. It's just a quick stopover; we're both flying out tomorrow morning. But we'll make the most of it, I promise.'

The girls settled themselves into the red leather seats. 'OK, ladies.' Katie picked up a menu. 'It's Friday night. Are we doing cocktails?'

Evie and Hayley cheered, and the table dissolved into excited chatter about which ones they wanted. Jenny couldn't help her mind drifting back to the night of the gala, when Jamie had made her that special cocktail. Her heart tightened at the thought of how happy she had been that evening, and how it had all ended.

Evie, sitting next to her, must have noticed her face, because she nudged Jenny gently. 'What's up?'

'Not much.' Jenny shrugged. 'Found a guy, loved him, left him, still wish it had turned out differently.'

'Have you not told them about what happened?' Katie's tone betrayed her surprise.

Jenny shook her head. 'I don't know why. I guess I never thought about it. It's not exactly a fairy tale.'

Reena was quick to jump in. 'You don't have to talk about bad things on your birthday.'

It was, Jenny realised, possibly the best time to talk about it. To share it among these four friends who were the best supporters she had in the world.

They were mainly silent as she told her story, but when she finished Hayley raised a hand, as if taking an oath. 'Me too.'

Evie put up her hand in a similar fashion. 'And me. And I wasn't strong enough to do anything about it like you.'

'Woah.' Katie leaned across the table. 'Now I feel incredibly lucky, because all I've ever had to deal with is the odd sexist comment.'

Reena gave a cautious smile, her eyes mischievous. 'Maybe your blinding beauty scares them off?'

'Oh yeah.' Katie's tone was full of mock sarcasm.

All of them burst out laughing, glad of the change in the mood.

'But seriously, both of you?' Katie shook her head. 'That's shit.'

'Yeah.' Evie nodded. 'It was the same conference, last year. Someone was really handsy at dinner and then when I tried to give them a brush off, they followed me to my room. I had to call hotel security. It was really scary.'

Katie looked towards Hayley, but the other woman just shook her head, eyes cast down. 'I haven't told anyone about what happened to me. Except Rajiv and my therapist. But I promise that when I'm ready to share my story you'll be the first to know.'

Evie squeezed Jenny's hand gently. 'You know that life sucks sometimes. But friends are here to make it better.' She smiled, and Jenny couldn't help smiling too. She was so lucky to have such good people in her life and she was going to make the most of every minute of this evening.

'Right.' Jenny plucked the menu out of Katie's hands. It was time to overwrite the bad memories with good ones. 'Is it margaritas all round, girls?'

By the time they left the bar Jenny still hadn't found out where they were going. But Katie promised it was only a short walk away, so they left, arm in arm, until grumbling passers-by made them split up into smaller groups.

Hayley linked arms with Jenny. 'So what's your latest project?'

'Project? What do you mean?'

'I remember you spent most of your spare time while we were together altering all those thrift store clothes. Don't tell me you don't have something on the go.'

Jenny smiled, the special smile that appeared whenever she thought about her latest creation. 'There's a red dress. I've cut it out, I just need to find the time to piece it together. There's couple of photos of the design on my phone. I'll show you when we get there.'

She lowered her voice. 'Where are we going actually?'

Hayley shrugged. 'Beats me. Katie wouldn't let us in on the secret.'

'I really wanted to pay for tonight, just to celebrate my windfall, but Katie wouldn't let me do that either.' Jenny pulled a face.

'Quite right too! Every cent of that money should go towards your studies.' Hayley wagged a finger at her, then couldn't help laughing. 'Goodness, I sound like my mom. What is the world coming to?'

'I still wonder if it was the right thing to do. To take the money, I mean. I can't help feeling as if I sold out.' Jenny wrinkled her forehead.

'I know what you mean.' Hayley's voice was serious. 'But I can totally see why you did it. Going through a public tribunal process would be just humiliating. And you can begin to move on with your life now, instead of focusing on that.'

'Exactly that. Thanks, Hayley.' Jenny squeezed her friend's arm gratefully.

As they turned down a back street, Jenny suddenly realised where they were and what their likely destination was. But how the hell had Katie managed to get them a table at a Michelin-starred restaurant that had a waiting list months long?

She was just going to call out to Katie when she saw someone waiting in front of the restaurant. Not the Grayson they had been talking about, but Mia instead. What was she doing here? It could hardly be a coincidence.

Katie held up her hands apologetically. 'When Mia tracked me down and offered to sort the table for us, I just couldn't say no. I hope you don't mind.'

Mia looked a bit uncomfortable, which wasn't surprising. 'I'm not staying. I just came to say hi to Jamie and make sure you got the table. He's working at the bar. It was him who sorted it really, he wanted to thank you, although he wouldn't tell me what for. And the food is on him too.'

Jenny let out a breath. Here she was, thinking that maybe Mia had used her family connections to secure her the gift, when it was just a nice gesture from Jamie. She gave Mia an impulsive hug. 'Thanks. And please stay. It would be great to catch up. I've missed you.'

She wouldn't get through the night without thinking about Nadeem a hundred times anyway, so having Mia there would hardly make a difference. It might even make her feel better, knowing that something good had come out of this situation.

Mia grimaced. 'Are you sure? I don't want to gate-crash. I mean the food here is totally out of this world, just well, after what went down with Nadeem...'

'Are we going to stand here all night, or what?' Reena's voice came from behind them.

Jenny slung an arm around Mia's waist. She couldn't blame Mia for her brother's behaviour, especially when she really liked the girl. 'Come on. You've got to go in anyway. And you can tell me all about how it's going with Jamie.' A knowing look crept across her face.

Smiling, Mia pushed open the solid metal door.

Chapter 15

Nadeem lay stretched out on the sofa in his boat, his head pounding. He had been going over things all day, trying to work out what to do.

There must be someone who could help him, someone who wasn't connected with all of this. The lawyer they had used already would know what to do, but it would just be embarrassing to go back to him. That wasn't an option until Nadeem was totally sure of his next steps.

Derek had called a couple of times that evening, but Nadeem had refused to pick up, not when he felt so conflicted. He had been so sure that he had put himself in a strong position this morning, and instead Derek had just made him feel like he was being immature.

He rolled over on his side, propping himself up on one elbow. All the stress was getting to him. First his father being ill, then having to step up to manage the company. Meeting Jenny had been unexpected and had totally bowled him over. And then for it all to go tits up like this...

It wasn't only about work. It was about Jenny too. He felt terrible for not giving her story at least some credit, despite what Dina had said that night, and shame at the thought of how he had hurt her. He'd seen her suffer through trauma responses and flashbacks; had he really just dismissed all of that as acting? Still, maybe he shouldn't be surprised. Making the wrong choices in life seemed to be totally his thing.

But what should he actually do now? That was the million-dollar question. He could call the police in and get them to investigate, but that seemed a bit extreme. And word would get out, which would be bound to have negative consequences for the company. What was the solution when two people you really cared about both said the other one was lying? It seemed like an impossible situation.

He suddenly realised he had other friends. One in particular who always gave him good advice. But at this time on a Friday night, they'd be out at the pub and would have had a few drinks by now. It was best to leave it until tomorrow. There was nothing that couldn't wait another twelve hours. Sean's sober perspective would help, being unconnected as it was to any family ties, and for the first time he understood what Jenny had meant when she talked about friends versus family. Guilt swept over him as he recalled how judgmental he had been about her choices.

He lay on the sofa, watching the reflection of the water on the ceiling, wondering how things had got to the point where he was totally out of his depth. From a purely professional point of view, losing Derek would be a nightmare with them all as stretched as they were. Melissa as well, if it turned out that she hadn't done her job properly. Two of his most senior people were caught up in a tangle which was going to be a nightmare to resolve. No matter which direction he examined the situation from, it wasn't looking good. Thank goodness he had a couple of precious days before everyone would be back in the office. He would need that time to think about what to do.

Even though it was only just gone nine he knew that he should probably try to sleep; his nights this week had been pretty broken up and he was totally exhausted. But sleep held no appeal for him because of the dreams. Last night had been even worse than usual. Somehow Jenny and Derek had been woven in alongside Nate, in a situation where he was supposed to protect them all but had totally failed in his duty. Added to that, he couldn't stop thinking about the betrayed look on Jenny's face across the table in that meeting room.

He knew what he really wanted most of all. If Nate would just walk through the door right now, somehow they'd manage to solve this together. Nate had always been the one who kept him going when things got tough. But now, out of the two people he most wanted to call – Jenny and Nate – one wouldn't pick up the phone and the other just couldn't. A flick of his arm sent the phone flying into a corner and as he heard the smash a small sliver of satisfaction speared through him. Damn them all. Damn everything. How had he thought that he could hope for happiness in his life when Nate wasn't there to share it with him?

He swore out loud as he remembered that there was one person he had actually promised to call tonight. Dina had specifically told him she needed his help with something, and it sounded serious. He reached for his laptop, knowing he could call her on that, but the bag it was supposed to be in soon followed the phone as he realised he had left the computer on his desk at work. A quick check of his watch showed that the building would be locked up by now. He could call the management company to be let in, but the number was on his phone which was now lying smashed in the corner.

This seemed to be the pattern which described his life. Making impetuous decisions which then hurt other people and let them down. Got them killed. Ruined their lives. Made them feel like he didn't love them. He tried to fight the voice in his head that was telling him he was useless, but as the waves of emotion crashed over him, he knew it was a lost battle tonight.

Jenny lay on her bed, lost in a haze of contentment. She was so lucky to have such good friends. She shouldn't really have been surprised that Katie had managed to pull together a birthday party for her that was both small and intimate whilst at the same time being incredibly impressive, but it still warmed her heart that they had done it all for her. And the restaurant had been amazing. She rubbed her stomach, sighing happily.

Her phone rang. At 2am? It was someone listed in her contacts as DE. She almost let it go but, fuelled by alcohol, her curiosity made her pick it up. 'Hello?'

'Jenny? Jenny? Is that you? Oh, I'm so glad I reached you, I tried to get hold of Mia but she's not picking up her phone and Derek's not answering either and I didn't know who else to ring and I'm really worried and I can't get hold of him and I don't know what to do...'

Jenny suddenly realised who it was. DE stood for Dina, Edinburgh; the initials put in quickly the night of the party. When they had been joking about kiddie pictures of Nadeem. It seemed a hundred years ago now. This night was full of surprises.

Did it sound like Dina had been crying? She sat up, instantly feeling totally sober. 'Dina? Is that you? Just slow down, take a breath and start again. Tell me what's going on.'

She heard Dina take a deep breath and let it out. 'Yes, it's me. I'm sorry. I'll start again. It's just that I'm so worried. I'm sorry for calling so late. And I'm really sorry for bothering you. It's just that I've been trying to get through to Deem, and I can't get hold of him. I'm really worried about him and I thought you might know where he is. Are you with him at all?'

This phone call was getting weirder by the minute. 'Dina, you do know that we're not speaking, right? I haven't seen him since I signed the papers.'

There was a long silence on the other end of the phone. 'Papers? What papers?'

Now that was interesting. The man who seemed so close to his family hadn't told them about a small sum of sixty thousand pounds. Jenny was about to open her mouth and then remembered the agreement that she'd signed. But Dina had been there that night and had heard her side of the story already, so did it really count? She took the risk. 'Your lovely brother decided he didn't believe me. But he was worried enough to buy my silence with a payoff of money from the company funds. And made me sign an NDA. So officially I shouldn't even be mentioning this to you.'

'He what?' Jenny could hear the surprise and anger in Dina's voice. 'Well, I hope they gave you enough money to make it worth it. I'm really sorry about all this, Jenny. I kind of assumed you guys had worked things out, seeing as I hadn't heard anything. I forgot to ask because I've just been so tied up with the baby and other things.'

The silence stretched out while Jenny tried to work out what to say next, but Dina got there first. 'Actually, to be totally honest with you, I've been suffering with post-natal depression which has just taken over everything. That's why I've been up at my parents so much these last couple of months; I've been hoping they could cheer me up a bit. It's been a struggle just to drag myself out of bed in the mornings, let alone think of anyone else's problems. It's no excuse, I know.'

This was turning into a very surreal conversation. Jenny had to pinch herself to check she wasn't dreaming. How could the women of that family be so nice, when the men were so clueless?

'Hang on.' Jenny suddenly remembered the purpose of the call. 'Are you sure Nadeem's not just out somewhere with his phone switched off?'

'I don't think so.' Dina sounded very definite. 'I – well, Mo and I have been having some issues lately, because of all my stuff that's going on, and Deem specifically said that he would call me tonight when he finished work so we could talk things through. We haven't caught up in ages, and now I know why; he'll have been afraid of telling me about this. I just left it and went to bed because I thought he maybe got stuck in the office until really late, but then I woke up to feed the baby and he hasn't replied to any of my messages.

They haven't even arrived at his phone. And he never breaks his promises. Especially not when it's family.'

Yes, his precious family. Jenny cut that uncharitable thought off; she was bigger than that. 'Surely he'll be fine. He knows how to take care of himself.'

There was silence on the end of the phone for a few moments, and when Dina spoke again Jenny could sense the hesitation in her voice. 'Look, Jenny, I don't know how much my brother has shared with you about his history.'

'A lot of it. Probably not everything.' Jenny forced herself to be honest.

'Probably not, although if he's shared anything with you at all it shows how much he likes you. He's normally a closed shop as far as feelings are concerned. Well, since he lost Nate, anyway.'

That didn't match Jenny's experiences, but she didn't say anything. How was she to argue with someone who had known him forever?

'Did he tell you he was suicidal back then? After Elaine left him?'

'No, he didn't.' Jenny could feel shock hit her, but then, given what he had said about the state he had been in at his lowest point, it wasn't really a surprise once she thought about it.

'So you can see why I'm worried about him. It's not like him to forget something so important.'

Jenny blew out a silent breath. She could totally see where Dina was coming from, but was this really her problem? Nadeem clearly had people who cared about him and he just wasn't her responsibility.

But Dina...well, Dina was the one who had actually believed in her. She couldn't hold her brother's actions against her. The real question was though, could she hold Nadeem's actions against him? Enough to refuse him help when he was maybe in serious trouble? With a sigh she realised that she couldn't. Damn her sense of civic duty. 'Do you really think that he might be in any danger?'

Dina hesitated. 'I can't say for sure. But I'm worried enough about him that I can't say no.'

It was decision time. 'Right, Dina, what do you really want me to do?'

Dina hesitated. 'Well – I've tried to call Mia but her phone's out of action. She must be somewhere underground or she's run out of battery.'

'She was with me tonight. She and Katie went on to a club. You won't catch up with her before morning.' She herself would probably never go to a club again. Even the thought of being amongst that press of bodies had been enough to start making her feel sick.

Dina let out a breath. 'Ah, that explains it. I'm glad she's in safe hands. I feel bad asking this now that I know what's gone down between you, but is there any chance of you going to check at his boat? Seeing as you're not that far away. If not, I'll just call the police, see if they're willing to do it. Don't feel like you have to.'

Jenny thought of how overstretched the emergency services already were on a Friday night. It was just a knock on his door. She wouldn't even have to talk to him. And if anything had happened then she would be calling the police herself. 'I'll do it.' It wouldn't take long. She would be in and out and home in bed before she knew it.

'Oh Jenny, I'm so grateful to you.' The relief in Dina's voice was obvious.

'Right. Give me the address. I'll take a taxi.' Jenny stood up, taking stock of what she was wearing. Her top was a little revealing for a rescue mission, but she threw a jumper and coat over it and pulled some trainers on. She left a note for Katie in the kitchen and ordered a cab, promising to text Dina when she had any news.

It was only a short ride away. Dina had given her a precise description of the boat and she picked it out easily from the ones moored alongside it. The canal was quite an eerie place at night time, Jenny decided, with the street lights shining off the murky water. She shivered, despite her warm coat, then told herself off for being so fanciful.

Crossing to the deck of the boat, she knocked quietly but firmly on the hatch, aware that there must be people sleeping in the next boat which nestled just behind her. There was no response, so she tried the handle, just in case it was open. The door swung upwards easily, and she found herself looking at steps which led downwards into the gloom. There was just enough light from the street to see where to place her feet, so she gathered her courage and climbed carefully down, closing the hatch behind her.

There was barely enough light inside to make things out, but it was more spacious than Jenny had expected, and much warmer than the air outside.

'If you're here to steal things, I haven't got any valuables.' A dry voice came from the darkness. 'Although I guess you might get a bit of money for the furniture and kitchen cabinets.'

Jenny squinted in the half-light. She could just make out a figure lying on the sofa at the end of the room. 'Nadeem?'

'Jenny? What are you doing here?' She saw a sudden movement; him sitting up, most probably.

'Dina was worried about you.'

'Shit. So she sent you to check if I'm still alive or not. What a fuck-up this is. How did she rope you into that one?'

'None of your business.' Now that she knew he was fine the adrenaline was beginning to seep away, leaving her tired and irritable. She started to move forward and bumped her shins on what must be some kind of coffee table. 'Ouch! Would you mind getting a bit of light in here?'

'The battery's gone. I've been so busy at work I forgot to charge it. There's candles and a lighter in the cupboard by the door if you want them.'

Jenny lit a small tea-light, using the torch from her phone to see what she was doing, and placed it on the coffee table.

To stall for time she lit another, and another, until the table was full of them and the light danced around the cabin. She could see his face more clearly now, and the lines of strain etched deeply around his eyes. Were those tear marks on his cheeks? 'So what happened to your phone?'

His finger pointed the way to where small pieces of technology littered the floor. 'Just can't get decent quality equipment these days.' An attempt at a laugh sounded more like a sob. Even in the dim light he looked pretty terrible but she found it hard to feel sorry for him. He had got his sister worried. Got herself worried. And now she was annoyed for caring enough to come.

'Dina was really concerned about you.' It came out more sharply than she had intended, but to hell with it. This guy had got her out of bed in the middle of the night. All for nothing. She had a right to be pissed off. 'She thought you might be suicidal. Like after Elaine dumped you.'

He froze. 'She told you about that, did she?'

'Not all of it.' She put her hands on her hips.

He rubbed a hand across his face. 'That was the night I was pretty close to the edge. If it hadn't been for Dina and Derek then I don't know what would have happened. But she's got nothing to be worried about. I've put all that behind me now.'

He sounded so confident that in that single moment she hated him. 'I'll just toddle on home then, shall I?' She turned towards the exit.

'Don't go. Please stay.'

There was such vulnerability in his voice that Jenny turned back, although her foot refused to move from where she had placed it on the first step of the stair. His eyes met hers and the look she saw there almost swayed her physically, such was its intensity. Her fingers clenched around the handrail to steady herself.

She knew she should give some sort of response, but there were just too many emotions in her head for her to think straight. And then one word popped into her mouth. 'Why?'

Nadeem looked at her blankly. 'Why?'

She carefully placed her foot back on the floor and stood, still gripping the handrail for support. It was either that or pick up something and throw it at him. 'Yes, why? Why do you want me to stay? Last time we met you couldn't get out of the room fast enough. So what's changed?'

Even in the dim light she could see him flush, and he shifted uncomfortably. 'I regret what I said that day. It was wrong to be so judgmental.'

'Thank you.' She couldn't stop the acid in her tone. 'Kind of you to realise it. But I have to ask you again, why?'

'Why what?'

Jenny sat down on the bottom step, hugging her knees to her chest. She could feel the cold October air that was filtering through the gaps in the hatch creeping down the back of her neck, and turned up the collar of her coat against the chill. 'What you've said doesn't change anything. Your company ruined my life. No, scratch that, you and your precious cousin, between you, ruined my life.'

He frowned. 'Ruined your life? You were the one who walked away with sixty thousand quid from it all.'

She found herself shaking, although whether it was from the cold, exhaustion, or anger, she didn't know. She would go with anger. It was more useful. More focusing. Still, even through her rage she could see where he was coming from. How it must have looked to him when she went back into that room and demanded that they double the amount they were offering. Only that fact kept her from getting up and leaving. Sometimes it was a real disadvantage to be able to put herself in someone else's shoes so easily.

She tightened her arms to stop the shivering. 'You still haven't answered my question.'

He scrunched himself into a corner of the sofa, tucking his legs up in a similar fashion to hers. 'Honestly? I really don't have an answer. I just hate feeling like this. As if I'm the bad guy.' A hand broke away to run through his hair. 'I really felt like we had something special together. But then I was forced into an impossible position where I had to pick between the two of you. I went for Derek because I've known him all my life and he's like a brother to me. But based on some new evidence that's come to me recently, I'm not so sure I made the right decision after all.'

Jenny's heart leaped at his words. He'd thought they had something special. Then it fell to the floor as she realised the implications of what he'd just said. 'You do realise that's possibly the most insulting thing you could have admitted to me?'

His head snapped up to meet her gaze, clearly bewildered by her statement. 'Why?' It was his turn to throw the word back at her.

She sighed. How could he be so dense? 'You've basically said that you didn't believe me. That you weren't willing to trust my word. But now that some other evidence has come to light from someone else, you may – *may* – have changed your mind.'

Curiosity overtook her anger and she couldn't help herself. 'What did you actually find out?'

'Someone else in the office has been saying similar things about Derek. Not as serious as you,' he added quickly as she sucked in a breath at the possibility, 'but someone that I trust.'

'Ouch.' The acid was back in her voice, and she didn't care one bit.

'Oh God, I didn't mean it like that.' He rested his head on his knees briefly, then lifted it again. 'Come on. You have to appreciate the situation I'm in. I met you on a plane, for Christ's sake. Knew you for two weeks. And then you asked me to weigh up your word against someone who I've known my whole life.'

'But I was telling the truth.' Even as she said it, she knew how trite it sounded. It was the same as it had ever been. Her word just wasn't good enough, and now she had lost someone else because of another person's lies. It was like history was repeating itself.

Nadeem blew out a breath. 'Yes, but that's what Derek said too. In fact, that's what he's still saying. I confronted him about this other stuff and he's still denying it.'

Her bum was getting stiff on the step and she shifted, trying to get the blood back into the right places. 'Well, that really doesn't surprise me. He's hardly going to give up now. Especially when he's cost your company sixty grand. Can you imagine him admitting to that? But then, you know him better than me.' She couldn't help the sarcasm which crept into her voice.

A faint smile appeared on Nadeem's face, the first she'd seen since she arrived. 'No, you're totally right there. He always has been a stubborn sod.'

There was only one thing left to say before she went. 'You know, you just have to trust yourself on this one. You need to work this out for yourself. Get an impartial investigation going. I can't help you, because I have too much of a stake in this situation. Derek won't help you, for exactly the same reasons. So you need to decide who you really believe.'

He looked at her as if she'd just asked him to divide a baby in half. 'But you don't understand.' His voice choked and he swallowed a couple of times before he carried on. 'Last time I abandoned a friend I've regretted it ever since.'

'*I* don't understand?' Maybe she really was wasting her time here. 'You think *I* don't understand tough decisions? Life-changing decisions? Are you kidding me? Laying aside how I had to leave my family, do you really think it was an easy decision to take your money and walk away? To sacrifice my reputation and a little bit of self-respect for the greater good?'

'I don't follow your reasoning.' His body posture was still defensive.

'Listen to me.' Jenny was really getting into her stride now. She had never thought she would have the chance to say these things to him, and now that she did it felt like squeezing the pus out of a particularly nasty zit. 'That money will let me carry on with my studies. Will let me help out a whole host of other people, once I finally qualify to be a solicitor. And the extra I asked for meant that I could give a big donation to Katie's women's shelter. Which helps out other women who've been in abusive situations. So yes, that's why I went for that. You say you're trying to do good things through your foundation. But that money you gave me can go so far. And do so many things.'

It was strange, sitting here having a conversation with someone who had hurt her so much. If it had been surreal having Hayley and Evie – and Mia – turn up at her birthday dinner, or Dina call her in the middle of the night, this had to top it all. She found herself yawning. It was all too tiring.

She looked down at her feet, not wanting to meet his eyes. If she did she might get sucked back in and do something she would regret. 'Look, I need to get home. You're just going to have to figure things out for yourself. But one thing I will say is, don't let the past influence your evaluation of the present. I can't tell if leaving Nate was the right thing to do or not, but it has absolutely nothing to do with what's going on right now. It's totally separate and not connected.'

She got to her feet, feeling as if she had left her heart still sitting on the step. 'I'm tired, Nadeem, so I'm going home. Have a nice life.'

Her eyes couldn't resist looking at him just one more time before she left, and because of that she saw the exact moment when the realisation hit him and a look of horror spread over his face. 'Oh shit. It's true, isn't it? You're totally right. I let my fears mess up my judgment.' He put his forehead down on his knees. 'Oh fuck. What have I done?'

When he lifted his head and looked at her she saw the certainty in his eyes.

'God. He...and you...' He jumped up, startling her into stepping back, and she almost tripped over the next step up, catching herself from falling just in time. Nadeem pointed a finger at her. 'It's you, isn't it? It's always been you that's been telling the truth.' He slapped himself on the forehead. 'How could I be so sodding dim? How can you ever forgive me?'

Jenny thought she should have been happy at his words, but all she could feel was a weariness just seeping through her body. She fished her phone out of her pocket and checked the time; it was almost four in the morning. No wonder she was so exhausted. 'Look, I'm really sorry, but I desperately need sleep. I just don't have mental space for all this right now. I'm going to go home, and when you've worked this all out in your head, then maybe we can talk.'

Nadeem stopped his pacing and looked down at her as if really seeing her for the first time. 'Stay here. Don't go wandering around in the middle of the night. Have my bed. I'll take the sofa.' As if realising what he'd just said, he shook his head. 'No. What am I saying? You hate me. Of course you won't stay.'

'I don't hate you, Nadeem.' Somehow she found that was true. The idea of staying here with a man who had hurt her so much seemed crazy, but the thought of going back out into the cold and waiting forever for a taxi, or walking home, felt like a mammoth task too. She looked at him, trying to weigh things up. Could she really trust him after all that had happened?

Exhaustion overcame common sense, and she nodded wearily. 'You know what? Screw it. I'll take the bed.'

Chapter 16

Nadeem awoke and checked his watch. Almost ten. He listened carefully, but he couldn't hear anything from Jenny. He would just check up on her, and then connect up the electricity and make a pot of coffee.

Totally shattered, she hadn't even remembered to close the bedroom door. She slept with one arm flung across the pillow, curls in a wild tangle. He suddenly realised that there was nothing he wouldn't do to protect her. Strange how things could seem to turn around in a heartbeat. But the real truth was that it had always been that way. He had just been lying to himself about how he felt.

Sort out your mess first, then maybe you deserve to have someone in your life. He turned and went to put the coffee on and got lost in his thoughts as he filled the cafetière and put it on the stove. It didn't take long to boil.

'Mm, is that real coffee?' Jenny spoke from behind him.

He turned to find her standing in the doorway. She had her jeans on, but was still wearing the t-shirt he had given her the night before. It was the one he had bought in Tanzania, with a silhouette of Kilimanjaro against a dusky red background. The colour suited her; it set off the grey of her eyes and the pink of her cheeks, although with the difference in their heights it looked more like a dress on her. He smiled at the thought.

'Yup, all ready to go.' He poured it out into the two small cups. 'Milk and sugar?'

'No, just black.'

She gave him a tentative smile as she spoke, and he couldn't help smiling back. Things were going to be OK between them. He would make sure of that if it killed him.

Jenny settled herself on the couch, curling her legs beneath her, although he could feel a slight unease radiating from her. He wasn't surprised; it was a strange situation they found themselves in. 'I can't believe I slept so well.' She sipped slowly from her cup. 'Either your bed is somehow magic, or there's something in the air down here.'

Nadeem shrugged. Either way, he was glad. Because a sleep as deep as hers meant that she trusted him around her. Which was at least a start. But how could he begin to bridge the gap between them?

'Jen.' He finally managed to find his voice. 'Things have been pretty tough lately on both of us, and I'm sorry for that, as a lot of this is my fault. I was the one who asked Derek to join the company, and I was the one who didn't believe you.'

He leaned back against the kitchen counter and curled his hands around his coffee cup, drawing strength from the warmth.

'I need to talk about things, Jen, but I'm searching for something to say right now that doesn't sound either horribly self-pitying or terribly clichéd.' He took another deep breath. 'That night at the party, it was just some tosser messing around with a shotgun. But by the time I'd sorted things out you were gone. I came straight back to you. I promise.'

'Derek found me in the garden.' He could see the pain in her eyes. 'Threatened me. I couldn't stay after that. It was more of a self-preservation instinct than anything rational, I think.'

'This is partly where I've been struggling with all this. You tell me things about him which I have a hard time believing. The thought that he might threaten someone – or do any of the other things you've described – just seems fantastical to me. It's just not the man I know and love.'

'I totally understand that.' Her voice was raw, as if it cost her to admit it. 'But I think that people always show just the parts of themselves that they want to reveal. And isn't it possible that he might have hidden this side of himself from you? Knowing that you would disapprove if he didn't?'

He nodded as her words sank in. 'I've wondered that myself. You could be right. What a cliché that would be. In fact look at me, an army veteran with PTSD' – he spoke the words with deep sarcasm – 'whose best friend turns out to be some kind of woman abuser. I am a total walking cliché.'

Jenny just looked down at the mug in her hands, as if she didn't know what to say.

Nadeem gestured with a hand. 'I don't know how to fix it, Jen. People seem to think that because I look alright on the outside that I'm alright on the inside, but really I'm barely keeping things together. I'm thirty-one, for God's sake. With plenty of money, and an amazing family, and everything that I could ever wish for. I should be able to hack it by now. And yet every day I just feel like a fraud. I'm not a good manager, not even a good brother, or a good son, or a good friend. And what I did to you just makes me ashamed.'

Jenny sipped at her coffee, obviously considering his words. 'Don't you think everyone is pretending to some extent? I know I am. I've been working for the past few years in jobs I don't really like, just to save money for a career that I'm not even sure I want to do any more. I now spend my time trying not to panic every time some strange guy brushes against me in a crowd, because I don't want everyone to think that I'm someone who can't keep her shit together.'

Nadeem reached out a hand towards her. 'You're doing great. Amazingly great.'

Jenny looked at him uncertainly and in that moment he saw all the pain he had caused her, and what it was costing her even to just be here with him. His heart shattered into tiny pieces of guilt and he knelt on the floor beside her.

'I need to apologise. Properly. I need to acknowledge how much I've hurt you, say how much of an idiot I've been, and to promise you that I will never do it again. Can you find it in your heart to forgive me?' He held his breath, desperately willing her to say yes.

Something softened in her eyes, and some of the tension left her shoulders. 'That's one heck of an apology, Nadeem.'

He shrugged, while inside he took a long sigh of relief. 'I'm sorry that I didn't believe you about Derek. I should have done, and I don't know how to make things right again.'

His hand rubbed across his forehead. 'It's just so hard, you know? I've known him my whole life. He's been like a brother to me. Every time I've needed him he's been there.' He hurried on. If he was going to apologise properly it wasn't about him. 'I know it took me some time to accept all this. But I'm really sorry I didn't believe in you. I know I hurt you, and I never wanted that.'

Jenny suddenly found she couldn't stay angry at him any more. She reached over and ruffled his hair gently. 'Thanks.' Her voice was soft.

'I've always been slow to trust people I don't know.' He rocked back on his heels, leaning against the kitchen cabinet. 'Anyway, I realised all of that is just bullshit. I should have trusted you.'

Jenny felt a tug of emotion; his words meant more to her than she would have expected.

He smiled at her. 'I really like you, Jen. I don't think I've ever met anyone as special as you. I know that after all that's gone down a relationship probably isn't on the cards for us, but I just wanted you to know that.'

'What do you mean, isn't on the cards? Have you still got doubts about me?' She had to get that one straight at least.

'Oh God, no.' A horrified look passed across his face. 'I'd have you back in a heartbeat if you could forgive me. But I worry that I've hurt you too much.' He ran a hand through his hair.

Was that true? She couldn't tell. She did still care for him, but one apology couldn't erase all the pain of the last two months. 'I can't tell you at the moment. I'm still catching up. It's going to take me some time to come to terms with all of this and work out how I feel about you.' She drained the last of her coffee and passed her mug to him. 'I really thought we had something special too. And then all this messed it up. I think we really need to talk about that.'

'Any chance you want to go for breakfast somewhere?' He sat down at the other end of the couch. 'You can have a shower here if you want.'

Jenny hesitated. Was she ready for this? She nodded. 'OK. I'd like that. Only issue is, if I'm going to have a shower, I'll have absolutely no wish to put on my skanky underwear from last night.'

'Go commando.' Nadeem's face was carefully innocent.

Jenny pushed at him. 'I'm sure you'd like that, wouldn't you?'

'Actually, not really. Thinking those kind of thoughts about you is...well, slightly painful.' The theatrical wiggle of his eyebrows completed the joke.

Jenny dissolved in helpless giggles, and Nadeem joined in with laughter too.

'You're not just one walking cliché, Nadeem, you're zillions of them.' She gestured expansively with her arms. 'I'm going to call you Mr Cliché from now on. It's like you're swimming in them.'

'So you're saying I should be proud of my clichés?' Nadeem flexed his biceps and pretended to admire himself.

'Yeah.' Jenny nodded. 'If they're part of who you are then why not?'

Jenny and Nadeem sat in the sunshine by the side of the canal, looking at each other across a weathered wooden table as the world went by. In the end they had gone via Jenny's flat, just to pick up some clean clothes and reassure Katie that everything was alright.

'How's the granola?' Nadeem seemed reluctant to start in with the heavy stuff straight away.

'Amazing.' Jenny waved her spoon. 'How's the toast?'

Nadeem just nodded happily, his mouth full.

'I can't believe I never found this place.' Jenny took a mouthful of her fruit.

'It opened pretty recently.' Nadeem waved a hand towards the tiny kiosk. 'But the food is great. And the coffee is out of this world.' He cleared his throat. 'I do believe you about what happened with Derek, you know. And I'm sorry it took me so long to come to that conclusion. But what do you want to do about it? Do you want your job back? Do you want to go to the police? I thought that confronting him would bring it all out, but it's totally not worked.'

Jenny pushed her bowl away. 'He's crafty, that's the problem.' Her mind was thinking slowly through all the possibilities. 'He's totally right that there isn't any proof. And now he knows someone is onto him he'll be even harder to catch next time.'

She fiddled with the jar of sugar. 'Sometimes I really wish I'd been able to go to the police that day. It would have taken all this out of my hands and then I wouldn't have had to make any decisions.'

'I've been wondering that. Why didn't you?' Nadeem's voice wasn't judgmental, just curious.

'A combination of things. But all my anxiety issues stem from the thought of being in a situation I can't control. I was really thinking about going to the police on the way home that day, but even the thought of it was enough to give me a panic attack.' She couldn't look at Nadeem. If there was pity on his face then she didn't want to see it. 'But if we get back to the real problem, your HR people – Melissa especially - should have at least done some sort of investigation into my complaint. There's definitely something fishy going on there.'

'Yeah.' Nadeem's eyebrows drew together. 'I asked Melissa about it. But she's sticking to the story that you were just spreading rumours.'

'OK.' Jenny leaned her elbows on the table. 'Firstly, Derek definitely did what he did, and that means Melissa, at the very least, is not doing her job properly, and possibly worse, could be covering for him. Even if Derek totally denied everything, she should have investigated it formally.'

'Yeah.' Nadeem's face was grim. 'She said she did, but somehow now I doubt that. She's worked for the company since we started up the office in London, and she's known my parents for way longer than that. So I don't have a clue what's going on. Melissa said her husband had his life messed up because someone accused him of something similar when he hadn't done anything, but that's still no excuse.'

Jenny bit her lip. 'I can totally understand where she's coming from. But you're still going to have to deal with that somehow. You have to have a complaints process that works. I lost my job for something that wasn't my fault, and not only that, she threatened Colin with dismissal if he helped me too.'

She could feel her anxiety rising and wrapped her arms around herself, counting her breaths until it lowered slightly. Looking at small details on people passing by seemed to help. A pink knitted flower on a hat. Purple laces on a pair of green trainers. The ladybird toy stored safely underneath a child's pram.

She looked back at Nadeem. 'What do I want to happen with Derek?' She thought back to what had happened that day, trying to remain objective. 'He'd been drinking, which I guess is one of the reasons why he dared to do it.'

'Hang on.' Nadeem leaned forward. 'You say he'd been drinking? At work?'

She nodded. 'I could smell the alcohol on his breath.'

Even thinking about it brought the taste of whisky back into her mouth. She rolled her neck, trying to loosen it.

Nadeem frowned. 'I'm so sorry to put you through all this.'

She rubbed her forehead. 'It's OK. I think it's got to be done. What were you going to say?'

'The alcohol, I was thinking about. I smelt it on him yesterday morning. He'd literally just got back from the States. I assumed he'd just had a couple of drinks on the plane to help him sleep or something, but he was pretty drunk at the party too. I thought that was just him taking advantage of my parents' whisky, but now I wonder.'

'Maybe you could ask around.' Jenny rubbed her forehead again. 'Didn't you say he left his previous job to come and work for you? Someone at his old company might have noticed something. Or one of his other friends. If he really has an alcohol problem, someone will be aware of it.'

'You're right.' Nadeem smiled for a moment, and then his face suddenly fell again. 'But this is all about him. When it should be about you. What do you really want out of all this?'

He was totally on her side now, Jenny realised, and that thought made her want to hug him and never let him go. But his question did make her pause and think. What did she really want out of all this?

'It's hard to say.' She spoke slowly, aware that parts of her brain were whirring away frantically behind the scenes. 'Part of me wants to lock him up forever and throw away the key. But honestly? All I really want is for him to understand exactly what he's done. For him to understand exactly what all this has done to me, and to all the other women he must have done it to. And never do it again.'

Seeing his expression, her mouth twisted wryly. 'Oh yes. There's no doubt that if he's done it to me then he's done it to others before. Maybe like you say, not as seriously, but that really doesn't matter. Any kind of behaviour that makes someone feel uncomfortable is totally unacceptable.' She shifted on the bench. 'What's your end game in all this anyway?'

'I just want him the hell out of my family's business.' Nadeem's jaw tightened.

It was then that Jenny realised she had been wrong about one thing. 'It's not working in the company that's dragging you down, is it? Just the extra responsibility.'

Nadeem looked surprised. 'Of course. That's what I've been trying to tell you all along. I love what we do. It makes me feel like I'm making a difference in the world. To bring medicine to someone who might not otherwise be able to get it, or to make sure that the people fighting for our country have the supplies they need? Now that I've really got involved in it, there's nothing I'd rather get up for in the morning. I'd do any-thing to make that work. It's just the worry that I might screw it all up that's been stressing me out. Especially with this latest news. Dad thinks the world of Derek. I'm worried finding out about this will quite literally kill him.'

He laced his fingers together, resting his elbows on the table. 'The four of us as kids were such a tight-knit group, we did everything together. Derek was a year older and always the leader, dreaming up the next ad-venture, while Dina was the one who'd come up with a strategy for what we were planning. I was exceptionally good at looking pathetic and innocent when we got found out, and Nate was just the laid-back one, willing to go along with whatever the latest escapade was.'

A smile cracked across his face. 'I think that's partly why Nate followed me into the Army; it was just an-other big adventure. He was the one right behind my shoulder when I had issues with with some racist bul-lies during our initial training. He was never afraid to get into a scrap for something he really believed in.'

The serious expression returned and he ran a hand through his hair. 'If I'm totally honest, my anger at Derek isn't just because of what he's done to you. I also feel betrayed; it's just not what I'd expect from a friend. I'd thought that Derek would always be there for me, and to lose him in this way is almost more than I can bear.'

What could she say to that? She was sorry that her actions had caused Nadeem so much grief, but it totally wasn't her fault. In fact, if someone else had said something sooner then they wouldn't even be in this messed up situation. 'If we can't involve your father, we're going to just have to confront Derek ourselves. Together. So that he realises this is serious.'

'You're using the word we, Jen.' Nadeem shook his head. 'It's not your problem. I'm the one who needs to make this right.'

Jenny smiled at him, finally sure of at least one thing. 'It is my problem, Nadeem. I really want to see him pay for what he's done. And given that we're dealing in honesty right now, I have to tell you that despite all the crap you've chucked at me, I do really care for you.'

Nadeem face softened and he touched her hand gently. 'I really care for you too.'

His voice was quiet, and the feeling she heard in it warmed her heart. Was there a possibility of a second chance for them both? Only time would tell.

Chapter 17

Nothing could be done until Monday, when Nadeem would have a chance to contact someone at Derek's old company. He headed into town to replace his phone, while Jenny turned, as she so often did in times of stress, to her dressmaking. She was ready to put the pieces of the red dress together and watch it take shape into a masterpiece.

Some time later, Jenny found her stomach rumbling and realised it was past seven in the evening. Katie, who would have normally disturbed her by now, was out working at a charity dinner. Four hours of work had turned the pieces of silk into something resembling a garment. Finishing and decoration would still take her a while, but it sat on the mannequin like a bold splash of hope.

She whacked a pizza in the oven, thankful for the need to not spend any more mental effort, and flopped on the sofa. Besides a message from Hayley reporting a safe arrival there was nothing important on her phone, which was a good thing. She desperately needed to catch up on sleep.

But then Jenny realised there was one person she did really want to talk to. Her sister.

She considered the idea as she munched her pizza. It was so long since they had last spoken, if you didn't count hanging up on her the last time. And even if she let her mother slip away from her, she had a duty to Bella, who had never done anything wrong. No, not just a duty. A wish. A wish to see her sister again.

With trembling fingers she picked up her phone and found the number. It rang for a long time and she was just about to hang up when someone answered. 'Hello?'

'Bella?' Jenny's voice was tentative.

'Jenny?' The voice on the other end sounded shocked. There was a lot of background noise; it sounded like a restaurant or something similar.

'If you're busy, I don't want to keep you.' Jenny suddenly wavered. This was such a bad idea.

'No way! Let me just find somewhere more quiet.' The noise suddenly receded.

'Are you sure I'm not disturbing you?'

'No, sure, it's all good. How are you? What's going on?'

'I'm fine.' It wasn't totally a lie. 'I just wanted to call and see how you're doing.'

She could tell Bella sensed the hesitancy in her voice, because the next words all came out in a rush, as if she was afraid that Jenny would hang up. 'Look, I can't tell you how great it is to hear from you. I really want to see you. When can we meet up?'

'Depends on your schedule.' Jenny felt a bit blown away by her sister's enthusiasm. 'I don't start my new job until Wednesday.'

'That'd be amazeballs.'

Jenny had to smile at Bella's choice of words. There were only six years between them, but sometimes she felt as if her sister spoke a completely different language.

'I've got a meeting just off Oxford Street on Monday morning.' Bella continued. 'We could have lunch after that if you like.'

Meeting? Jenny was surprised. Her little sister had something serious enough to be called a meeting? 'Sure.' Jenny couldn't see a reason to say no. 'You can tell me all about it afterwards.'

They spent a couple more minutes making arrangements. Just before she hung up, Jenny said quickly, 'Promise you won't-'

'I know, tell Mum. I won't. I know you'll make it up with her someday. See you soon.' Bella rang off.

Jenny's heart swelled at the words; how could her sister trust her like that without any explanation? It made Nadeem's earlier disbelief all the more insulting.

She rolled over on the sofa and stared at the ceiling. She would be seeing her sister in less than forty-eight hours. It all seemed quite unreal. Jenny couldn't help hugging herself at the prospect, and then a big yawn split her face. It was time for a bath and then she would try to get some sleep.

Jenny had picked her favourite noodle place in Soho, knowing that Bella loved Japanese food. Or used to, she reflected ruefully. How long was it since they had even spoken? Probably that awful day four years ago when they had just argued. About nothing in particular. Or maybe, about everything.

It was the day she had finally plucked up the courage to go and find her sister. Knowing she wouldn't be welcome at home, she had gone to visit Bella's school. The teachers had recognised her and welcomed her with open arms, but the reception from her little sister had been far from friendly. Alternately petulant and sullen, the sixteen-year-old had acted as if Jenny was the villain in the whole story. When Jenny had tried to explain her decision to leave, Bella had been unwilling to listen to anything she had to say.

It had ended in a ferocious slanging match that was not something Jenny was proud of, which made Bella's eagerness to meet up seem all the more precious.

Bella breezed in bang on time, looking every inch the confident businesswoman in a smart grey trouser suit. Jenny had to blink and remind herself that her sister was only twenty; the suit and some careful makeup made her look much older, which was probably on purpose if she'd had a business meeting. The years had turned her sister from a hesitant teenager into a young woman, and Jenny liked what she saw. Despite the posh outfit, Bella still gave her a warm hug in greeting.

'You have no idea how good it is to see you.' Bella sat down in the chair opposite. Jenny's throat grew tight; how could she have left it so long to call?

Ordering food took them a couple of minutes, and then they were free to chat. Jenny scanned her sister's face and then laughed; Bella's dark brown hair was cut in a practical bob very similar to her own. She did envy her those smooth waves though; so different from her daily wrestle with her own wild tangle.

'I'm so glad you rang the other day.' Bella dived right in at the deep end as usual. 'I've wanted to call you for so long. Well, as soon as I realised how childish I was that day. But I was afraid that you'd never forgive me for what I said. And then afterwards I thought you might be angry that I hadn't called earlier. And...well, screw it. You're here now. How is everything?'

Jenny had to smile; she realised she had been so busy thinking of her own insecurities recently that she had forgotten to remember others might have them too. She found herself telling Bella all about the trip to

Scotland and what had happened with Nadeem. Bella took it all in, nodding slowly. 'It sounds like you've had a really tough time. Do you really like this guy?'

Jenny sighed. 'Yes. I'm afraid I do. Does that make me naive?'

Bella shook her head. 'He has put you through a lot. But really, isn't it good in some ways that he stuck by his friend? I mean, I always thought that if Ivy had been a bit less ready to believe that you stole her boyfriend, you wouldn't have lost her friendship.'

Ivy. Jenny blinked. She had even mentioned Ivy to Nadeem in passing, but in truth she never really thought much about her childhood friend at all these days. The two of them had been best buddies for a while until her stepfather had managed to fabricate a lie that Jenny had made out with Ivy's boyfriend; all part of his manipulative plan to isolate Jenny from anyone who could help her. Maybe if Ivy had possessed a bit more trust in Jenny's character then she wouldn't have believed him. But then, life at eighteen was tricky enough. She couldn't judge her former friend too harshly.

'You're right.' Jenny smiled wryly. 'I guess that could be why I was willing to forgive Nadeem. I just hope-' The longing she felt in her chest made her breath catch suddenly. 'I just hope the two of us can put all that behind us now and finally move on. I don't know if a proper relationship is on the cards, but we're friends at least so far, which is something.'

'I'm sure you'll work it out.' Bella took another mouthful. 'This is good stuff! Great choice of a place to eat. Nice one.'

'Anyway, that's enough about me.' Jenny leaned forward. 'What about you? What's this mysterious meeting you had this morning?'

'Ah.' Bella gave a small satisfied smile. 'I forgot that you didn't know anything about my latest project.' She smoothed down her jacket unconsciously. 'You remember how I always said I'd never go to university?'

Jenny nodded; Bella had always declared it 'boring' and 'useless'. It was one of the things they had argued about that day, among many others.

'I know you were disappointed, but really it was the best thing for me. Anyway, much to Granny's horror, I spent six months working my way around bars and nightclubs in Europe.'

Jenny wasn't surprised at this. Her sister had always been a bit of a rebel.

'I did a couple of months in a swanky bar in Monaco, which was just full of people with more money than they knew how to spend.' Bella gave a sigh. 'But the experience made me realise that I'd gathered a lot of connections, both through our family and while I was at that posh school they paid for, and it would be possible to shamelessly use them to help other people who needed it.'

'Like Princess Diana.' Jenny raised an eyebrow. 'Or Jameela Jamil.'

Bella laughed. 'Don't compare me with them. I don't think I'm quite in that league.'

Jenny shrugged, but couldn't stop herself from smiling.

'It took me a long time to work out what I really wanted to do with my life, but eventually I realised that my heart is here in London.' Bella placed a hand in the centre of her chest. 'I still remember that weekend we went to Buckingham Palace together.'

'You remember that?' Jenny was surprised. It hadn't been long after they had moved back in with their grandparents. Their mother had been hopeless at the time – prostrate with grief, Jenny now recognised with hindsight – and their grandmother had volunteered to take them to London. For the two young girls the sights had been exciting and the crowds bewildering. 'I remember the amazing paintings in that gallery.'

'I don't remember that.' Bella shook her head. 'I just remember you buying me that red bus money box full of toffees. I still have it on my bedside table.'

Jenny found herself suddenly unable to speak; hearing that made her realise that even throughout all these years then her sister had never given up on her.

Bella just smiled at her, but Jenny could see the depth of emotion in her eyes. 'So anyway, I came back to London and convinced a few rich philanthropists to donate some money to help me set up a hairdressing salon. We give apprenticeships to people who are trying to rebuild their lives after suffering from domestic abuse.' She grinned mischievously at Jenny's obvious look of surprise.

'And I suppose that all your rich acquaintances get their hair cut there, even if only because they feel like they should?'

Bella winked at her, the grin still on her face. 'Exactly! And it's been really popular. We've got plans to open up two more in the next six months, in different areas of London. My meeting today was actually with a huge hair care company to see if they'd be willing to supply us with their shampoos and stuff at a massively discounted price. I won't tell you who it is yet because I don't want to jinx it, but I think it's pretty much in the bag.' She leaned back in her chair with an air of great satisfaction.

Looking at her sister sitting in front of her, Jenny felt nothing but pride and admiration for the young woman she had become.

'How is Mum, actually?' Jenny bit her lip.

Bella tugged at one ear. 'She's doing pretty good, actually. Since Richard left, much better than she was.'

'Wait.' Jenny couldn't believe it. 'He's gone? When did this happen?' Her palms suddenly prickled with tension and she rubbed them together to try to calm herself down.

Bella sat back, the surprise evident on her face. 'Shoot. I assumed you'd have heard. But then, why would you?' She took another sip of her green tea. 'It was about a year ago. Basically, once the main money ran out he didn't have any reason to stay. He tried to get half the house with the divorce, but luckily that one got thrown out.'

A feeling that was a mix of both relief and anger swept through Jenny. That Bella had pegged their step-father correctly as a freeloader made her happy. But her anger came from knowing that he had been able to get away with it for so long. 'So what did happen to all the money?'

Bella shrugged. 'I think it was already on its way out. A lot of Grandfather's investments went slowly bad as the recession really set in, and then when he died there was inheritance tax to pay. I think he always meant to put everything in a trust fund but never really got round to it. The upkeep of the house swallowed every-thing else. I think Mum's planning to sell it to some rich Russian or something.'

'Oh! Grandfather would turn in his grave.' Jenny laughed, and her sister joined in.

Then Bella sobered, leaning forward and putting a hand on Jenny's arm. 'She's doing alright, Jin-Jin.' Jenny felt her eyes prickle at the use of her childhood name. Bella spoke casually, but Jenny could see the effort it was taking her. 'She's got herself on some decent medication and she's doing OK. But it's been a long haul.'

Jenny reached over and took her sister's hand. 'I'm really sorry I ran away.'

Bella smiled faintly, her eyes dangerously watery. 'It's alright. I think I would've done the same if I were you.'

Jenny bit her lip. 'Bella, even though he's gone, I still don't think I'm ready to see her yet.'

Bella pursed her mouth up, looking so like their grandmother that Jenny just had to smile. 'Seriously, I can understand that. She was the one who didn't even try and keep in touch with you when you left.'

Jenny nodded, her throat tight. This news was pretty earth-shattering. The man who had terrorised their whole family was gone from their lives. Suddenly the air felt lighter and colours seemed brighter. 'This is a lot to take in.' It seemed somehow slightly inadequate, but it was all she could find to say.

Bella squeezed her hand again. 'I think we both had to grow up too quick, the both of us. So just take your time and think about what your next step is going to be. You've earned it.'

'Yeah. I have to say I'm pretty happy right now, apart from all this recent stuff that's been going on. I've got some great friends here in London.'

'Tell me about them.'

'Well, there's Katie, for starters.' Jenny told Bella about her flatmate.

'Oh wow.' Bella was impressed. 'I could really do with someone like that. I'm arranging this charity auction the second week in December, and it's turning out to be a nightmare. Do you think she might be able to help? I can pay her, of course.'

'Sure, I can ask. I think she'd love to if she's not too busy.' Jenny smiled happily. 'But I think you should definitely meet her anyway. She volunteers at a women's shelter, so you'd probably have a lot to talk about.'

The two girls ended up wandering through the shops together for much of the afternoon. When they parted at the station Bella hugged Jenny tightly. 'Don't you leave it so long next time.' She wagged a finger in warning.

'Pah!' Jenny scoffed. 'Don't you leave it so long either; now that I know you're in London you won't be able to get rid of me.'

They parted with promises that Jenny knew they would keep. She had to thank Nadeem, she thought ruefully, for bringing her back together with her sister. She would never have done it without him.

Jenny had put her phone on silent, not wanting anything to interrupt her time with Bella, but when she checked it there were two missed calls from Nadeem. She rang him straight back. 'Any news?'

'Yeah. You were totally right. He didn't get fired from his old job, but he did get persuaded to leave. Due to his drinking apparently. He missed one too many important meetings.' Nadeem was silent for a moment. 'I can't believe it. An alcoholic too? How blind have I been?'

In that moment Jenny wanted to be right beside him and put her arms around him, so raw was the emotion in his voice. 'You aren't the first, and you won't be the last.'

'I don't know.' He did sound really depressed now. 'Most of me is totally pissed off at him, but in some ways I just feel sorry for him. I mean, he's clearly got problems. And it's not as if I haven't had my own demons around drinking.'

Jenny could totally see where Nadeem was coming from, but still, the man was a creep, and had to be stopped somehow. The beginning of a plan was starting to form in her mind. 'Can I call you back when I get home? I might have an idea about how to handle this.'

Chapter 18

Jenny sat next to Nadeem in the swish boardroom. It had taken them a few days to finalise their plans for this meeting and now she couldn't wait for it to be over. If she actually made it and didn't expire from the stress. Even just coming back to the office had been enough to send her anxiety sky high, although the warm smiles and handshakes from her ex-colleagues had helped somewhat.

Nadeem's hand settled on her shoulder. 'Everything alright?'

She looked at him sitting beside her. He must be going through his own roller coaster of emotions. Somehow the warmth of his touch gave her the courage that she needed. She nodded, smoothing down the jacket of her suit for the fifteenth time. It was the suit she had been wearing when all this had started, now carefully laundered and pressed, which felt right somehow. As if by claiming back her suit she was claiming back her life.

It also helped that yesterday had finally been her first precious mental health appointment. It had left her drained but positive that there might be light at the end of the tunnel. She clasped her hands and placed them deliberately on the table. 'Let's do this.'

Germaine poked her head around the door. 'He's on his way. Are you ready?'

Nadeem nodded, his face grim.

Germaine settled in beside him just in time as Derek came through the door. The smile on his face faded as he became aware of the setup of the room and the looks on their faces. When he registered Jenny sitting beside Nadeem his eyebrows lifted, but he said nothing.

'Close the door and have a seat, Derek.' Nadeem politely indicated the other side of the table.

Derek sat, a puzzled look on his face. 'What's she doing here?' He pointed a finger at Jenny.

'Look, I'm not going to play games.' Nadeem's voice was flat, but Jenny could sense the anger he was hiding. 'We know what you did, and we don't care why. You lied to me. And those lies cost the company a lot of money.'

Derek gaped at him. 'Don't be ridiculous. You-'

Nadeem cut him off. 'Enough of your protests. It's too late for that. I want you to apologise to Jenny. And you're going to pay back every penny of that money from your own account. I'll escort you personally to the bank to do it.'

Derek just sat back and laughed. 'Sixty thousand pounds? Now why would I do a thing like that?'

'Because.' Jenny spoke up. 'If you don't, I'm going to the press about what you did to me.'

'The press? And what exactly would you accuse me of?' Derek laughed again. The sound sent shivers down her spine, and it was only Nadeem's solid presence beside her that made her keep her cool.

'Sexual harassment and bullying. There are three other women in this company who will back me up on that.' Jenny tried to match her tone to Nadeem's, even though she was screaming inside.

'Don't be ridiculous.' Derek tone was disparaging. 'Who's going to believe your stories?'

'He believes them. She believes them.' Nadeem nodded at her words, while Germaine inclined her head in assent. 'Besides, with the gossip rags the way they are these days, you don't need proof to get a story. Most of them are quite happy to run with hearsay.'

Derek leaned back in his chair, crossing his arms. 'This is ridiculous. Nadeem, you're not going to let her ruin my good name, are you? Don't just give into her threats. She signed that NDA. If she does this, we can sue her into the ground.'

'I've torn it up. It's the one thing in my life that I'm truly ashamed of.' Nadeem's voice was hard.

Derek froze, the colour draining from his face.

Nadeem leaned forward, resting his arms on the table. 'I trusted you, Derek, and you lied to me. I'm not only going to make you give me that payment, I'm going to ask you to resign your director's position.'

Derek shook his head. 'Ridiculous. I refuse. I'm going to talk to Alan about this.'

Jenny looked at Nadeem. It was time. She picked up her phone. 'Germaine, please thank your assistant for me, for getting such a convenient list of numbers. I'll just dial the first on the list and see what they say, shall I?'

She punched in the number on speakerphone, watching Derek's face growing redder as she did so. It rang a couple of times, and then a cheery voice answered. 'Good morning, Daily-'

'Wait.' Derek's voice interrupted.

Jenny's heart leaped in triumph, and then she realised the receptionist would be waiting. 'Sorry, wrong number, apologies for that.' She hung up, and looked expectantly at Derek. 'Well?'

He leaned back in his chair, a satisfied smirk on his face. She knew it wasn't over yet; he thought he had a get out clause. 'I'd love to do what you're asking, but, you know,' he patted his pockets theatrically, 'I didn't bring my ID to work today. I can't authorise such a big payment at the bank without it.'

Jenny couldn't help a small smile; she had anticipated this move and knew what to say. 'I don't know if you remember, but you asked me to bend down that day to put some papers in the bottom drawer of your filing cabinet, just so you could ogle my bum. But I saw your cheque book lying in there too. So you can just write out a damn cheque.' To turn this small thing against him suddenly felt like flying free.

'God.' Derek suddenly crumpled, placing his head in his hands. 'Deem, please, don't do this to me. It'll wipe me out. That's all the money I've saved to rebuild my flat.'

'You need to get some help, Derek.' Nadeem sagged in his chair too. 'We know about the drinking. You need to get yourself into some kind of rehab.'

Derek looked up, his expression betraying his surprise at the words. 'God. I'm fine. So I have a few drinks every now and again, so what?'

'You know that's not what it is. You've been in this office drunk on more than one occasion. Think about your parents. They'd be horrified if they knew what you've been doing. Think about how you ruined Jenny's life. She still has sleepless nights because of what you've done. Think about your sister. About Dina and Mia too. How would you feel if it happened to one of them?'

When Derek didn't reply, Nadeem spoke again. 'Please, DK. Do it for me.' His tone was soft.

'Fine.' Derek suddenly spread his hands out in acceptance. He looked totally crushed.

It didn't take long to write out the cheque. Jenny scanned it swiftly, just to make sure that there were no mistakes, but it all looked correct. He could still stop it before it cleared but somehow she knew he wouldn't.

Derek stood, his mouth stretched in a fake smile. 'Well, it's been lovely seeing you all.'

'Wait.' Nadeem slid another piece of paper across the table to him. 'You still need to sign this.'

'What's is it?' Derek frowned.

'Your resignation letter. Citing your inability to continue due to other unavoidable commitments.'

Derek just signed the paper and left, slamming the door as he went.

Nadeem turned to Germaine. 'Go and make sure he really leaves, if you don't mind. And make sure that the instruction to revoke his pass and IT access has gone through. I'll call his parents and let them know what's happened.'

Germaine just nodded quickly and disappeared. Jenny sagged back in her chair, one hand to her mouth. Nadeem was instantly beside her, kneeling on the floor. 'Are you alright?'

She just shook her head. 'I think I'm going to throw up.'

Nadeem grabbed the waste paper bin which stood in the corner. 'Here you go. Do whatever you need. You were amazing. Oh, and just be thankful we invested in good solid stainless steel bins, instead of some plastic crap with holes in it.'

Jenny looked at Nadeem, and then back at the bin, and started to laugh. It was so similar to what Katie had done that she couldn't help it. She laughed until the tears came, but instead of feeling embarrassed about them she was glad when Nadeem pulled her in and held her close. She felt some of his tears falling on her head too, and didn't mind; if he had been more matter-of-fact about losing his best friend then she would have thought less of him.

'Sorry. I still feel slightly bad for him, even though that makes me feel really guilty.' His voice was muffled in her hair.

'Don't worry.' She lifted her head. 'It's like breaking up with someone. It hurts at first even though it's the right thing to do.' She sniffed loudly.

He pulled a clean handkerchief out of his back pocket. 'Here, blow.'

Jenny took it gratefully.

'You were amazing.' Nadeem touched her shoulder gently.

'You were pretty amazing too.' Jenny sniffed again, then blew her nose loudly. 'I couldn't have done it without you.'

'But still. Have you never thought about becoming a barrister? You could really take them all to the wringers.' Then he paused, considering. 'Or do you want your old job back? We need all the good people we can get at the moment.'

'Not going to happen.' Jenny shook her head. 'I have other things I want to do with my life now.'

Nadeem gave her another squeeze and kissed her gently on the top of her head. 'I'm looking forward to hearing all about them. Can I take you out for dinner tonight?'

Jenny should have seen the request coming, but it still threw her slightly, because she already knew what her answer had to be. She turned to him, her heart breaking. 'You know I had my first appointment with mental health yesterday, right?'

Nadeem nodded, his face obviously puzzled at the sudden change in topic.

Jenny tugged at her hair, then realised what she was doing and clasped her hands together instead. 'We talked over everything that's happened, and how I felt about it. Especially about you. And how you got caught up in everything.' She bit her lip, willing herself to hold his gaze. Doing this to him was just as bad as she had imagined. 'She didn't exactly warn me off a relationship with you, but she did say I should consider things very carefully before stepping back into one, given the circumstances.'

Jenny could feel herself beginning to shiver at the thought of what Nadeem might say, but a deep breath helped to steady her. 'I've been thinking a lot since then about what she said, and, much as I like you, I think she's right. The last couple of months have been a bit of a mental rollercoaster, and I think I need to go away and process some of it before I jump into anything else.'

Nadeem rocked backwards onto his heels, disappointment plain on his face. He opened his mouth and closed it a couple of times, clearly unsure of what to say. Finally he spoke very quietly. 'I understand. Much as I like you, I'm not going to try and change your mind if that's how you really feel. I don't want to be yet another man trying to pressure you into something you don't want to do.' He rubbed his forehead with both hands, then looked back up at her. 'But please just tell me one thing. Is that a definite no to something happening in the future, or is it a not sure?'

Jenny shook her head, swallowing to try and clear the lump in her throat. 'I can't tell you that. And if I'm totally honest with you, some part of me is still pretty angry at you for how you acted, and I don't think that's any basis for a good relationship. Don't wait around for me, Nadeem. It just wouldn't be fair when I can't promise you anything.'

She got up from her chair and smoothed down her skirt one last time. 'Take care of yourself. I'll always remember those magical two weeks we had together before everything exploded apart.' Stifling a sob, she fled from the office, and Nadeem was left gazing after her, a stricken look on his face.

When Jenny got home she and Katie snuggled up on the couch with large glasses of wine.

'Give me Thor.' Jenny flexed an arm theatrically. 'Screw the real men. Nothing less than a god is enough for me.'

They both giggled hysterically, and Katie hugged her tightly.

It was the right decision, Jenny thought, as the familiar music of her favourite film started. Being single would give her more time to spend with Bella. Getting to know her sister again was really important. Reena and Katie would see her through all this, and she had another mental health appointment next week. Slowly but surely, she would survive.

The film was great as usual, but Jenny found her thoughts wandering elsewhere. As the credits started to roll, she turned to Katie. 'I've been thinking.'

'Yes?' Katie looked at her enquiringly.

'What would you say if I spent the money I got on starting up my business instead of going back to study?' Jenny pressed the pause button on the remote. 'Would you say I was crazy?'

Katie pursed her lips. 'I'd say it was risky, but not totally crazy. Why, are you considering it?'

'I don't know. I still have moments when I wonder if selling out was the right thing to do. But I guess I can't change that now, so I need to forget about it. It's just...' Jenny tried to search for the words that would express how she really felt. 'It's just I'd feel a bit guilty spending the money on something that seems so selfish. I desperately want to make a difference in the world, and being a solicitor would be a great way to do that.'

She took refuge in another sip of her wine, savouring the tart taste as it slid down her throat. 'But part of me is thinking that maybe it isn't for me. I've been realising lately that I went for that because it was safe. It was something I could control. A tidy, ordered job with tidy, ordered tasks. I want to do it because of what happened with my family, and because of Alison, but I've realised that what I said to Nadeem applies to me too. I shouldn't let the past define what I do in the future.'

She shifted on the sofa. 'What I really want to do is design amazing clothes. And make them too. But then, I don't want to regret it later if I do spend the money on that. I mean, how is that going to make a difference in the world? Normal people aren't going to be able to afford the things I make, if I do go ahead with it.'

'Probably not.' Katie shrugged. 'But if that's what you're passionate about then I think you should go for it. I think there's always other ways to give back. You could make sure you only source from small suppliers, for example. And look at what Bella does with her business. I've been trying to get some kind of creative classes set up for the women at the shelter so if you wanted to help out with that it would mean a lot.' She took a sip of her own wine. 'Also, one of them who's there at the moment desperately needs a job to support her two kids. She's having problems finding work that's flexible enough to fit in around school hours and will accommodate her when they're sick. If you could even give her a few hours a week it would make a shedload of difference. And, you could keep your supermarket job for now and just see how it goes. Shift work would mean you'd be free during at least some of the office hours.'

'Yeah, I'd thought about that.' Jenny bit her lip, considering. 'But I'd have to do it from here to start with. It would mean fabric everywhere.'

'I wouldn't mind that, if it's really what you want to do.' Katie shrugged, her face serious. 'But there's also that place down by the canal that rents out studio space to artsy people. They might give you a decent price to rent a worktable for a few hours a week. I could help you with all the accounting and stuff as I have to do that already for my business.'

'Stop that suggestive waggling of your eyebrows! It just looks weird.' Jenny couldn't help a laugh. 'Let me think about it. You're right, I could do it alongside other things.' Then she registered something Katie had said. 'Artsy people? Is that what you call them?' She started to tickle Katie, who pretended to look horrified.

'My wine! For goodness sake!'

'Don't be ridiculous, it's almost empty.'

'Every drop is precious.' Katie drained her glass and set it on the floor. 'So how about it? Do we have a deal?' She stuck out her hand.

Jenny considered for a moment. 'I'm scared, Katie. This feels too much like losing control of my life.'

'I don't know.' Katie poked her gently with a finger. 'Isn't it more like taking back control? Refusing to let the past define you?'

Jenny frowned; she had never really thought of it like that. Then she nodded and clasped Katie's hand firmly. 'You're right. It's a deal. Let's do this.'

Chapter 19

Nadeem sat in their weekly ops meeting as his staff went through the security plans for their latest set of shipments to Nigeria. They had finally managed to recruit an operations manager who was doing great things, which had eased the workload somewhat over the last few weeks, but Nadeem had come to realise that he himself wasn't cut out for this job. His mind was wandering and he knew it was rude, but he couldn't help it.

Also, there was Jenny. He missed her. Badly. Christmas wasn't that far off, London was already splattered with lights and he felt like happiness was being stuffed down his throat. The staff had decorated the office and every time he looked at the festive display he just thought about how he had hoped to take Jenny back home for the holidays.

'Sorry, Idris. You were saying you're not a hundred percent sure that the arrangements will cover the journey to the final destination?'

Idris nodded. 'Yes. We think we should ask for another car from our police escort, just to be on the safe side.'

Nadeem's phone bleeped before he had the chance to reply. There were only a few people who were on his silent bypass list, and none of them usually called him during the day. He turned back to his team. 'Sorry people, I have to take this. How about we take a five minute break?'

The expressions of relief on a couple of people's faces told him it was a good idea. As they all filed out, he pulled out his phone. It was Mia. What was she doing calling him at work? His stomach clenched in sudden worry. Had something happened to his dad? Forcing himself to be calm, he took the call.

'You're a total tosser, Nadeem.' She sounded as if she meant it.

'Hello to you too, sis.' For some reason he found he was amused instead of annoyed.

'I mean it. Why didn't you tell me you and Jenny never managed to work things out between you? I only found out because I ran into Reena by accident this morning.'

Nadeem rubbed his forehead. 'Come on, Mia, you know what work's been like. I've been run off my feet in here.'

'I don't care. You've got people to do things for you. Don't screw it up with the only decent girl you've ever dated.'

He could feel a headache building. 'I really don't have time to talk about this now. I'm in the middle of a meeting.'

Mia ignored him. 'I called because I've just managed to get you a ticket to Bella's charity event next week. Don't ask me how, these things are like gold dust. I had to call in a lot of favours to get it.'

Relief that it wasn't about their dad and puzzlement as to why she was calling him about something so insignificant made him irritable. 'Why the hell would you think that I might want to go? You know I hate those kind of things.'

'Oh purlease. Get your work brain off and your thinking brain in.' He could almost feel Mia rolling her eyes at him. 'Jenny will be there. Don't screw it up.'

'Come on. That ship has sailed. She told me she doesn't want a relationship with me. Why would she change her mind?'

'She loves you, Deem. It was obvious the night you brought her to the party. And do you really think she would have come to your boat to rescue you if she didn't?' He heard some shouting in the background and her voice was muffled for a few seconds, then she came back on the line. 'Sorry, that was someone asking me if I'm coming. I've got a class in three minutes.'

'You'd better go then. Thanks for trying anyway, but I'm not going to hassle her. She told me she needs space and I have to respect that.' Nadeem rubbed his forehead, trying to suppress his annoyance. He was fond of his little sister, but sometimes her interfering was just too much.

'She needs someone who will stand by her no matter what.' Mia was insistent. 'Did you ever tell her how much you love her? No? I thought not. You should do. It would change everything.'

Hope flared in his heart and then quickly died. 'Even if that was true, you know what things are like since Derek and Melissa left. When would I ever get the time to see her? If she did want me back.' His tone was wistful.

'You're the boss, Nadeem. Delegate. That's what bosses do. Do I have to spell it out for you? D-E-L-E-G-'

'I know how to spell.' He interrupted her. 'But I don't have anyone to-'

His mouth stopped working as he saw what he should have done from the start and found that the decision he had to make was no decision at all. 'I'll take it. The ticket, I mean.'

'Don't thank me or anything.'

'Thanks, sis.' A grin split his face from ear to ear. 'Name your price and I'll pay it.'

'I'll cash it in later.' Mia laughed. 'You can name your first baby after me if you really like.'

Nadeem sobered instantly. 'Let's cross that bridge when we come to it.'

'OK, got to go, I'm really going to be late now.' She hung up on him before he had the chance to say good-bye.

Jenny looked up as she heard the key in the front door. Katie and Bella tumbled through the doorway laughing, their noses bright from the cold.

'Everything set for tomorrow?' She shivered as a blast of freezing air from the doorway went straight through her pyjamas.

'Yes. As ready as we'll ever be. This is going to be the party of the century.' Bella turned shining eyes on Katie and squeezed her hand. 'And I wouldn't have been able to do it without Katie's help.'

Interesting. So that was the way things might be going? She hadn't even considered the possibility. But her sister and her best friend? She couldn't ask for a better person to take care of Bella's happiness, if that was how things did turn out. She wouldn't say anything though. It could just be a really good friendship and if that was the case it made her really happy too.

'Dinner's keeping warm in the oven. A customer left a few tubs of mascarpone cheese under one of the self-checkouts today and no-one noticed until they'd been there for at least a couple of hours so I've made us a lasagna. Let's get it dished up, I'm starving.'

'And Thor is waiting.' Katie flashed a wicked grin at Jenny, then turned back to Bella. 'I can't believe you've never seen any of the films.'

Bella shrugged. 'I've never been much of a Hemsworth fan. I'm more of a Hiddleston.'

Katie gave her a puzzled look. 'But he's in them all too.'

'You're kidding me. As who?' Bella's disbelief was clear on her face.

'Loki.' As Bella continued to frown at her, Katie pulled out her phone and tapped a few times. 'Here, look.'

Bella took the phone for a closer look. 'Shit. I never noticed. That dark hair makes him look totally different.'

'I can't believe you didn't realise.' Katie took her phone back and threw it onto the sofa.

'So what are we waiting for?' Bella grabbed the oven gloves from their peg and struck a superhero pose. Katie burst out laughing and Jenny joined in.

Bella opened the oven door and placed the lasagna on the table. 'This looks amazing. Is Reena not joining us?'

'No, she told me she's got a hot date tonight.' Jenny couldn't help smiling. 'She's promised to text me and let me know how it goes.'

'And what about Nadeem? Is he really out of your life for good?'

Jenny frowned and shook her head. 'I still haven't seen him since that day we got rid of Derek. I did tell you, right? Exactly what happened?'

Bella nodded. 'Yeah, you told me. But I just kind of hoped that you guys would have worked things out by now. I mean, after all the nice things you said about him, have you just given up on him?'

Jenny frowned, trying to consider her answer. This conversation had taken a very unexpected turn. 'I don't know. I think it's just easier this way. It still kind of hurts that he didn't believe in me, even though I can totally see his reasons.'

Bella took the steaming plate Katie handed to her. 'Wouldn't you think less of him if he'd just given up on his cousin at the drop of a hat? I mean, would you believe it if someone from your supermarket said that Katie had got high on drugs and beaten them into a pulp?'

'No, of course not.' Jenny's reply was so automatic she didn't even stop to think about it. Then she held up her hands. 'Alright, alright. I can see what you're trying to do. But it doesn't solve anything.'

Bella turned to Katie. 'Don't you agree with me?'

Katie hesitated, obviously torn between Bella's enthusiasm and the knowledge that the situation was complicated. 'I don't know. It's more tricky than that.'

'I don't want to talk about this right now.' Jenny balanced her plate on her knees and reached for the remote. 'Let's just watch the film.'

There was no more said, but later that night when she was tucked up in bed she couldn't help thinking about the conversation. Did she have any right to judge Nadeem for how he had acted? Was she still angry at him? And was that a bad thing?

She rubbed her eyes. She'd had enough of feeling bad about things. There was no shame in anything that she had done in the past. But what about the future? What did she really want from her life? The question went around in her head as she considered the answers.

Time spent with friends, of course. She loved Katie and Reena to bits and she was so happy to have Bella back in her life. If she was honest with herself she should probably try to build bridges with her mother too.

What else?

A job she loved was really important. She had already started planning out her new business.

Her brain was circling around the most important question and she forced herself to confront it head on. She wanted Nadeem. Even though it seemed crazy after all they had been through, if she really considered things properly he was just a good guy who had tried his best to navigate through a difficult situation. Expecting him to be perfect wasn't going to help them both, and allowing Derek to come between them would mean that in some way the guy had finally won. She couldn't imagine what the solution was to the situation, but there must be something they could do. Maybe she should call him. Try to talk and work this out somehow.

At the thought of seeing him a strange ache invaded her chest. Was it a crime to lie to yourself? Because that's what she had been doing these last few weeks, pretending that she was happy without him.

Jenny was awoken by a scream of anguish from the living room and sat bolt upright in bed, peering blearily at her clock. It was just typical that on her day off something would wake her up. She wrenched open her bedroom door to find Katie kneeling in the living room, staring at her phone with a horrified face.

'What is it?' Jenny could feel her heart thudding in her chest.

Katie just groaned theatrically. 'Tina's gone and got the flu. She looked a bit tired yesterday, but I thought it was just because we've been working so hard to set all this up.'

Jenny didn't quite know if that warranted an early morning banshee scream, but it was pretty serious. Tina was Katie's right-hand woman, and was supposed to not only be helping her with all the last-minute arrangements for Bella's event that evening, but also to be one of the models for the fashion show. Lots of celebrities had donated designer clothes and were going to be there. It would also be packed with journalists so they couldn't afford for anything to go wrong.

'I can help you with all the pre-arrangements.' Jenny had intended to use the event to network with some of the designers that were going to be there, but she could maybe squeeze that in after dinner when everyone would be more relaxed anyway.

Katie looked up at her as if she was a rescuing angel. 'Really?'

Jenny shrugged. 'I don't see why not. Being backstage will be interesting too.'

Katie eyed her up speculatively. 'I would ask you to take Tina's place in the fashion show, seeing as you're pretty much the same size, but I know how you hate being in the limelight.'

'Same size, but not the same height! You'd have to find me a pair of very tall platforms.'

Katie eyed her speculatively. 'That could be arranged. Besides, most of the dresses are short anyway.'

Jenny realised that Katie was actually being serious. She considered for a moment, waiting for the anxiety to start swelling in her throat at the thought of being up in front of all those people, but nothing happened. Maybe it was time to show off a little, and what helped

Katie would also help Bella. Phoning Nadeem could wait until tomorrow.

'Sure.' She gave a wide smile, extending her hand to help Katie up from the floor. 'I think this calls for pancakes. We'll need some fuel before we get going.'

'Are you sure you really want to do this?' Nadeem's mother asked the question for what seemed like the thousandth time. He was sitting with his parents in the boardroom, and there were only a few minutes before the meeting was due to start.

'Yes.' He nodded definitively. 'Germaine will do a far better job than I will. She's got the right skills, and even more importantly, the passion to succeed. She's been with the company for so long that she knows it inside and out. You need me as your man on the ground where I can do what I love and play to my strengths, and it will let you both step back from the company permanently and enjoy an early retirement. Now let's get this over with and then everyone can go and enjoy the Christmas party.'

The meeting dragged on interminably, but the only decision Nadeem was really interested in was passed unanimously. He skipped the company drinks afterwards; there was somewhere far more important he had to be.

Jenny stood still as the makeup artist put the last touches in place. She had thought she would feel nervous, but in actual fact she was elated. Some day she would be one of the designers who was auctioning off an outfit for charity while everyone tried to outbid themselves on the price. She was sure of it. And to have some of the major names in the industry around tonight, to be able to listen in on their conversations? It was stunning. She had already learned a load of useful things from the discussions that had been going on around her.

Backstage was crowded with men and women, some of them standing around waiting to go on, and others having final makeup done and hair twisted into place by staff from Bella's salons. She identified clothes from several famous French and American big names, and a number of British designers too. Bella had really pulled all the strings she could to put together something special in this glamorous West End venue.

'Two minutes.' Someone murmured in her ear. She nodded, smoothing her fingers over the gorgeous white folds of the knee-length halter-neck dress and fingering the matching pearls at her throat.

She could hear Bella giving the introduction she knew that her sister had been practising for weeks, and then a polite ripple of applause. The music started up.

The first model exited onto the runway, and Jenny joined the line to wait her turn. Then she was off, out into the glare of the lights and the crowded room. She hadn't expected the lighting to be so bright actually; it was hard to see anything beyond the first row. It took all her concentration to stay upright in the mega-heeled shoes she had been given to wear.

And then, as she turned to go back up the stage, there he was. Halfway up the front row sat Nadeem, looking exactly the same as the night he had taken her to the party. Their eyes locked and at the shock of see-ing him she almost stumbled. The initial surprise in his eyes faded to a teasing grin and he gave her an appre-ciative nod. Jenny tore her gaze away and carried on past him, her heart pounding.

Chapter 20

By the time Jenny reached the dressing room her palms were damp and her legs were trembling. She still had two more outfits to go and she honestly didn't know if she could walk past Nadeem two more times. Her attraction to him still ran as deep as ever, so much so that she was disturbed by her strength of feeling. Why was he even here? What if they couldn't work things out between them? Where would that leave her?

She swayed, and one of the other women put a hand on her shoulder. 'Are you alright?'

'Yes...yes. It's just the heat.' Her voice was faint and it sounded slightly pathetic even to her ears.

Someone brought a glass of water, which she sipped at gratefully while they helped her into her second gown. This was a gorgeous midnight blue dinner dress, with a scandalously low-cut neckline that enhanced even her relatively modest bust. The thought of

Nadeem seeing her in the dress sent a flush of heat up the inside of her thighs.

As soon as she stepped out her eyes locked on his again, and it was as if there was no-one else in the room but the two of them. His gaze held a message that was unmistakable. Daringly, she winked at him as she passed in front of him, causing his lips to curve upwards in response. The third time she went out she didn't dare to look at him, although she could feel his gaze heating her like a blazing sun.

There was a huge round of applause as the last model left the stage, and Jenny knew that people would be moving towards the dining area. Bella had arranged a seat for her at one of the tables, so she had to move fast.

Jenny changed quickly into her beautiful red dress, giving herself a swift check in the mirror. Her hair and makeup would do very well just as it was. The high modest halter neck combined with the tapered waist and bare arms left just enough skin showing to tease but not to show off, and she knew that it was definitely her best work to date. No better way to display it than to wear it. She wanted to look her best tonight. And especially now that she knew Nadeem was here. This was a perfect opportunity to talk to him.

Standing on a step so she could see, she scanned the room. A touch on her elbow made her turn, and there he was. Her heart thudded at the sight of him.

She was wondering how to open the conversation, but Nadeem got there first. 'I need to apologise to you one more time.' He pressed his hands together, as if in supplication. 'I started off our relationship apologising, so it's only fitting that I do it again. And as many times as you need me to.'

Jenny couldn't help teasing him just a little. 'If I remember rightly, you actually started it off by scowling ferociously. For at least twenty minutes. Are you going to do that too?'

Nadeem's solemn face cracked into a wide smile, and in that very moment Jenny knew that her instincts were correct and he was the man she really wanted by her side. 'Oh, Jen. I love you. And I want you back in my life.' Then his face sobered again. 'I promise you that I'll do anything to make this work out between us. All you have to do is name it.'

He held her gaze, as if willing her to believe his sincerity. 'I've realised that in trying to support my family, I threw away the one thing that made my life really special, and that was you.' His back straightened a little, as if he was bracing for her reaction. 'I did consider asking you to be part of my family, to show you how much you mean to me, but knowing your history I was worried that you might see it as too invasive and controlling.'

Her breath caught and she found herself lost for words. He understood. He really did. A great weight lifted off her shoulders and she finally felt like she could breathe again.

Nadeem shook his head. 'I've been over that night you left a million times and all the things that happened after that, and I know that in spite of my best efforts not to screw things up, I totally did. But life is short and I can't help trying just one more time.'

As his words filtered through to her brain, she realised that he hadn't been the only one to mess up. She had been too judgmental of his choices. Too untrusting of his intentions.

'Nadeem -' Words failed her as he swept her a deep bow, the same as he had done for her that first morning at the beach, and she almost thought she could smell the salty tang of the sea as the memory passed through her head.

'May I escort you to your table, madam?' He formally offered her an arm. If it hadn't been for the emotion she saw in his eyes, she never would have guessed what lay beneath his polite exterior.

He was right, that life was too short. And in that minute, she knew what she wanted her answer to be. But she would keep that to herself for the moment. Words were all very well, but until they were borne out by actions then they didn't mean a thing. She just smiled and placed a hand lightly on his arm as they started walking. Even that slight contact set her heart racing.

'I do have something to thank you for.' Jenny kept her voice low. 'You showed me the importance of family. I would never have got in touch with Bella if it weren't for you, and I'm so happy to have her back in my life.'

'I'm happy for you too. You've been through so much, I'm just amazed you found it in your heart to help me in the way you did.' Nadeem's tone was serious. 'I still can't quite believe it. You're such an incredible woman.'

Jenny looked into his eyes and what she saw there warmed her heart. She leaned her head briefly against his shoulder, feeling the strong curve of his arm under the soft wool of the suit.

They stopped in front of the table list and she released him reluctantly. 'I need to leave you for dinner, unfortunately. Bella said she would put me next to someone I would really want to talk to.' She scanned the list. 'Ah. Now I see what she meant.'

She pointed to the board where their names were written next to each other. 'I'll wait to kill her until later.'

Nadeem laughed out loud at the expression on her face. 'I'll be my most likeable self, I promise.' His hands were raised in surrender.

Jenny led the way to their table, a smile playing on her lips. 'Fine. But don't complain when you find you can't keep up the pretence for long.'

Over dinner they chatted with the other six around the table, all of whom had interesting stories to tell. As coffee was served and people started to drift off Jenny filled Nadeem in on her news. 'I'm still working at the supermarket. I kind of like it now I've made up my mind about it. It's local, and the people are friendly. And it fits in with my plans for my new business.'

It took a moment for her words to sink in, but when they did his face lit up. 'You're really going for it? That's so exciting!'

'It's just from my bedroom at the moment, but I've already had orders from a couple of Bella's friends, so at some point I hope to be able to expand into my own space.'

Nadeem nodded thoughtfully. 'Seems like there's been a lot of change. I've quit my job as director. I finally persuaded my parents to let Germaine take over because I just wanted more time doing what I really enjoy.'

'Really?' Jenny smiled, feeling her fingers tingle with emotion. 'What are you going to do instead?'

'I've agreed to go and work for our foundation. Which means, among other things, another trip to Tanzania to check up on the medical centre. The salary's not that big, but then living on the boat I don't need much.' His voice betrayed his pleasure. Jenny reached across and squeezed his hand gently. She was so happy she thought her heart would overflow.

'Look.' Nadeem leaned across close enough so that only she could hear his voice in the noise of the room around them. 'You're the person who means the most to me, and I'll do anything for you. I think you should know that I've cut off all communication with Derek. I've just been too angry at him for what he did to you. No-one should do that to anyone. I will forever regret that I didn't believe you straight away, but the honest truth is that it was all tied up with my guilt over what had happened with Nate. It was a dick move, I know, and if you never forgive me I'll understand.'

Jenny turned her head and looked at him. His serious expression showed how worried he was that she would reject him again. She brought up a mental image of Bella in her mind and that gave her the strength to say her next words. 'You were just trying your best to do the right thing. Nobody's perfect.'

She gripped the edge of the table tightly and took a deep breath. 'He's your cousin. You'll always be related to him, and you'll never get away from that. But if we're together, then we can find our way through this together somehow, and don't they always say that two heads are better than one?'

Nadeem pulled her close and kissed her on the top of the head. 'I do love you, you know that? You're amazing.'

She looked up at him. 'I love you too. Otherwise I wouldn't have been able to say all of that.'

The staff were starting to usher the guests towards the ballroom area, and Jenny pointed towards them. 'Would you like to dance?'

Nadeem's hand touched her shoulder. 'Actually, I don't think it would be a patch on last time.' His voice was a murmur in her ear. 'Would you like to escape this crowd? I know a little romantic place by the side of a canal where we could stay the night?'

She turned her head. Their lips were almost touching. A couple of centimetres would close the space between them, if that was what she wanted.

'When I say stay the night, I mean...' His voice trailed off.

It was time to make her choice one way or another, and this time she knew what she was going to say. 'I'd love that. But could I just leave you for an hour or so? This is a chance to network that I won't get again for a while.'

'I'll come with you.' Nadeem's response was quick. 'I'll lure in all the women with my rugged good looks and charm.'

Jenny laughed. 'Now that is a cliché. Although I'll be expecting you to flirt with the men too, just to keep things even.'

She gestured towards a man with large glasses who was clearly making his way towards them. 'You can start with him.'

Nadeem looked over. 'Isn't he someone famous? His face looks very familiar.'

'Really?' Jenny couldn't help teasing him again. 'Are you sure?'

Jenny washed her hands in the sink. It was well past time to leave. She had picked up a stack of tips from various people who seemed only too happy to pass on their knowledge to someone who was just starting out. The crowd was beginning to thin now and she couldn't wait to go home. Well, it wouldn't be home, but something like it. She loved the little canal boat. And Nadeem would be there with her, which was all that mattered. She knew some people would say she was a fool for trusting him with her heart again, but sometimes you just knew. Some things were worth taking a chance on. She hummed happily to herself as she dried off with a paper towel.

'I'm sorry to bother you, but I just have to say that I love your dress. Who is it by?'

Jenny turned to find a grey-haired woman standing behind her, who was dressed in a floor-length black gown. It was an expensive brand, but also a few years old. That was interesting. Someone who bought quality and then hung onto it. Or maybe even bought second-hand.

Jenny smiled. 'Thanks. I designed it myself.'

The woman pressed her hands together in delight. 'Oh, I knew it! You're one of the designers. Which company do you work for?'

'I actually have my own.' She didn't yet, but if everything went to plan then she would do soon, so it was only a small bending of the truth.

'Oh, that's amazing.' The other woman leaned in confidentially. 'Tell me. Do you also design business wear? I've just started a new job which is a bit of a step up and I've discovered that my current wardrobe isn't working for me. And with my shape as rotund as it is then I'm finding it really hard to get things which suit me, but that still look right for the office, you know?' She gestured to her figure, which looked more curvy than rotund, but Jenny didn't want to argue. 'I can see you've worked wonders with that dress, and since you're short like me...' The woman's voice trailed off.

'Oh.' Jenny reigned in her surprise, and set her business mind to work. 'Of course. I could maybe work up a few basic sketches for you, and you could see if there's anything which catches your fancy?'

'Oh, that would be wonderful.' The woman fished in her handbag and pulled out business card. 'If you call the number on here, my assistant will arrange a time for us to meet. Would you mind coming to my office? Or would you prefer me to visit your studio?'

Jenny had to smile at the mention of a studio; at the moment all she had was heaps of material piled around her bedroom. She took the card. 'No, I'm happy to come to you, it's no problem.'

The other woman held out a hand. 'I'm Grace Walters.'

'Jennifer Lang.' Jenny took the hand and shook it firmly.

'Well, I'll let you go. Looking forward to hearing from you soon.' The woman disappeared into one of the toilet cubicles.

Jenny could barely stop herself from jumping up and down as she made her way back into the main hall. Her first proper commission. Or at least, the distinct possibility of one. Curious, she turned over the card. The logo of a well-known pharmaceutical company was printed on the front, and the card read, 'Grace Walters, CEO'.

'Wow, Bella, you really did pull out all the stops tonight.' This could change everything.

Stopping only to collect her day clothes, Nadeem and Jenny made their way towards the exit. Jenny suddenly spotted Bella waving at them. 'Don't tell me you were going to leave without saying goodbye.' She looked at them both with a satisfied smirk on her face. 'Mum's here, and she wants to say hello. If you're OK with that.'

Jenny hadn't expected her mother to be here tonight, but she supposed that she should have. Seeing Nadeem had driven everything else quite out of her mind. Jenny looked at him and felt him take hold of her hand and squeeze it gently.

Bella led the way to where their mother sat in an elegant green dress at an empty table. She rose to meet them as they came towards her. Jenny found that Nadeem was still holding her hand and she was glad of his implicit support. There were more grey hairs and a few more lines on her mother's face than when she had seen her last, but otherwise she seemed to have barely changed. Actually, that wasn't totally true. Jenny couldn't remember the last time she had seen her mother looking so happy.

Natalie eyed them up, her keen eyes not missing anything. 'I see you've found yourself a half-decent escort then.'

Jenny bristled, ready for a snappy retort, but then realised that her mother's eyes were sparkling. A quick glance at Nadeem showed he was trying to bite back a smile as well. She decided a shrug was all she could do. 'Well, he's kind of decent when you get to know him.'

'I'm looking forward to doing more of that.' Natalie came forward and gave her a hug, and Jenny felt herself melt into those warm arms as if the intervening years had never existed. 'I'm so glad you're happy.' It was barely a whisper in her ear.

Natalie stood on tiptoe to kiss Nadeem on the cheek. 'You just take care of her, young man, alright?'

'Yes ma'am.' He gave her a salute.

Nadeem's arm stayed wrapped around Jenny throughout the ride back. The taxi dropped them off at the top of the steps, and they walked hand in hand down onto the canal towpath.

They finally stopped at the green boat which gleamed in the lamplight. Nadeem jumped on board and held out a hand for her and she stepped across carefully, lifting her long skirt with the other hand.

He caught her close and touched his lips to hers. The kiss was all the sweeter for having waited so long. He broke off suddenly, fumbling in his pocket for the key, and she swayed against him, feeling bereft. Their breath steamed in the cold night air.

Nadeem looked down at her. 'I'm sorry I couldn't provide romantic moonlight and stars, but the good old British weather just wouldn't oblige.'

'I don't care. All I want is you.' She could barely see his eyes in the darkness, but when he bent his head and kissed her again she could feel what her words had done to him. He hastily unlocked the hatch, and they descended into the cabin.

Nadeem stripped off his jacket and flung it over a chair. 'Would you like a drink?'

Jenny shook her head. 'I can't believe you're offering me a drink when all I really want to do is strip those oh-so-sexy clothes off.'

His lips curved upwards with that smile she loved on him and he crossed the two paces to her in a heartbeat. He cradled her face between his hands, tangling his fingers in her hair. 'Oh Jen.' His kiss contained not just passion, but also deep tenderness. Breaking off, he drew her by the hand towards the small door which led to the bedroom. But once inside, he hesitated.

'What's wrong?' She smoothed back his dishevelled hair.

He smiled again. 'I just can't quite believe that you're really here, that it's really you. If you knew how many times I've dreamed of making love to you in this very bed.'

Jenny laughed. 'I assure you, it is really me, and I am really here. But if you wait much longer to give me what I want then I might just to have to reconsider my options.'

His face took on a look of horror for a split second until he realised that she was joking. Then he took a mock swipe at her, she dodged, and they both fell together onto the lush puffy duvet. Jenny landed on top of him heavily and they both collapsed into helpless giggles.

'What is it with you, making me laugh when I'm doing my best to try and turn you on?' Jenny sighed.

Nadeem's eyes suddenly took on a dark intense look. 'Sweetheart, you don't even have to try for that one.'

He slid her dress up her thigh with a murmur of appreciation, and then she heard his sharp intake of breath as he realised what she had known all evening.

Nonchalance was quite hard to come by, but she did her best. 'Well, they would have shown through the fabric of the dress.'

Nadeem groaned aloud. 'God, Jen, if you only knew what you're doing to me...'

She quickly undid the buttons of his shirt so she could run her fingers down his body and unzip his trousers.

'Are you sure you're ready for this?' Nadeem drew back and looked at her. In the darkness she could barely make out his face, but she could feel his eyes looking at her.

'I am.' She nodded. 'I've still got a long way to go on some things, but with you I've put those demons to rest.'

He just kissed her tenderly, and she felt a single tear fall gently onto her face.

Afterwards they both stripped off their clothes and lay cradled in each other's arms, snuggling up under the covers. Jenny didn't wake again until the dawn light started creeping in around the curtains, and as she stirred sleepily she felt Nadeem do the same beside her. They lay in bed, listening to the birdsong coming from outside the boat.

Nadeem spoke suddenly. 'So is this our future now? Are we all good? Because I'm lying here desperately hoping you'll say yes.'

'I don't know.' Jenny spoke from her heart; there was nothing else she could do. 'I've got a lot of history. Are you sure you want to take that on?'

He cupped her cheek gently with his palm. 'We've both got a lot of history. And some shared history that I'm not so proud of, but we've still managed to get through that.'

She felt the weight of the past lift just a little, but before she could open her mouth he spoke again. 'I could ask you the same question. Are you sure you really want me? I don't know if I'm worthy of your love after everything that I've done.'

She studied him for a moment, and lifted a hand to smooth out the small crease in his forehead. 'Well, you didn't exactly cover yourself in glory. But I know that through everything you were desperately trying to do the right thing. No-one's perfect, not even you, although I know you do your best to try. So there's only one answer to your question.'

Nadeem raised an eyebrow with a smile. 'And would you care to actually share it with me?'

'The answer's yes, you dipstick.' Jenny punched him softly on the shoulder. 'But only if you promise to make me laugh every day of the week.'

Nadeem pretended to consider for a moment, stroking his chin, then reached an arm across and took her hand. 'There will always be laughter in our lives, I promise. Any other important requests?'

Jenny propped herself up on one elbow. 'I want a massive cup of coffee every morning. Hand delivered to me in bed.'

Nadeem's eyes sparkled. 'In that case, it's a good thing I bought a bigger coffee maker a few weeks back.' He looked slightly embarrassed. 'I pretended to myself it was for when friends came round, but I think part of me was just hanging onto the hope that one day you might forgive me. Do you forgive me? I mean, really?'

His face was serious now, and as she looked at him lying there she knew there was only one answer to that question too.

'Yes. I do.' Her eyes brimmed with tears as she spoke. And as he wrapped his arms around her, she knew that she would never doubt him again.

THE END

Acknowledgements

Every book has a journey, and this one's journey has been particularly long, so there are a large number of people I need to thank.

Some people were directly involved in the finalising of this book and these I owe the greatest thanks to, although any remaining errors are entirely my own. Ali Williams, for her excellent editing skills, and Fully Booked, for the amazing cover. Kritika Narula, for her sensitivity read; Cliff Johnson, for giving me insights into PTSD; Paul Knight, for detail about British Army procedures; and Elizabeth and Amanda, for some nifty proofreading.

I also have to thank Kate Walker and the Walker's Stalkers writing group, for reading the very first chapter I wrote, and convincing me that it was a story worthwhile writing. The Romantic Novelists' Association New Writer's Scheme gave me further feedback which helped to shape the story. Donna Hillyer, a freelance editor, gave me advice at a critical point when I was confused about how to make it really work, and for that I will be forever grateful. Also Charlotte Ledger, who taught me so much about writing when I was working with her at One

More Chapter. Additionally, without all the knowledge gleaned from other members of the RNA and the Bestseller Experiment podcast I would never have had the courage or the contacts to self-publish this story.

The usual thanks go to my family and friends, who have given me so much support and encouragement on my writing journey. I have to particularly mention the following people: Diana and Alan, as without their invitation to stay with them in the Highlands this book would never have existed; Mairi and Laura, who distracted me from the tribulations of lockdown with numerous discussions about what makes a good story; and Donna, who kept bringing me food and reminding me what laughter is.

I have one last thank you for all the people who have so generously shared details of traumatic experiences and what it is like to live with the impacts of these; without them this book would not be what it is.

If you enjoyed this book, you might like Sasha's other book, *Something Like Happy*:

Jade is just trying to get by. She doesn't want to talk about it. She doesn't want a fuss.

But one day she meets Nick and everything changes.

Out of the most difficult of situations, Nick and Jade's friendship grows into something both of them never knew they needed.

Jade used to be sure that she was better off alone. But could it be that together, with Nick by her side, she can start to feel something like happy again?

Available from all major paperback and eBook retailers

Lightning Source UK Ltd.
Milton Keynes UK
UKHW011011290921
391376UK00001B/28

9 781739 936907